Save a kingdom? Seriously
barely save himself from at
save a kingdom. And then only by running and hiding.

But six months ago, Greg played a role in an unlikely prophecy foretold on the magical world of Myrth. Against all odds he managed to survive. Now a second prophecy has been revealed, one featuring the "Hero Who Slayed Ruuan," and Greg is once again pulled into Myrth.

Only Greg and a small band of friends know Ruuan still lives and Greg is no hero. Meanwhile, hundreds of thousands of Canaraza warriors will soon gather outside Pendegrass Castle to settle a score with King Peter and his army. Greg will be there too. With three generals battling by his side, he is expected to fight with the strength of ten men and make the difference that will lead the king to victory.

It seems impossible, but Greg should have learned from his first trip to Myrth that just because it's impossible doesn't mean everyone won't expect him to succeed. After all, everyone already knows he's a hero and prophecies are never wrong.

How to Save a Kingdom

JOURNALS OF MYRTH

Book Two

Bill Allen

Bell Bridge Books

Bell Bridge Books
PO BOX 300921
Memphis, TN 38130
Print ISBN: 978-1-61194-091-6

Bell Bridge Books is an Imprint of BelleBooks, Inc.

We at BelleBooks enjoy hearing from readers.
Visit our websites – www.BelleBooks.com and www.BellBridgeBooks.com.

10 9 8 7 6 5 4 3 2 1

Cover design: Debra Dixon
Interior design: Hank Smith
Photo credits:
Kingdom (Manipulated) © Annnmei | Dreamstime.com
Background: Debra Dixon

:Lshk:01:

A Hart Day at School

Short of a valley full of purring shadowcats, nothing could drain away a boy's consciousness faster than one of Mrs. Beasley's seventh-grade algebra lectures.

"Did you not get enough sleep last night, Mr. Hart?"

"Wha-huh?" Greg's head snapped up and tottered about in a fair imitation of a bobblehead doll. Greg had once faced an ogre in an enchanted forest, a mysterious witch in the gloom of her decrepit shack and a dragon at the center of its white-hot lair. None offered the same level of intimidation as Mrs. Beasley could muster.

Eventually, the snickering of his classmates reached Greg's ears. He ran his fingers through his hair, but the unruly nest, now bent further back off his forehead from resting his head in his arms, refused to lie flat. "Oh, no ma'am . . . I mean, yes . . . er, I'm fine."

Mrs. Beasley peered at him over her spectacles, her lips scrunched up smaller than a dime. Rumor was, the woman possessed no sense of humor, but before that could be proved, she would have to listen to at least one thing a student had to say. Her cold stare never wavered as she spoke, and her voice dug under Greg's skin like a rusty knife.

"Why don't you come to the board, Mr. Hart, show us all how to solve this equation?"

Greg's stomach knotted even tighter than Mrs. Beasley's lips. The laughs took up again, which was bad enough, but one booming chortle lingered long after all others died away. Greg turned to see Manny Malistino, or Manny Malice, as he was better known, sneering one row over and two seats back.

Slouched as deep in his chair as he could go, his knees propped high into the air, Manny looked as though he was trying to lie on his back and suck in his stomach so he could strap on his desk like a belt buckle. He was an anomaly, way more mass than any one boy his age ought to have, or any two grown men for that matter, and all of it seemingly bent on making each day of Greg's life more miserable than the last.

"What are *you* laughing about, Mr. Malistino?" Mrs. Beasley's shrill voice rang out. "Perhaps you'd like to demonstrate *your* keen wit for us instead?"

The usual murmuring ceased, as not a single boy or girl in class dared make fun of Manny Malice. Manny's eyes darted toward Greg for an instant, but Greg wisely chose that moment to wipe up the large puddle of drool on his notes.

"I'm waiting," said Mrs. Beasley.

"Uh, no, ma'am," said Manny.

"I mean, I'm waiting for you to come to the board."

Throughout the room students threw hands over their mouths or raised books in front of their noses. It was the type of silence that could make ears bleed.

With a grunt, Manny slid upright in his chair and screeched around the hardwood floor, struggling to pry himself loose from his desk. By the time he broke free, the unnatural silence had grown so thick it was a wonder Manny managed to wade through it. Greg was afraid to smile for fear Manny might somehow hear him. Still, it was all he could do not to stab out a foot as Manny passed.

Mrs. Beasley's voice pushed past Greg's smugness. "And you can help him, please, Mr. Hart."

As if a floodgate had been opened, the entire class erupted. Greg winced. He glanced across the room to see if Kristin Wenslow was among those laughing. As crushes went, the one he had on Kristin could have flattened just about anything, maybe even a brute like Manny. She caught his eye and swept a strand of light brown hair from in front of her face. Greg's breath caught in his throat.

"We don't have all day, Mr. Hart."

"Sure seemed like it when you were lecturing," Greg said too softly for anyone to hear.

"What was that?" Mrs. Beasley's voice rang out. The woman could hear a feather drop at fifty paces.

"I said, 'I'm coming.'"

Greg glanced one last time at Kristin, climbed out of his chair with un-Manny-like grace and trudged toward the front of the room, where Manny stood staring dumbly at the whiteboard. The mutant boy's frame rose like a mountain, growing higher and higher the nearer Greg approached, until finally Greg reached the board and Manny's navel turned to greet him.

"I'll get you for this, Hart."

"Me? What did I do?"

"I don't see anyone writing," observed Mrs. Beasley.

Manny stared at the board as if it were covered with hieroglyphics. Greg watched him struggle a few seconds, then snatched up a marker and scribbled the answer to the problem Mrs. Beasley had posed the class.

"Not bad, Mr. Hart," said Mrs. Beasley. It was possibly the nicest thing she'd ever said to him. She turned then and asked if everyone understood Greg's solution. Greg suspected she was hoping they didn't.

"You tryin' to make me look stupid, Hart?" whispered Manny.

"No need for that."

Manny couldn't have possibly picked up the insult, yet his single brow bent itself into a vee. "After school," he growled. "I'll be waiting outside."

Mrs. Beasley whipped around and glared over her spectacles at the two of them, her eyes wide and calculating. Greg stared back, afraid to move. Finally her frown began to straighten. Soon Greg barely recognized her.

"You may sit down," she informed them both. She then walked to the board, scratched out another problem and directed her wrath at another student.

Greg exhaled slowly and returned to his seat, preoccupied now with the clock. Time passed so slowly, he half expected to witness the hands creeping backward, but in the end, the bell rang and Mrs. Beasley granted everyone permission to leave. Even so, Greg stayed put while the others packed up their books and spilled out of the room. Math was the last period of the day, and Manny was sure to be waiting outside.

"Aren't you going home?"

Greg's eyes snapped forward, where Kristin Wenslow's freckled face hovered high above him. His heart lifted. For a second he forgot Manny was waiting to pulverize him. "Kristin?"

"The bell rang. Didn't you hear?"

"Yeah, I . . . uh . . . just wanted to finish jotting down some notes before I left."

"But your books are all packed up."

"Huh? Oh, right. I'm done now."

Kristin continued to stare down at him, the overhead lights framing her soft hair like a halo. Greg considered reaching up and touching her cheek, but stopped when he imagined her shrieking and knocking over desks trying to lurch out of his reach.

"Well?" she said.

"Well what?"

"Are you going to leave or what?"

"Oh, yeah," said Greg. "I mean, no. I just remembered I need to jot down a few more notes first. Don't worry. I'll make the bus."

Kristin bit her lip in the cutest way. "If you say so. I . . . um . . . guess I'll see you later." And just like that, she wriggled her shoulders to center her backpack, offered a confused smile and ambled out of the room.

Greg stared dumbfounded at the door. He'd have given anything to go with her—anything at all—but if he had to be flattened by Manny Malice, he could at least do it without Kristin watching. Again he checked the clock. Three forty. He'd need to leave soon or miss his bus and have to walk home. On the other hand, if he stayed put, at least he'd be able to walk . . .

Finally he arrived at a decision. He reached behind his chair for his backpack and jumped when something coarse and wet streaked across his knuckles.

"Rake. You scared me."

Displaying the same reluctance Greg had been feeling, a small creature never before seen in Mrs. Beasley's classroom peered out from the pack and gradually emerged to explore Greg's fingers with its tiny pink tongue. Greg nearly smiled in spite of his impending doom.

Roughly the size of a squirrel, but with shimmering blue-black fur and a long tail that could easily wrap twice around its body, Rake was a shadowcat, the only one of its kind on Earth. More importantly, he was Greg's closest friend. The two had spent nearly every moment together since they first met six months ago on the distant world of Myrth, a land of monsters and magic where Greg had once gone to slay a dragon.

Okay, technically Greg didn't go to Myrth to slay a dragon. He went because he was too slow to react when the magicians there opened a rift between worlds and snatched him out of the woods behind his house. But *they* had done so with the intention of having him slay a dragon, so Greg felt that should count for something. If nothing else, it made for a better story—or at least it would have, if he could have ever risked telling anyone. He'd tiptoed around the subject with Kristin once, but quit when she felt his forehead and asked him to lie down until she could bring the school nurse.

Still, it was the only time she'd ever touched him, and Greg couldn't say he hated the feeling. In fact, he'd give anything to feel it again.

Telling her more about Rake just probably wasn't the best way to go about it.

"Come on, Rake," Greg said with a sigh, "get in the pack. We don't want to be late for our beating."

The shadowcat stared at him quizzically, leaned forward and smashed a furry cheek into Greg's hand.

"Not now. We're going to miss our bus."

As if understanding, Rake crawled obediently into the pack. Greg quickly cinched up the straps. If anyone were to ever see Rake . . . well, Greg didn't know what he'd do. Then again, if he didn't figure out a way to slip past Manny Malice and onto his bus, what difference would it make? Just because he was going to die didn't mean the secret of the shadowcat had to die with him.

After a few whispered reassurances to his backpack, Greg headed for the side exit, slipped outside and scurried along the wall toward the front of the building, all the while thinking about that one miraculous day last fall when he'd fought Manny Malice and actually won. Using his skill in *chikan*, an ancient martial art he'd learned on Myrth, Greg had tripped Manny with a stick and sent him cartwheeling into the bushes. For months afterward, Greg had viewed that as the happiest moment of his life. Today it seemed the stupidest. Manny would be ready this time, and Greg didn't have a stick.

At the edge of the building, he paused to peer around the corner. The first of the buses, lined up across the lawn about a hundred yards away, was already beginning to pull out from the curb. No problem. The coast was clear, and while he had never thought so at the time, Greg was lucky enough to have spent much of his life as the smallest boy in school, which meant he was far more experienced at running than most boys twice his size, a necessity, since that was normally who he was running from.

With the same determination he'd once shown when chased by a fifteen-foot-tall ogre, he abandoned the safety of the wall and darted across the lawn. Not a bad effort, really. He made it nearly halfway to the curb before Manny stepped out from behind a large tree trunk to block his way.

So, this time the ogre is ahead of me.

Greg managed to grind to a halt an instant before his face collided with Manny's stomach, but his pack was slower in stopping. Despite a lot of frantic flailing and grabbing, Greg felt the bag fall from his shoulder, tossing a bewildered Rake onto the lawn.

"Going somewhere, Hart?"

Greg didn't hear. His only thought was to dive on top of Rake, who let out a panicked screech not of this Earth.

"What a baby," Manny jeered. "You scream like a girl. Get up and fight like a man."

With Rake barely hidden beneath one shoulder, Greg didn't dare get up. He reached blindly backward for his backpack, managed to snag one strap . . .

Manny casually stepped on the fabric before Greg could reel it in. "What's the matter? Too weak to wift your wittle backpack?"

With a maniacal laugh, Manny slid his foot away, taunting Greg to try again. Greg took a deep breath, gripped Rake's fur and squirmed to his knees, yanking on the pack as he went. This time Manny was less subtle about stomping on it.

Aw, man.

Greg stared at the enormous legs before him, fantasizing about how they'd look dangling from a dragon's jaws. He followed them up to Manny's even larger torso, where Manny's giant hands were forming into fists. Before Greg could look much higher, a bright pinpoint of light suddenly split the air behind Manny with a loud sizzling *zap*.

Manny's smile faded. He started to turn to see what Greg was looking at.

Greg needed only one glance. He had seen this phenomenon twice before. He had an idea Manny shouldn't be seeing it now. Panicked, he jumped up and reached for Manny's shoulder.

He probably should have let go of his bag first.

The backpack whirled through a wide arc that struck Manny squarely in the ear. Manny let out a yowl befitting his size and dropped to his knees, but Greg took little notice. He barely got out one hysterical screech himself before the space ahead burst wide-open, roaring louder than a dozen angry Manny Malices, and sucked him off his feet.

A Hart Act to Follow

Greg felt Rake's rough tongue probe his ear. He opened his eyes to find himself lying on his back, staring toward a ceiling barely visible within the gloom of a cold chamber. The stone floor pressed hard against his shoulders, and shadows flickered from the fires of torches hung in sconces lining the walls.

Greg knew immediately where he was. He'd been in this room twice before—two more times than he ever wanted. Of course, the *second* time he'd come here so the magicians of Myrth could send him home, so he supposed being here only once before would have been worse. But now he was here a third time, and that thought made his stomach clench even more than the long, magic tunnel he'd traveled through moments ago.

"Hey, Greg," a familiar voice greeted him.

Greg turned toward a boy's face beaming beneath a shock of bright red hair. It, too, was familiar, and part of him was happy to see it, but a larger part of him knew he was only seeing it because he had literally landed in a world of trouble.

"Lucky?"

"You were expecting someone else?"

Greg shook his head. The first time he met Lucky Day, the boy had just advised the king's magicians when to open a portal between this world and Greg's own. Lucky had been looking for a Greghart, and out of the infinite times and places when and where the portal could have opened, by chance it miraculously picked the exact spot Greg had been standing. Now it looked as if Lucky had proved himself worthy of his nickname again.

Greg had to wonder if being lucky all the time was a good thing.

"Sorry for the small welcome," said Lucky, "but everyone's really busy, and we just recently found out we needed you again."

"Needed me?" Greg asked with the same enthusiasm he'd shown over leaving Mrs. Beasley's classroom. "For what?"

"A fight with the Army of the Crown."

Greg felt a horror he hadn't experienced since last leaving Myrth, except possibly for his occasional dealings with Mrs. Beasley. "I don't want to fight the king's army."

Lucky laughed. "Relax. I said a fight *with* them, not against them."

"Oh." Greg liked this idea only slightly better. "Who are we supposed to fight?"

"The spirelings."

"What?" He would have preferred an army of Mrs. Beasleys. The spirelings were fierce warriors with razor-sharp teeth who could run much faster than a man . . . or more to the point, much faster than Greg. On Greg's last visit, the entire spireling race, hundreds of thousands in all, had grouped for battle outside the dragon's lair. Fortunately Greg had needed to fight only two of them. Even so, it was only a matter of chance that he hadn't been killed. "Why would anyone want to fight the spirelings?" he asked with a gulp.

Lucky offered a warm smile, which, next to his bright red hair, was his most distinguishing feature. "You tell *me*. As I understand it, you fight 'with the skill of ten men.' And somehow you're going to make the difference that leads the king's men to victory."

"Don't tell me Simon screwed up and named me in another of his prophecies?"

"Well, he didn't exactly name you outright. He just said the army would be joined by 'the Hero who slayed Ruuan.'"

"But nobody slay—"

Lucky's hand flew up and clamped over Greg's mouth.

"—dwoon," Greg finished.

Lucky glanced over his shoulder. For the first time, Greg noticed several mysterious figures in black robes lurking in the shadows, peering his way. Seeing few other options, he peered back. He couldn't distinguish any features beneath the hoods, but he recognized these men. King Peter's magicians. Last time he'd been dragged to Myrth, the men had clapped and cheered, amazed that Lucky had managed to kidnap his intended target. Now, having witnessed that miracle once before, they remained motionless in the gloom, saying nothing.

Lucky shot Greg a scolding look. "What do you say we go see how the preparations are coming?"

While the question was worded much like a suggestion, Lucky's tone left no room for argument, and Greg would have found it hard to argue anyway, what with Lucky's hand still clamped over his mouth. He barely had time to scoop up Rake before Lucky whisked him toward a heavy oak door set in one wall of the small room.

Greg cringed as Lucky grasped the handle and swung the door open. After all, the last time he'd stepped through this door, the thousand people waiting outside had cheered so loudly Greg had thought he'd be crushed by the sound.

But today the Great Hall stood empty. Not a single person had come to greet him. Not even King Peter or Queen Pauline. Sure, Greg felt relieved, but still . . . he'd always known he'd eventually be forgotten, even if he had fulfilled the last prophecy, but he'd thought his fame might at least last longer than six months. *Wait, the magicians probably moved me through time.*

"How long has it been since I left?" he asked hopefully.

"Well, let's see," said Lucky. "Bart went to Simon's shortly after we returned from the Infinite Spire, and he returned directly to the castle after he learned of the next prophecy. Since then we've been struggling to figure out what he was trying to say, so . . . about two weeks."

"Two weeks?" Greg couldn't believe everyone had already forgotten him. He eased Rake onto his shoulders and tried not to sulk as Lucky dragged him out of the Great Hall and along passage after passage. Eventually they reached a set of huge double doors dividing a wide stone wall.

"This way," Lucky said. He pushed open the doors and stepped outside.

Greg followed, eyes cast to the ground, but took only two steps before a thunderous clap erupted. Claws dug deep into his shoulder, and Rake rocketed into the shadows as only a shadowcat can, while Greg screamed and took in the scene, mouth agape.

"Greghart! Greghart! Greghart!"

No wonder no one was waiting inside. The Great Hall could hold only a thousand people or so, making it completely inadequate for today's crowd. At least ten times as many people were here—possibly everyone on Myrth. They clapped and hollered and cheered Greg's name again, and the deafening noise left Greg even more speechless than when his mouth had been clamped shut by Lucky's hand.

"Surprise," said Lucky.

Greg continued staring dumbly for several seconds until the cheers died away and his heart slowed to twice its normal rate.

"Say something," Lucky whispered out of the corner of his mouth.

"Oh . . . right. Uh . . . hi, then."

As one, the crowd whooped and hollered even louder. When the noise finally died away again, a beautiful girl in an elegant gown strode forward and regarded Greg with what might have been considered a smile from a greater distance. Greg observed the flowing red hair and recognized her immediately as the king's eldest daughter, Penelope.

"Welcome back," she told him rather flatly. Not exactly a warm welcome, but far friendlier than she'd ever offered before. Perhaps he'd stepped up a notch in her eyes when he'd rescued her sister, Priscilla, from the dragon last fall. Or, considering how the magicians had changed the time, just two weeks ago.

"Thank you, Your Highness," Greg answered meekly.

Penelope scowled. "Father asked me to inform you that he and Mother will come as soon as they are able. Oh, and Priscilla should be around here someplace, too."

"Er . . . thank you," Greg mumbled again.

"You are quite welcome," she replied stiffly.

With that, the princess turned and strode off through the crowd. Dozens of others rushed to take her place. Soon Greg found himself shaking hands with hundreds of men and accepting hugs from the women. He even kissed a baby or two before he learned to keep an eye out for them.

He had just paused to wipe a sticky handprint from his cheek when the noise fell to a hush. The crowd parted. Men dropped to one knee and women bowed as King Peter and Queen Pauline, both dressed in elegant magenta robes and sparkling, gem-encrusted crowns, glided up through the gap. The only one left standing was Greg. For the first time in his life, he felt uncomfortably tall. He stooped awkwardly, struggling with his head bowed to watch the king and queen approach, until King Peter, an enormous man who made even Manny Malice look small, reached him and used one hand to lift Greg's shoulders.

"Greghart, my boy, why are you bowing? It's just us, remember?"

"Sorry, Your Majesty," said Greg.

"Peter," the king reminded him.

"Greghart, my dear," said Queen Pauline in a soft, lilting voice. "How splendid to see you again. A shame it must always be under such dire circumstances." She smiled at him with warm blue eyes, and Greg had to admit she was pretty, even with the wisps of gray peeking through her otherwise red hair. "Did Penelope fill you in on all that is transpiring?"

"Not really. She said you'd be here soon. That was about it."

The queen frowned. "That girl, I swear . . ."

"Simon's made another prophecy," King Peter said.

"About the spirelings," interrupted Greg. "Lucky told me." Just off to his left, Lucky beamed proudly.

"Then I suppose he also told you about the three generals."

Greg shook his head.

"I didn't have time, Your Majesty," Lucky blurted, his cheeks reddening.

"Call me Peter, Lucky. No one around here is going to get it right until you, of all people, do."

Queen Pauline curled an arm around Lucky's shoulders and assured him he'd done nothing wrong, while the king turned back to Greg.

"I'm talking about Generals Hawkins, Talbout, and Bashar," King Peter said. "They're mentioned in the prophecy as well. All three are supposed to be fighting at your side during the upcoming battle, but that's about as much as we know. I've had my best men working on it for days, but . . . well, they just can't make a bit of sense out of Brandon's handwriting. Understanding the rest of the prophecy seems a lost cause at best."

Brandon, Greg knew, was the name of King Peter's scribe. Greg also knew Brandon had a drinking problem, so it wasn't surprising his handwriting might be hard to decipher, but there was one thing Greg didn't understand. "Why can't Brandon just *tell* you what it says?"

"He's not here," King Peter said, frowning.

Queen Pauline rolled her eyes at her husband's expression. "He's gone on holiday," she elaborated. "And he certainly deserves it. The man works so hard."

"Yes, well, we all work hard," said the king, "but he certainly picked a fine time to disappear, didn't he?"

"Brandon did not just disappear. He's been planning this trip for months. And we know where he is. He went to see his dear old mother in Pillsbury."

Those kneeling in the crowd had waited awkwardly to this point, but now apparently decided it would be all right to stand. Some even dared to press close—so close, Greg found them impossible to ignore. Even King Peter was forced to pause long enough to smile and shake a young woman's hand, although he did cleverly look away just as she was about to hand him her baby.

"So we know where Brandon is," he said to his wife. "That doesn't help us, does it? Pillsbury is over six hundred miles distant. By the time my runner gets to him and brings him home, at least five weeks will have passed. Holiday or not, I'm not sure we have that kind of time."

"But Lucky said Bart just got back with the prophecy a few days ago," Greg said, struggling to see past the huge baby one woman was thrusting out at him. Only on Myrth could a child be expected to grow into a head like that. "Brandon can't have been gone long. Won't your runner be able to overtake him sooner?"

"Ha. I'm all for taking a holiday," said King Peter, "but not for months at a time. No, Brandon didn't hike to Pillsbury. Mordred popped him there."

"The magician Mordred?"

"You know another Mordred who could pop a man across a kingdom?"

Greg breathed a nervous sigh. He didn't know many of the king's magicians, but he had an idea even if he did, Mordred would be his least favorite. The man considered Greg an impostor who should never have been brought to Myrth to slay the dragon Ruuan. Of course he was right, but it's not like Greg had *asked* for the job. And even if Mordred didn't have it out for him, if Greg were to choose an enemy, he'd want to make sure none of King Peter's magicians were among his choices.

"Why didn't you just have Mordred pop your runner to Pillsbury?" Greg asked.

"I'm afraid we couldn't do that," King Peter said. "It seems Mordred has disappeared too."

"Disappeared?" said Greg.

"Oh, not in the sense you're thinking. We just don't know where he is."

"Then why not have one of the other magicians do it?"

King Peter's face reddened. He lowered his voice, though with everyone crowded so close, they might have heard his thoughts before he spoke. "I'm afraid they don't know how."

Greg remembered his trip to the Infinite Spire last time he was here, when one of King Peter's magicians had moved the entire Army of the Crown halfway across the kingdom. "Agni knows."

"Agni isn't here either. And the others claim he and Mordred are the only two who can do it."

Only two magicians knew how to transport someone to another place? And both thought Greg was an impostor. And both were missing now, when Greg needed their help.

It had to be more than coincidence.

Greg had another thought. "Why not just have your magicians pop Brandon back here?"

Again, King Peter reddened. "I'm afraid they don't know how to do that, either."

"But they just brought *me* here," Greg argued.

"Yes, of course, but they already knew how to set up that spell. They did it once before, remember?"

As was often the case on Myrth, Greg felt the entire task of pointing out the obvious fell on his shoulders alone. "So how is this different?"

King Peter offered him a sympathetic look. "According to Mordred, the two spells aren't the same. The one they used for you is meant to move people here from distant worlds. To retrieve Brandon, we need something that will work on Myrth."

"Wait a minute. Are you saying Mordred was the one who set up the first spell?"

"Of course," said the king. "Why do you ask?"

"Because he hates me. Why would he help you bring me here?"

With a frown, King Peter placed a hand on both boys' shoulders and announced to the crowd that they should continue to enjoy themselves while he spoke to Greghart in private. "Don't worry," he said in answer to the countless groans that echoed through the courtyard, "I'll bring him back soon."

King Peter led the two boys back inside the castle and into a secluded, torchlit room. Queen Pauline stayed behind to entertain the crowd. The last Greg saw of her, she was smiling widely and reaching out to kiss her first baby.

"Mordred doesn't hate you," King Peter said once they were alone. "Why would you say that?"

"Because he hates me," said Greg.

"He does not."

"Yeah, he does," Lucky told the king. "He doesn't think Greg is the right Greghart from the prophecy."

"Nonsense. Mordred holds you in the highest regard, I can assure you. He's been a great help to me in all matters where prophesies are concerned."

"Yeah, well, then why isn't he here?" Greg asked. "And you never answered my question. Why would a portal that could open up anywhere and anytime in existence not be able to open on Myrth? Doesn't that sound suspicious?"

"Not at all," insisted the king. "It's hard for you and me to understand the intricacies involved in casting spells, but Mordred's one of the most skilled magicians this kingdom has ever known. I hold the utmost trust in his advice. Now, let's not waste time arguing. We have far bigger concerns, don't you think?"

"Yeah, like why Mordred has conveniently disappeared right when Greg needs him the most," mumbled Lucky.

King Peter frowned.

"And why, just before he left, he sent Brandon away so no one could ask him about the prophecy," Greg added.

"As my wife told you before, Brandon planned his trip for months. And I'm sure Mordred had a legitimate reason for leaving when he did. I think we have more important issues to work out."

Now it was Greg who frowned. The fact Mordred might be out to kill him seemed more important than most things *he* could think of.

"First off, there's the matter of the three generals," King Peter continued. "We know about Talbout. His troops left a couple of weeks ago to check out a disturbance near the border to the north. This morning I sent one of my runners to find him and turn him back, but the general has a good head start, and he commands nearly a thousand men. It could be months before he can bring them all back home.

"Then there's General Hawkins. He took his men south soon after you left—"

"Hawkins?" Greg interrupted, remembering the army captain who'd escorted him halfway across the kingdom to slay the dragon Ruuan. "Any relation to Ryder?"

"Oh, right, you don't know, do you? I promoted Captain Hawkins after his success in the recent prophecy."

"You're kidding?"

"No, why?"

"Oh . . . no reason." *Because Ryder didn't do anything,* Greg couldn't help thinking. True, the captain and his men had gone with Greg to the Infinite Spire to battle the spirelings, but Greg and Lucky had ended up sneaking into the spire on their own. Ryder and his men never fought off anything more threatening than a sunburn.

The king smiled, and in the same tone he used whenever he boasted to others about what a great hero Greg was, he added, "I can't think of anyone who deserved it more."

With a jerk, the door opened, and Princess Penelope stuck her head into the room. "Oh, there you are," she said, exasperated.

King Peter scowled. "What have I told you about knocking?"

"Sorry. Mom says everybody's wondering why you took Greghart away—I know, I can't see why she cares, either—but wait till you hear this. She wants you to bring him back."

"Tell her we'll be along in a moment," King Peter said. "Right now we have important matters to discuss."

Penelope crossed her arms over her chest. "What am I, a messenger?"

"*Penelope.*"

"Yes, Father, I'm going."

"Anyway," King Peter said after the door closed, "Ryder and his men headed south to rout out a band of trolls reported to have been terrorizing the locals near the bridge over to the Styx."

"Isn't this whole area the sticks?" Greg asked.

"Heavens no," said Princess Penelope, who had just stuck her head back into the room. "The Styx is a lovely area south of the kingdom where old people go to die."

"What are you still doing here?" her father asked.

"You haven't seen Prissy have you? Mom's looking for her, too."

"No. Now go. Please."

"All right. You don't have to yell." She slipped the door closed again, and this time the king waited to make sure she was truly gone.

"Okay, back to the matter at hand. The runner I sent for Brandon is to pick up Ryder and his men, too, but they've been gone about two weeks. He won't catch up before they reach the southern border and split off to the west. That means he'll have to wait until after he finds Brandon to hunt for the army. Honestly, I don't expect any of them back for close to two months."

"Two months?" Greg liked the idea that Ryder would be on his way back to help, but two months seemed a long time to wait, even if the months on Myrth did last only three weeks. Greg was reluctant to ask the one question pressing heaviest on his mind, but it was a big question, and the pressure proved unbearable in the end. "When am I supposed to . . . meet the spireling army?"

"We don't know exactly," admitted King Peter, "but I'm going to have to guess it will be at least a few weeks off, since that's the soonest all the key players could possibly get here."

"So you do think Ryder and this General Talbout will make it back in time?"

"If we can believe the prophecy, yes."

"If?" Greg felt sweat trickle down his back, all the way to his heels. He had been told that prophecies were fragile things, that if you stopped believing in them, even for a moment, they might not come true. Now here King Peter was, clearly having doubts, and well—even though Greg never really believed in prophecies, he'd at least feel better not believing in one that might be true rather than one guaranteed to get him killed.

"It's General Bashar who concerns me most," King Peter said in a somber tone.

"Why, where's he?" Greg asked.

"We don't know," said the king. "Truth is, I've never even heard of him."

"What?"

"Now don't worry, we're still working on it. As I told you before, we're having a bit of trouble deciphering Brandon's writing. It might not have been 'Bashar' at all. Maybe 'Dasher' or 'Bashire' or something. It's hard to tell."

"But don't you have just one other general in your army?" asked Lucky.

King Peter frowned. "Yes, General Stefanopolis. Brandon's writing is bad, but, well . . . we're just not sure what he was trying to say."

"So what are you going to do?" Greg asked.

"I'm already doing it. First, as I've told you, I sent a runner for Brandon and Ryder. Hopefully Brandon will return in time to tell us who we're dealing with. But in the meantime I've sent a tracker to find Bart, the bard, as well. He delivered the prophecy to us right before Brandon left on holiday, and if we can find him first, he should be able to shed some light on the situation for us. Maybe my magicians will need to open a portal to bring this General Bashar here from another world, as we did with you. I can't say. The real question is: Will we find out soon enough to get him and his men to the battle on time?"

"And if we don't?" Greg asked hesitantly.

The king wiped his palms on the rich cloth of his robe. "No need to bother ourselves with *what ifs*. Remember, we have the prophecy to back us up on this."

Greg caught himself rubbing his own palms on his jeans. He felt an overwhelming desire to run back to the courtyard, where he might find at least one person who had confidence he would survive the next few weeks.

As if reading Greg's thoughts, King Peter sighed and said, "Perhaps you boys should get back to the celebration. My wife is right. A lot of people have come to support you, Greghart, and you shouldn't disappoint them." He guided the boys to the door and opened it for them, but then paused and regarded them with a troubled expression.

"What's wrong?" Lucky asked.

What isn't? Greg wondered.

"Nothing," said the king, when he clearly meant *everything.* "I suggest you enjoy yourselves tonight while you can. Just put on a brave face and try not to worry too much about the prophecy. After all, there'll be plenty of time for that in the weeks to follow."

Greg and Lucky found Rake cowering in the courtyard, trying to protect his long tail from thousands of boots and heels. The shadowcat quickly leapt up to Greg's shoulders and hid under Greg's shirt. Unable to hide themselves the same way, Greg and Lucky were forced to endure nearly an hour at the celebration, dodging questions and graciously accepting praise for things they'd never done, before Princess Priscilla finally arrived to save them.

While all the ladies in attendance wore their most elegant gowns for the occasion, Priscilla wore a pair of torn pants over muddy boots. Her soiled tunic hung loosely off one shoulder, as if she'd recently survived a fight with a bobcat. Greg knew the princess well enough to know she might have done just that.

Much like her father, Priscilla held little interest in acting like royalty, but while she might not look like a princess, the others recognized her station and kept their distance.

"Are you listening to me?" she demanded.

Greg smiled. In spite of the horror of his predicament, he felt it was nearly worth the hardship of facing another prophecy to see Priscilla again. He suddenly realized he was staring. "Oh, sorry. You were saying?"

"I couldn't find out much—Brandon's writing is awful—but I did discover one thing."

"I would hope so," said Lucky. "You've been gone for hours."

Priscilla frowned. She and Lucky had a habit of rubbing each other the wrong way.

"Forget him," Greg said. "What did you find out?"

The princess glared at Lucky as she answered. "While everybody was busy struggling over this new prophecy, I got a peek at the last one."

"You're kidding," said Lucky.

"Well, I had to do *something* in all that time."

"I meant, why bother?"

"Come on, you guys," said Greg. "Tell us what you learned, Prissy."

"Priscilla," the princess snapped.

"Sorry."

"Oh, no, I'm sorry," she said, taking Greg's hand in her own. Greg had to admit, he liked her touch nearly as much as Kristin's, back home. "I didn't mean to snap. But this is really important. Everything Brandon wrote about Simon's last prophecy came true—the Molten Moor, and the stampede in Fey Field and the whole trip across the Smoky Mountains—all of it."

"Big deal," said Lucky. "We never doubted the prophecy was true."

"Speak for yourself," said Greg. "Remember, it said I was going to slay Ruuan."

"No, it didn't," said Priscilla. "That's what I'm trying to tell you. It said you were going to *sleigh* Ruuan."

"That's what I said."

"No, not slay, spelled *S-L-A-Y*," she explained. "Sleigh, spelled *S-L-E-I-G-H*. Simon knew the whole time that you weren't going to kill Ruuan."

"Or maybe Brandon just doesn't know how to spell," Lucky said, stifling a laugh.

"Oh, like you do?" Priscilla snapped.

Greg groaned. "Would you two stop? What are you trying to say, Priscilla?"

"Don't you see? Simon's last prophecy was exactly right. And now that he's made another, we should expect it will be right, too."

"I never expected it wouldn't be," Lucky replied smugly.

"No, you still don't understand," Priscilla said, effectively wiping the grin off Lucky's face. "It should be right, but it isn't."

"How's that?" both Lucky and Greg asked in unison.

"This new prophecy is about 'the Hero who slayed Ruuan.' That's slayed, *S-L-A-Y-E-D*, not sleighed, *S-L-E-I-G-H-E-D*."

"Shouldn't it be *slew*?" asked Lucky.

"But nobody slayed Ruuan," Greg argued.

Priscilla offered him her most exasperated look. "Exactly. That's what I've been trying to tell you. Simon's latest prophecy can't possibly be true."

Priscilla's Dis-Hart-ening Plan

Lucky's jaw fell slack. "This is horrible."

"No," said Greg, "this is great. If the prophecy is wrong, maybe now we won't need to fight the spirelings."

Priscilla shook her head. "Nobody except us knows it's wrong, and we can't say a word to anyone."

"Absolutely," said Lucky. "We can't have people thinking one of Simon's prophecies isn't true."

"But it isn't," Greg nearly shouted.

Priscilla and Lucky both looked up sharply to find several of the guests staring their way. The two smiled and chuckled as if Greg had just finished telling a good joke. Then each grabbed one of his arms and pulled him off to an isolated corner of the yard.

Priscilla had just started to scold him for his loose lips when Greg noticed a movement over her shoulder. It would have been hard to miss. It looked a lot like a fifty-foot-wide dragon trying to hide behind a twenty-foot-wide pillar.

Greg blinked, but the image didn't change. The dragon, an enormous beast that easily stood as tall as a football field was long, scampered on tiptoes to a closer column and peered out at the three of them.

Unless he was mistaken, Greg recognized this as Ruuan, the dragon he was supposed to have slain on his last visit to Myrth. Of course, Greg had never seen another dragon to make a decent comparison, but he had an idea he was probably right, especially since Ruuan had claimed to be the last of his kind, and because this dragon wasn't torching everything in sight.

The dragon leaned his ridged head above the gathered crowd and placed one heavily clawed finger over his enormous lips. ***"PSSST,"*** he whispered, rattling the courtyard enough to cause several punch glasses to topple over.

"Uh—ah—" Greg said, pointing at Ruuan.

Priscilla looked over her shoulder and then back again, puzzled. "What is it, Greg?"

"Yeah, what's wrong?" said Lucky. "You look like you've seen an ogre."

"But, the dragon—"

"What are you talking about?" asked Priscilla. She reached for Greg's forehead. "Are you feeling okay?"

Greg ducked her hand and stretched up to stare over Priscilla's shoulder, only to witness Ruuan peering out from behind the pillar again. The enormous dragon jumped into the open with a boom, waved his arms desperately to capture Greg's attention and then jumped back in behind the pillar.

What is Ruuan doing? He was supposed to be dead. If anyone saw him jumping about . . . well, even these people might get suspicious. The results could be disastrous. At least that's what everyone had said when Greg was on Myrth the first time. "Uh, could you excuse me a minute?"

As Greg edged past the princess and rushed toward the pillar, Ruuan turned and scampered out of the courtyard, creating a minor earthquake. It bothered Greg that no one else seemed to notice.

Outside the courtyard, the temperature dropped a full forty degrees. When Greg had left Myrth before, the cold weather was just settling in. Now two weeks had passed. While everything looked just as green as before, winter was clearly coming into its own. No doubt King Peter had asked his magicians to regulate the heat in the area of the celebration, but out here on the lawn, Greg needed to wrap his arms about his chest and jog to stay warm. Trembling footsteps echoed from the south. He set out in that direction.

Softer footsteps could be heard rushing up from behind.

"Where are you going?" Priscilla called out.

"Yeah, what's up, Greg?" Lucky said. "It's freezing out here."

Greg didn't bother answering. He suspected they would understand once they saw Ruuan for themselves. He found the dragon hiding unsuccessfully behind a tall tree near the edge of the Enchanted Forest.

"Ruuan, what are you doing? Someone will see you."

"SHHH." The dragon's head towered above the trees as he strained to see if anyone had heard. Then his neck swung downward, until his enormous face blocked Greg's view of the entire forest behind him.

"Ruuan," Lucky and Priscilla both shouted. "Where did you come from?"

"KEEP IT DOWN. IF I USE TOO MUCH MAGIC, THE KING'S MAGICIANS MAY SENSE MY PRESENCE."

"But what are you doing here?" Greg asked again.

"I CAME TO WARN YOU ABOUT THE SPIRELINGS. THEY'VE BEEN AMASSING OUTSIDE MY SPIRE FOR WEEKS. I FEAR THEY WILL SOON MARCH UPON THE CASTLE."

"We already know," Priscilla told him. "Simon's come out with another prophecy."

"I KNOW ABOUT SIMON," said Ruuan, **"BUT YOU MUST KNOW . . ."** The dragon hesitated. His head surged above the trees to scan for eavesdroppers, then sank again. Greg's stomach heaved. He wished Ruuan would quit doing that. **"THE PROPHECY IS . . . WELL, IT'S . . . WRONG,"** the dragon finished. **"*SHHHH.*"**

"We didn't say anything," Priscilla argued. "You did."

"We already know about the prophecy being wrong, too," Greg informed Ruuan. "It's supposed to be about the one who slayed you, but obviously that can't be right . . ."

"YES, THAT WOULD BE *SLEW.*"

"No, I mean because you're still alive."

"Unless Greg's supposed to . . ." began Lucky, but Ruuan stifled him with a jet of scalding steam strategically aimed inches above the boy's head. "Uh, never mind."

"WE SHOULDN'T BE DISCUSSING THIS HERE. I ONLY CAME SO I COULD TELL YOU TO ASK YOUR KING TO LEND YOU HIS AMULET. IF YOU GIVE IT TO THE SPIRELINGS TONIGHT, THAT SHOULD STOP THEM FROM ATTACKING UNTIL WE CAN LOCATE THEIRS."

"What are you talking about?" Greg asked. "What happened to the spirelings' amulet?"

"IT DISAPPEARED THE DAY YOU CAME TO MY LAIR. THEY'VE BEEN UNABLE TO LIVE IN THE SPIRE SINCE, BUT NOT UNTIL RECENTLY DID THEY DISCOVER EVIDENCE SUGGESTING WHAT HAPPENED TO IT. SOON THEY WILL COME FOR RETRIBUTION."

"What evidence?" Greg asked.

"IT SEEMS THEY FOUND A BOOK INSIDE THEIR TUNNELS . . . SOMETHING OF YOURS, AS I UNDERSTAND IT."

"My journal," said Greg, remembering the book of fabricated adventures he'd lost on his last visit to this world.

"AT FIRST THEY THOUGHT THE BOOK PROVED THAT THE SMALL BOY THEY'D SEEN IN THEIR TUNNEL WAS JUST A VERY TALENTED THIEF WHO HAD MANAGED TO SEPARATE THE MIGHTY GREGHART FROM HIS JOURNAL.

"BUT THEN, WHEN THEY CONSIDERED THE THIEF'S MIRACULOUS DEFEAT OF TWO OF THEIR WARRIORS, THEY COULD COME TO ONLY ONE POSSIBLE CONCLUSION. THE SMALL BOY COULD BE NONE OTHER THAN THE MIGHTY GREGHART HIMSELF—DISGUISED BY POWERFUL MAGIC, OF COURSE."

"That's ridiculous," said Lucky.

"It sure is," said Priscilla, "and it doesn't explain why they want to attack Daddy's castle."

"BECAUSE THEY KNOW FROM THE LAST PROPHECY THAT KING PETER WAS THE ONE RESPONSIBLE FOR BRINGING YOUNG GREGHART HERE. THEY CAN ONLY ASSUME HE DID SO WITH THE INTENTION OF STEALING THEIR AMULET."

"I can't believe this," said Priscilla. "It's not our fault. Greg put the amulet back."

"Yeah," said Lucky. "I saw him place it in the alcove with my own eyes."

"I DO NOT QUESTION THE FACT THAT GREGHART RETURNED THE AMULET. BUT STILL IT SEEMS IT DISAPPEARED AGAIN SHORTLY THEREAFTER. THAT IS WHY WE NEED TO GET THE OTHER AMULET FROM YOUR KING. IT IS THE ONLY WAY TO APPEASE THE SPIRELINGS."

"Then we're in real trouble," said Lucky. The dragon shot him a displeased look—never a good look on a dragon.

"He's right," said Priscilla. "Because Daddy's amulet is missing, too."

"THIS DOES NOT PLEASE ME," Ruuan said, stroking his chin with a claw twice as long as Greg. **"NOW WE MUST HUNT UP ONE OF THE OTHER TWO."**

Greg knew from his last visit to Myrth that there were four identical amulets in all. He had held each in his hand at one time or another. If the spirelings' amulet was gone, and so was King Peter's, that left only two: one belonging to Marvin Greatheart, the most popular dragonslayer on Myrth, and one owned by Witch Hazel, a horrible hag with dark powers who lived at the center of the Shrieking Scrub. "I recommend we get Marvin Greatheart's," he quickly suggested.

"A WISE CHOICE," said Ruuan. **"HOP ON MY SHOULDERS. I WILL FLY US THERE AT ONCE."**

Greg strained to catch a glimpse of the dragon's shoulders amidst the dark silhouette of trees. "Um . . ."

"We can't go to Marvin's now," said Lucky.

"He's right," Priscilla said. "They're throwing a party in the courtyard for Greg this very moment. Mom would be mad if she knew we'd been gone even this long."

"And the king is expecting to see us off on our journey in the morning," said Lucky. "He told me that according to the prophecy we'd leave by the same route as before. That means we'll need to start off through the Enchanted Forest."

"Maybe we *should* go now," Greg blurted. The last time he'd ventured into the Enchanted Forest, he'd barely escaped with his life. "I mean, we know the prophecy is wrong anyway."

"NO, YOUR LITTLE FRIENDS ARE RIGHT," said Ruuan. **"EVEN THOUGH IT SEEMS THE PROPHECY IS WRONG, YOU MUST FOLLOW IT TO THE LETTER. UNFORTUNATELY, I WON'T BE ABLE TO HELP. THE FOREST PATHS ARE TOO NARROW FOR ME."**

"Wait, I have an idea," said Priscilla. "Ruuan, go back to your lair for tonight, then come back and wait for us at the arena in the morning, okay? We'll meet you as soon as we can."

At first Ruuan didn't look as if he appreciated a human telling him what to do, but once Priscilla shared her plan, the dragon did as she suggested and took to the air, bending some of the closer trees under the buffeting wind stirred beneath his wings.

Greg struggled to keep his feet. Then he thought of returning to the castle, and his legs finally failed him. How was he supposed to smile and nod for the crowd when they all expected him to champion their army in the upcoming battle against the entire spireling race?

"Well, here we are again," said King Peter.

He stood before Greg and Lucky on the manicured castle lawn at the edge of the Enchanted Forest, where a large crowd watched from a polite distance. Greg shifted his weight from foot to foot. The morning air hung colder than yesterday, even though he now wore a heavy gray cloak draped over a drab tunic and tights that Lucky had provided for him.

Lucky, too, wore a heavy cloak over his usual bright orange tunic and tights, although his cloak was an even brighter orange, suitable for scaring away monsters. Underneath he carried a pack slung over one shoulder, putting Greg in mind of a flamboyant hunchback.

"I said, 'here we are again,'" the king repeated.

"Oh, right," said Greg. "I'm afraid so."

"Why so pensive, Greghart?" said Queen Pauline, who stood at her husband's side. "You should be an old hand at this by now."

Greg attempted to match her smile, but his heart wasn't in it.

King Peter leaned close. "I'm afraid I have no amulet to give you this time, and Bart isn't even here to send you off with a song."

"Oh, that's okay," Greg said. Bart was a traveling bard who enjoyed writing ghastly ballads, all of which involved Greg narrowly escaping mutilation in one fashion or another. He doubted the musician had written anything he'd want to hear at the best of times, let alone just before stepping into a forest where the trees were known to funnel travelers straight into the awaiting jaws of ogres, and worse. "Do we even know where we're supposed to go this time?"

King Peter frowned. "Sorry. All we're certain of is that you will be starting off at this point. Beyond that, well . . . I was hoping you might have some ideas."

Greg matched King Peter's frown. If he had to do this—and by the looks on everyone's faces, it appeared he did—he'd at least like to have a plan. "We thought we'd start off by going to Marvin Greatheart's to get his amulet."

"A splendid idea." He offered Greg a wink. "You should probably bring back Marvin, too."

"Why? Is he mentioned in the prophecy?"

"With Brandon's writing, it's hard to tell, but if we take a lesson from the past, well, those Greathearts always seem to have their role to play."

Princess Penelope stood at her mother's side. She stepped forward now and offered her own frown. Greg probably wouldn't have recognized her if she'd used any other expression. "Good luck," she said, the way one might say, "Nice weather," or, "Pass the catsup."

"What about you?" King Peter said to Priscilla, who also stood by her mother's side. "Aren't you going to say good-bye to the boys?"

"Oh, right." Priscilla scurried forward and, after a quick wink at Greg, performed a melodramatic farewell that rivaled anything Greg had ever seen at the movies.

King Peter eyed his daughter suspiciously. "Are you finished?"

"Yes, yes. They can go now. If they must."

"Very well," said the king hesitantly. "Then I suppose it's time these men were off."

As Lucky and Greg moved closer to the edge of the Enchanted Forest, the leaves began to rustle and pull back, revealing a wide path that extended as far as the eye could see. Clearly the forest was anxious to lure them inside, and even though Greg had witnessed the sight before, he found it about as inviting as a quiet evening alone with Manny Malice.

Lucky, however, was clearly eager to go. Boldly he stepped into the forest, prompting the crowd to clap and cheer. Greg followed, though perhaps less boldly. Still, the crowd's reaction was no less exuberant. For the sake of those who'd come to honor him, Greg tried his best not to cringe as the trees slithered back across the entrance, cutting off his only avenue of escape.

The first thing Greg did was scan the ground for a good walking stick. On his last visit to Myrth, he and Lucky had traveled with a mysterious man named Nathaniel Caine, who had used a staff as a focal point for his meditation. After returning to his own world, Greg had taken to carrying a stick with him wherever he went, though the teachers wouldn't allow it at school, and his mother wasn't too crazy about him bringing yard debris into the house. He spotted a branch about the right size and picked it up, but dropped it rather quickly when the wood snaked up his arm and slapped him across the cheek.

"Ow," Greg said, backing away. "It hit me." He eyed the branch as it slithered away. "What do we do now?"

"Sit and wait, I guess." Lucky settled onto a nearby log. "Want a snack?"

"We just had breakfast."

"What's your point?"

Greg shrugged. "What do you have?"

Lucky dug through his pack. He found a large fruit pie, handed it to Greg and started looking for something for himself.

"How long will we have to hang out here?" Greg asked. Rake peeked out from under Greg's cloak to investigate the food, and Greg fed him a small bite of pie.

"Just till everyone outside the castle goes home," said Lucky. "Priscilla will let us know when the coast is clear."

"Well, I hope it's not long. This place gives me the creeps."

Lucky happened across a second, larger pie within the folds of his pack and pulled it out, along with a gleaming sword that was easily four times longer than the bag that held it. He used the sword to cut a small slice of pie, which he then stuffed back into his pack along with the magic sword before he started gnawing on the rest.

"Relax, Greg, we're perfectly safe here. As long as we don't make the mistake of following this trail deeper into the forest, we shouldn't run into any trouble."

Greg would have liked to believe Lucky, but when a sudden roar echoed down the path, shaking the trees and rustling bushes, he started to have doubts. Rake abandoned his bite of pie and shot down inside Greg's tunic, justifying his name with the series of claw marks he left across Greg's chin.

"What was that?" Greg asked.

"Not sure," said Lucky, "but don't worry. I'm betting we'll know soon enough."

Again a roar shook the air, so loud Greg thought the forest was crashing in on him. "Lucky, what should we do?"

"This doesn't change anything. We still have to wait."

Greg wasn't content to sit idly by while anything that could make that much noise made its way closer. "Give me that sword."

With a sigh, Lucky retrieved the magic sword from his pack and handed it to Greg. "Good luck. Don't go far with that thing. We might need it."

This time the roar toppled one of the smaller trees, nearly flattening the two boys. Thinking he was being attacked, Greg swatted at the trunk. The tree grunted and swatted back. Before the battle could build further, a boom sounded deep within the woods. Greg jumped at the sound.

"Did you hear that? Sounds like something exploded."

Lucky shook his head. "Not an explosion, Greg. A footstep."

A second boom shook the forest, and Greg tried not to think about the foot that might cause such a sound. He tried not to think about the third and fourth explosions as well, but the next three were hard to ignore, as they were quickly growing closer, and each was accented by the reverberating boom of trees crashing to the ground.

"Hmm," said Lucky.

"What?" Greg cried. "What is it?"

"Nothing really. Just a giant."

"A giant. Lucky, we've got to get out of here."

"Relax, Greg, no giant's going to notice us way down here . . . Of course, you might want to watch for falling trees." At precisely that moment a three-hundred-foot-tall timber dropped from the sky with a boom. Its tip vibrated to a stop just inches from Lucky's nose. Lucky offered Greg the briefest of smiles. "See what I mean?"

Greg froze with his chin pointed at the sky. One thing that amazed him about Myrth, aside from Lucky's annoyingly carefree attitude, was that the trees there grew three to four times taller than they did back home. Now, as he stared at the imposing figure hovering above him, it bothered him that anything could peer over those treetops without at least having to stand on tiptoes.

He screamed then, louder than he'd ever screamed in his life. Luckily it wasn't loud enough to capture the attention of a giant. The creature took two crashing steps forward and stopped just short of the edge of the forest.

Greg exhaled shakily as he contemplated the two enormous toes rising high on either side of him. Surely he'd have fainted dead away if the trees hadn't pulled back at that instant, revealing a bright green patch of castle lawn.

Princess Priscilla stood in the center of the gap. "What's with all the racket?" she said, apparently too close to the giant to notice. "Come on. The coast is clear."

The Agreement

Morning was already waning before Greg, Lucky and Priscilla reached the arena where Priscilla had asked Ruuan to wait. Greg recognized it as the spot where families had gathered for a celebration last time he was here. In front of him stood the dais where Princess Penelope, or at least an image of her, had waited for Ruuan to swing by and carry her off to his lair. Just behind the dais, Ruann—his scales shining brilliantly blue-and-gold—lay in the center of the arena. Most of him, anyway. His tail actually extended to the edge of the clearing, and then about another fifty feet into the surrounding forest.

"ANY PROBLEMS?" Ruuan asked.

"Nah," answered Lucky.

Greg would have disagreed, had he been able to find his voice.

"THEN WE SHOULD GET MOVING BEFORE SOMEONE HAPPENS ALONG."

"Wait," said Lucky, "you're not going to fly in broad daylight, are you?"

"I'M AFRAID I HAVE NO CHOICE." Ruuan crawled to his feet and stretched his legs, towering high above the tallest trees. **"WE DON'T HAVE MUCH TIME."**

"But someone might see you."

"DO NOT WORRY. MY MAGIC SHOULD KEEP THEM FROM NOTICING, AND ONCE WE'RE IN THE AIR, I SHOULDN'T NEED EVEN THAT. IF I FLY AS HIGH AS I AM ABLE, I DOUBT ANYONE WILL BE CAPABLE OF SEEING. BESIDES, I MUST FINISH THIS AND BE BACK AT MY LAIR BY NOON."

Greg looked at the sky. "But," he finally managed to say, "that can't be long from now."

"Yeah," said Lucky, "why so soon?"

Ruuan looked somewhat annoyed over the question—not a good look on a dragon. **"IF YOU MUST KNOW, I HAVE A MEETING TO ATTEND."**

"Who would want to go meet a dragon?" Priscilla asked, peeking up at Ruuan through the raised collar of her heavy cloak. The lime-green fabric was as gaudy as any Greg had ever seen, but he preferred it to the monster-colored fur she had worn last time they traveled together. "Oh, no offense, Ruuan," Priscilla added.

The dragon scowled. **"I MUST NOT SAY, NOR AM I SURE WHAT THE MEETING IS ABOUT, JUST THAT ALL OF OUR FATES MAY DEPEND UPON IT."**

"Then we better make sure you get back in time," Greg said.

Ruuan nodded. He stooped so the three of them could board, but even so, it was like expecting them to scale a fifty-foot rock wall. In the end he helped them each up in turn by wrapping his serpentine tongue around their waists and hauling them off their feet.

"Yuck," cried Priscilla at the stench.

"You should be thankful he's letting you ride up here instead of in his mouth," Greg said, remembering the time Ruuan carried him down the long, spiraling tunnel out of the Infinite Spire.

"And you should both be glad we're riding on top rather than underneath," Lucky added, obviously recalling how he'd barely survived being dragged out of the same tunnel while pinned beneath Ruuan's belly.

When everyone was in place between the golden spikes protruding from atop Ruuan's neck, Ruuan took to the sky with a single flap of his giant, leathery wings. The dragon glanced over one scaly shoulder to see that he hadn't lost anyone, then soared upward at blinding speed, rising higher and higher, until he shot into the clouds and out the other side. The only time Greg had been as high was when his family had flown to visit his grandmother in Florida. How much less intimidating it had seemed, being safely buckled inside a plane.

"So Greg," Lucky said, "what have you been up to since you left?"

Greg felt Lucky had no right to sound calm under the circumstances, but talking might help take his mind off his troubles. He started by telling of his immediate encounter with Manny Malice and Kristin Wenslow when he reappeared in the woods behind his house.

Lucky laughed when Greg described how he'd used his chikan training to sweep Manny's legs out from under him. Priscilla, on the other hand, did not seem as pleased.

"Who is this Kristin Wenslow?" she asked, the pitch of her voice far higher than usual.

Greg's face reddened. "Kristin? Oh, she's . . . just a girl . . ."

"I see," said Priscilla. She took to brooding for several seconds. Then just when Greg thought it safe to return to his story, the princess surprised him by blurting out again. "I suppose this Kristin girl wears all sorts of frilly dresses and things and behaves like a proper lady."

"What? Oh . . . ah . . . sometimes, I guess."

"I see," Priscilla repeated. She returned to brooding, and Greg was unsure whether to speak or not for fear of setting her off again.

"WE'RE HERE," Ruuan announced. He descended through the clouds as quickly as he'd risen, leaving Greg's stomach several thousand feet in the air.

"What?" said Lucky. "We just left."

"NONSENSE," said the dragon, dropping through a break in the trees and alighting as softly as a feather. **"IT HAS BEEN NEARLY A MINUTE."**

Greg scanned the area. True to his word, Ruuan had set them down just in front of the run-down hovel where Marvin Greatheart and his family lived, clear on the other side of the Enchanted Forest from Pendegrass Castle.

"I'LL JUST LIE FLAT AND HIDE WHILE YOU TALK TO THE ADVENTURER," Ruuan said as Greg and the others hiked across his back and down his tail to the ground. **"COME GET ME WHEN YOU ARE THROUGH. AND PLEASE DON'T DALLY."**

Greg seriously doubted Ruuan could hide just by lying flat. He thought it unlikely anyone who glanced this way would overlook what appeared to be a new mountain range to the east. Even so, he knew better than to argue with a dragon.

Luckily, both Marvin Greatheart, the greatest dragonslayer on Myrth, and his little brother, Melvin, already knew Ruuan hadn't been slain by Greg. But their parents were a different matter. Greg suspected that neither Edna Greatheart nor her husband, Norman, would approve of the course that Simon's first prophecy had taken.

Then again, according to Priscilla, that prophecy had been completely accurate. Still, Greg suspected it would be difficult to get the Greathearts to agree.

"Hullo," Lucky called. "Anyone home?"

Within seconds, Edna opened the door and stepped out onto the walk. Greg quickly sidled in front of her, as if he could possibly block her view of Ruuan.

"Greghart. What are *you* doing here?" Before Greg could even say hello, the woman turned her back on him and shouted into the house. "Norman, come see who's here."

Out from the shack wafted a deep, rumbling groan, which Greg recognized as the sound of Norman Greatheart struggling off the couch. Edna turned back to Greg. She clamped her hands over his cheeks and stared into his eyes, as if greeting her long-lost son, and then dragged him inside, leaving Lucky and Priscilla alone on the walkway. The two of them shrugged and followed.

Inside, Norman Greatheart shuffled over to where his wife stood fawning over Greg. Although now retired, Norman had once been a great dragonslayer like his son, which explains why he wore a patch over one eye and walked as though each bone in his body were waging war with all the others to be the last to cross the room. His jaw popped loudly as his mouth drew itself into a smile.

"Greghart, what brings you back to Myrth?"

"Another prophecy," Priscilla answered for him.

"Princess Priscilla," Edna said, as if noticing her for the first time. "Oh, and Lucky Day, too." She pointed at a threadbare sofa that took up half the room, even though it was the smallest sofa Greg had ever seen. "Welcome, both of you. Come, have a seat."

"Simon's made another prophecy?" said Norman. He staggered back to the sofa and dropped into it much the way an old building eventually drops into a pile of rubble. "Why haven't I heard?"

"It's rather new," said Greg, moving nearer. While it looked as though he was trying to hear Mr. Greatheart better, he was really just making it possible for Lucky and Priscilla to come in out of the cold. The room was that small. "King Peter just found out about it a few days ago."

"Yes, well, news does travel a bit slowly this way, now that people quit traveling the Enchanted Forest so much."

"People used to travel through the Enchanted Forest?" Greg asked, amazed. He shuffled further forward, bumping into the couch so Mrs. Greatheart would have room to close the door.

"Before it was enchanted, yes," said Norman.

"You mean it wasn't always?" Priscilla said. "Daddy never mentioned that."

"Heavens no, child" said Norman. "Hazel just cast that spell of hers about twenty years ago."

"The witch, Hazel?" Lucky asked.

Edna squeezed by him on her way to the kitchen. "Well, the only other Hazel I know is Hazel Biffington, and I can't see her enchanting a forest."

"But why?" Greg asked.

Edna laughed. "Why would she want to?"

"Privacy," said Norman. He blinked his good eye. "Hazel used to live at Pendegrass Castle until she had some sort of falling-out with the folks there. Not sure what happened, but she was madder than a wounded griffin when she left. Took up that spot of hers in the Sunshine Shrub and—"

"You mean the Shrieking Scrub," Greg corrected.

"What? Oh, sure, now, but then . . . quite a pleasant place really, before Hazel took up residence there and started practicing her magic. Now she's got her life, and the castle folk have theirs, and to be sure the two never mix she's got her Enchanted Forest and the Molten Moor to keep things separate."

"Don't tell me Hazel's responsible for the Molten Moor, too?" Priscilla asked.

"You mean the Miracle Marsh," Edna called from the kitchen. "That used to be such a lovely place, too."

"Still is," said Lucky.

Greg groaned. Only Lucky could enjoy negotiating the sea of molten rock that surrounded the Shrieking Scrub where Hazel lived. Greg was sure he wouldn't have liked the place even if the paths between lava pools hadn't shifted positions while he was trying to cross them.

"So, tell us about this new prophecy," Norman said to Greg. "Are you going to slay another dragon? I didn't think there were any left."

From the back room stepped Norman's eldest son, Marvin, dressed in a loincloth and carrying a battle-worn sword. His bronzed muscles rippled like a sail sheeting in a heavy wind, even after he stopped to regard the company. That, along with his curly blond hair, crystal-blue eyes and square jaw, caused Priscilla to release a quiet whimper. He gave a curt nod and called toward the kitchen.

"Mum, have you seen my amulet?"

"It's in the cabinet where it always is," Edna replied.

"No, it's not. I checked twice and looked everywhere else, too. It's not here."

Greg, Priscilla and Lucky all exchanged concerned glances. "*Your* amulet is missing too?" Greg said.

"Why *too?*" asked Norman, his neck crackling like a string of firecrackers as he craned his head toward Greg.

"Daddy's amulet disappeared a few days ago," Priscilla said. "He thinks someone stole it."

"You mean that other amulet Greghart had with him last time we met?" Norman's head pivoted back with a chorus of creaks and pops to meet her two eyes with his one. "Why would anyone want that?"

Priscilla skillfully transformed a grimace into a smile. "We don't know."

"Well, I must say, that is quite a coincidence."

"Now, before you go jumping to conclusions . . ." said Edna. She drifted over to the rickety old cabinet along the far wall, pulled open the drawer and rummaged inside for several seconds. "It's gone."

"Told you so," said Marvin.

"Not so fast. Melvin," Edna called.

Greatheart's little brother trudged into the room. Though no less than two years younger than Greg, Melvin already stood as tall. He was too young to possess Marvin's muscular physique, but he sported the same blond hair and blue eyes, and his jaw, while slightly rounded, showed a lot of promise. He was deep in thought until he spotted Greg.

"What's *he* doing here?"

"Hush, boy," said Norman. "Greghart's our guest."

"Have you been playing with your brother's amulet again?" Edna asked.

"Haven't seen it," Melvin answered. He glowered at Greg. "Maybe he took it."

"Melvin," Edna scolded. "We'll have none of that."

Marvin placed his hands on his hips. "Mum, I need that amulet."

"Well, don't blame me. I wasn't the one who lost it. Okay, we'll all just have to pitch in and look. I'm sure it's around here someplace."

But try as they might, they could not locate the amulet anywhere. Exhausted, Greg plopped down in one of the kitchen chairs, which just happened to also be one of the living-room chairs. Though grateful for the break, he was struck by a sudden thought.

"Ruuan."

"Ah," said Norman, "still having nightmares about your battle with the dragon, are you? Well, don't worry." He rubbed his patched eye. "The bad dreams will go away in ten or twenty years."

"No," said Greg, "it's not that . . . it's just . . . oh, never mind. Could you excuse me? I need to go outside a minute."

"Is something wrong, dear?" said Edna. "Are you feeling okay? You look a bit flushed."

"I'm fine," Greg assured her. He looked to Priscilla for help.

"Oh," she said, struggling for an excuse to help him slip away. "Ah . . . weren't you supposed to bring in my backpack?"

"You're wearing your backpack," Melvin observed.

"What? Oh, no, that's Lucky's backpack."

"He has one on too."

"Did I say Lucky?" Priscilla chuckled nervously. "I meant Greg. He's got mine and I've got his."

Greg took advantage of the distraction to slip out and run to where Ruuan lay as flat as possible in the field outside, nearly blocking out the midday sun.

"WHERE HAVE YOU BEEN?" the dragon scolded. **"I NEED TO GET BACK."**

"Sorry," said Greg. "We've been looking for Greatheart's amulet. I think it's lost, too."

"THREE AMULETS MISSING? THIS DOES NOT BODE WELL."

"Not if you're going to suggest we go ask Witch Hazel for hers."

"THE WITCH WOULD NEVER GIVE HERS UP FREELY. AND EVEN MY MAGIC IS NOT STRONG ENOUGH TO TAKE IT FROM HER IN HER OWN LAIR. I KNOW NOT WHAT WE CAN DO, BUT THIS WILL HAVE TO WAIT. I HAVE MY MEETING TO ATTEND. I SHOULDN'T BE GONE LONG. PERHAPS YOU SHOULD KEEP LOOKING. I'LL TRY TO RETURN FOR YOU ONCE MY BUSINESS HAS CONCLUDED."

"Okay," said Greg. "You should probably go before someone notices you." He glanced at the Greathearts' shack to see if anyone was watching, then turned back to say good-bye, but Ruuan had already leapt to the sky. "Good-bye then," Greg mumbled, just before the rush of air knocked him off his feet.

"Where's Priscilla's knapsack?" Edna asked when Greg made his way back inside.

"What? Oh. Uh, she must have left it back at the castle."

"Sorry," Priscilla jumped in, "I could have sworn I brought it with me."

"Maybe that's because you have one on your back," Melvin pointed out helpfully.

"Yeah, maybe."

"Mum," cried Marvin, "I've got to go. What am I going to do about my amulet?" In his desperation he searched the same areas everyone had covered earlier.

"Well, don't yell at your mother," Norman scolded. "Maybe next time you'll be more careful with your things."

"Where are you going?" Greg asked Marvin.

The dragonslayer paused in his search and met Greg's eye. "To the southern border of the kingdom. We've had reports of trolls amassing out that way."

"And you're going anyway?"

Marvin laughed. "That's *why* I'm going. Someone needs to rout them out, send them back under their bridges where they belong."

"Didn't King Peter say he sent Ryder and his troops down south to clear up those trolls?" Lucky asked Greg.

Marvin grunted. "Well, last I heard, Ryder Hawkins commanded only five hundred men. I'm sure they'll appreciate it if I go down there and handle things for them. Hey, maybe I lost the amulet when I wrestled that wyvern last week. I'll bet I dropped it on the trail."

Greg shook his head. "I doubt it. I'll bet this all has to do with the prophecy."

"There's been another prophecy?" Marvin said. "Why wasn't I informed?"

"It just happened," said Priscilla. "Besides, I don't think it mentions you at all. It just talks about Greg here."

"No," Greg corrected, "it talks about the Hero who slayed Ruuan."

"But no one slay—" Marvin said before his little brother had the foresight to kick him. Though the tactic worked, Melvin paid dearly for the effort. He screamed so loudly, dust drifted down from the ceiling. Tears welled in his eyes as he grabbed his toes and rubbed them.

"What'd you do that for, you little brat?" Marvin snapped, and for emphasis punched Melvin's shoulder, launching him across the shack.

"Boys," Edna shouted.

"What are you talking about, Greghart?" said Norman. "You *are* the Hero who slayed Ruuan."

"Of course I am," Greg said, forcing a chuckle. "I just meant it didn't mention me by name. And it also doesn't say I'm going to work alone. King Peter thinks I should bring Marvin along."

"I'll bet you'd like that, wouldn't you?" said Melvin.

"Now, Melvin," his mother scolded, "that's not polite."

"No, he's right," said Greg. "They say there's no one on Myrth who knows more about fighting than Marvin."

The dragonslayer shoved the sideboard closed and abandoned his search. "What is it you're supposed to do?"

"He's going to fight the spirelings," Lucky answered.

"Oh? That could be fun."

"And my dad's army is going to help," Priscilla added.

Edna stepped over to the counter to stir a huge steaming pot. "That should even up the odds a bit," she called over her shoulder.

Norman started to laugh, but then stopped abruptly and held his ribs, a pained expression on his face. "I wouldn't count on it. There's never been a kingdom army that could stand a chance against the spirelings. We've got no more than a couple thousand men against hundreds of thousands of them. And I'd guess we'd have a battle on our hands even if the odds were reversed."

Greg felt his stomach twist. "Then how am I supposed to survive?"

"Does the prophecy actually say you'll survive?"

"Melvin . . ." Mrs. Greatheart warned.

"I didn't say it, Marvin did."

Greg gulped and looked to Priscilla, who shrugged. Melvin crawled to his feet, noticed Greg's expression and snickered quietly enough that his mother didn't hear.

"Oh my. Maybe you *should* help him, Marvin," Edna suggested.

The dragonslayer nodded. "I suppose I could. But I still need to rout out those trolls first. Say, I'll tell you what, Greghart. If you want to come along and help me with the trolls, I'll help you with the spirelings when I'm done, okay?"

"Oh, I don't know. We need to get back."

Priscilla stood staring at the dragonslayer with a glazed-over expression. "Hang on, Greg. Just how long would this little side trip take?" she asked Marvin.

He thought a moment. "Would you want to go the quick way or the safe way?"

"The safe way," said Greg.

"The quick way," Lucky said, drowning him out.

Greg scowled at Lucky. "We're not that pressed for time. King Peter said he didn't expect the spirelings to attack for at least a few weeks."

"Well, the safe way's out, then," said Marvin. "Do you still have that eternal torch you got from Witch Hazel last fall?"

Lucky checked his pack and verified he had remembered the torch. "Great. The quick way it is."

"Maybe this isn't a good idea," said Greg. "We should head back. We never got Marvin's amulet, and we still need time to come up with a plan."

"We can do that on the trail, can't we?" suggested Priscilla. "We could really use Marvin's help. Even King Peter said so."

"I suppose," said Greg. He turned back to Marvin. "But I don't know anything about routing out trolls."

"What's to know?" said Marvin. "They swing a club at your head. You duck. Anyone with half a mind knows that."

Melvin snorted. "Anyone who doesn't might end up with half a head."

"Melvin," his mother scolded, "I'm not going to warn you again."

"So, what do you say, Greghart?" Marvin asked. "We got a deal?"

Greg really felt he had no choice. It was a feeling he'd come to expect on Myrth. "Okay, let's do this."

Marvin smiled, and with none of the face crackling Greg had come to associate with the dragonslayer's father. "We best get going. Amulet or not, I shouldn't be dallying around here."

"Nonsense," said Edna. "It's noon now. You'll eat first. Then you can go."

"But Mum—"

"Uhp," she said, cutting him off in an instant. "You have weeks to finish your little errand. Sit yourself down. I'll have lunch on the table in a minute."

Clearly the Mighty Greatheart knew better than to argue with his mother. He and the others moved to the table, and true to her word, Edna had a meal in front of them in a minute. It just wasn't the minute immediately following her promise. Still she was a great cook, and Greg finished off everything she placed before him, except one small portion he squirreled away for Rake. Soon the food was gone, and it was time to hit the trail.

"I want to go too," whined Melvin.

His mother dismissed the notion with a wave. "You're too young to be out fighting trolls."

"But Mawwwm . . ."

"It's okay, Mum," said Marvin. "I'll watch after him."

"Oh, I don't know . . ."

"Pleeeeease?" said Melvin.

"You won't let him out of your sight?" Edna said, staring into her eldest son's eyes.

Marvin shook his head and winked at his younger brother. "Not for a minute."

"Very well. I suppose it'll be okay," Edna said, though her face indicated she clearly didn't think it would be.

"Yeah!" Melvin shot Greg a smug look, as if he'd just won some sort of duel. Odd, because while Melvin had once set out to kill Greg to stop him from interfering in the last prophecy, the younger boy had eventually given up his plotting, so Greg no longer found him nearly as annoying. He really didn't care if the boy came along or not.

"Well, gather your things," said Marvin. "We need to hit the trail."

Melvin beamed even brighter than the sunlight that peeked in through the many holes scattered about the ceiling. "This is great. I can't wait to see the Mighty Greghart go up against his first band of trolls."

"You pay attention, son," advised Norman. "It's not every day you get the chance to see a true hero at work."

Melvin caught Greg's eye and tried not to let his parents witness his smirk. "No, no, I can't argue with you there."

Trolling for Trolls

Edna made everyone wait while she threw a few things into a sack for Melvin. Then Norman escorted them to the door, though the entire way Greg had serious doubts as to whether the retired dragonslayer would survive the full distance. He thought he understood now why Norman and his wife were willing to live in such a tiny shack. Norman would never have been able to negotiate a larger room.

The good-byes lasted longer than Greg would have liked. If he had been on his own world, Greg wouldn't have been surprised to see Edna rush inside to get her camera, but on Myrth she was forced to settle for a long gaze into the faces of each of her boys—not a bad idea when he considered they might come back looking like their one-eyed father.

Greg studied Marvin's attire, or lack thereof. "Is that what you're wearing?"

Marvin looked down at his bare chest and loincloth. "This is what I always wear."

"But it's freezing outside."

Marvin scoffed at the notion. "And you call yourself a dragonslayer." He picked up his sword and shield and stormed out of the house.

"Actually, I don't," Greg called after him, but Marvin didn't seem to hear.

At last the five were on the trail. Before long they stopped so each could pick out a suitable walking stick. Greg used extra caution, but this time his stick did not fight back. Then they headed south, taking advantage of the quiet to discuss their options for the upcoming battle.

"We don't have any," said Lucky. "You heard the prophecy, Greg. The battle must be fought."

"We have one," Greg argued. "We can get Witch Hazel's amulet and give it to the spirelings."

"Ha." Melvin could barely talk, he was smiling so widely. "You think Hazel's going to give you her amulet? She's furious with you for messing up her plans with the last prophecy."

"He's right," said Lucky. "She tried to kill you, remember?"

Of course, Greg remembered. He could think of nothing else since he'd started considering the witch as a serious option.

"But she gave Greg her amulet when he needed it last time," said Priscilla. "Even Hazel won't stand against a prophecy."

"But that's just it," said Greg. "Last time the prophecy said I needed the amulet to defeat Ruuan. This time it just says I'm going to battle the spirelings. She's never going to give me an amulet that could stop the fight."

"Told you so," said Lucky.

All morning they tossed out ideas for how to proceed once they got back to the castle, but no one came up with an idea that didn't deserve to be tossed out. Marvin had said nothing for a while. Greg looked up at the mighty dragonslayer's face and discovered why. Even he would have been hard pressed to talk with his teeth chattering so violently.

"Starting to reconsider the outfit?" Greg asked.

"Nonsense."

Ten minutes later Greg caught Marvin scooping up a handful of leaves and stuffing them down his loincloth.

"Sure you're not cold?"

"Ridiculous."

"You starting a scrapbook, then?"

Marvin tried to flash a carefree smile, but had to stop when his teeth started chattering again. "Fine. So I'm a bit chilly. It's not my fault. Normally my amulet protects me from the elements."

"But didn't you notice the moment you stepped outside?"

"Sure, but I guess I just figured I must be getting soft, sitting around the house all morning."

Marvin may have been getting soft, but he still marched on in only his loincloth for another hour before admitting he was ill prepared for the trip. Actually he didn't so much admit it as stow his sword and shield in Lucky's pack and chase down a small bear he draped over his shoulders.

At least the bear was the only beast they encountered in the woods.

"I don't get it," said Marvin. "These woods are usually loaded with monsters."

Greg let out a grunt. "You've never traveled with Lucky before, have you?"

He was quite content not to see any monsters himself. Well, perhaps *content* was the wrong word. Nothing could quell the fear he felt over his upcoming battle or the queasy feeling he got when he thought about how the prophecy predicting his success had already been proven wrong.

Melvin, on the other hand, was oddly exuberant, so much so, he even started being civil toward Greg. "Why so glum, Greghart?" he asked.

"You kidding?" said Greg. "You forget about the prophecy?"

Melvin looked back at him, confused. Then recognition seemed to strike. "Oh, yeah. Don't worry. We're gonna go back and fight the spirelings as soon as we finish with these trolls."

Greg returned to brooding, but Melvin was in a rare good mood and seemed determined to lift Greg's spirits, although after the first two hours of having his spirits lifted, Greg decided the boy was most likely only in a good mood because he knew he was annoying Greg to no end.

"What do you call a dragonslayer who gets sliced by a swinging dragon's tail?" Melvin asked now. It was just one of dozens of horrible dragonslayer jokes Greg had been forced to endure for the past two hours. Greg refused to bite, but Melvin was not put off.

"Twins."

Marvin chuckled, as he had with each of Melvin's jokes. Lucky and Priscilla, on the other hand, seemed no more impressed than Greg was.

"Don't you get it?" said Melvin. "He got sliced in two, see."

"Yeah, yeah, I got it."

"Well, how about this? Did you hear about the dragonslayer who forgot to jump out of the way of the swinging dragon's tail?" Greg pretended he wasn't listening, but still Melvin continued. "He was beside himself over his mistake."

This time Marvin openly snorted, while Melvin flew into a fit of laughter over his own joke. Greg tried to ignore the two of them but failed miserably, just as he failed to ignore each of Melvin's next twenty-nine swinging-dragon's-tail jokes, each remarkably worse than the last. Finally, to Greg's relief, darkness settled in and forced the group to look for a place to camp.

Dinner did not take long to prepare. Lucky pulled everything they needed, hot and steaming, from his pack.

"Oh, no," said Greg, as he sat down on a log to eat. "I forgot about Ruuan again."

"What about him?" asked Marvin.

"We were supposed to wait for him back at your parents' house. He was going to come get us once he finished his meeting."

Marvin looked puzzled. "I thought you wanted me to go with you."

"I do."

"So, what did you think? That we'd all just hop on the dragon's back and he'd fly us back to Pendegrass Castle?"

"Sure. That's how we got to your place. There was plenty of room."

"You do know I'm a dragonslayer, right?"

"Oh, right."

When Greg traveled the woods of Myrth on his last visit, each night after dinner he and the others had gathered with their walking sticks and honed their battle skills until they were too exhausted to stand. Tonight Greg was too exhausted to stand before they even finished dinner. The others agreed.

"You carry a bedroll?" Marvin asked when Lucky began to unpack his magic knapsack.

"You sound surprised," said Lucky.

"Well, being a famous dragonslayer, I have my pick of accommodations whenever I stop in populated areas," he boasted, "but when I tour the back reaches, as we're doing today, I live off the land. We dragonslayers have to know how to make do with what little we can find."

Greg looked Marvin over. He supposed with a sword in one hand, a shield in the other and wearing only a loincloth and a bear, it would be difficult to carry much more. "Did you pack a bedroll for me too?" he asked Lucky.

"Of course," Lucky said, pulling a second from his bag and handing it to Greg. The two laid out their bedding close together, but not so close, they soon found, as to prevent Priscilla from rolling hers out between them. The Greathearts gathered enough leaves to pad the ground and block out the wind, but within seconds Melvin's teeth were chattering so loudly, it would have been impossible for anyone to sleep.

"Want my bear?" Marvin asked, but Melvin wasn't having any part of it. Besides, the critter ran off as soon as Marvin set it down. "How about my shield?"

Melvin accepted the shield and curled up under it, looking quite snug beneath the unsurpassed protection of its insulating dragon scales. But that left Marvin to tough out the cold without even his shield to block the wind. He nestled as deeply as he could in the gathered leaves, but even Myrth's greatest hero had his limits. In the end he squeezed inside Lucky's pack, and the others didn't hear from him again until morning.

Snug within the heavy bedroll Lucky had provided, Greg could still feel the frigid wind whipping through their campsite. He was even gladder than normal when Rake snuggled up beside him, and he longed for morning, when the sun would bring an end to the paralyzing cold.

But the following day dawned colder than the night.

"I'm not coming out till you light a fire," Marvin called from the depths of Lucky's pack. When he finally did emerge, he brought with him a coil of rope and used it to cinch the boys' bedrolls around himself for warmth. Then the five travelers huddled together for breakfast, exposing their bare fingers only long enough to eat a large stack of blueberry waffles, also from Lucky's pack.

"You have waffles here?" Greg asked.

Lucky grinned. "You mean there's a name for these? I just used my talent to prepare something I thought you might enjoy."

"Hey, mine are full of dents," Melvin said. "What'd you do in there, Marvin, walk all over them?"

"Waffles always look like that," Greg explained, after which Melvin seemed to enjoy them more.

After breakfast they had no more than started out before they approached a cave cut into a huge wall of rock. Marvin stopped just short of the entrance and asked Lucky for the eternal torch.

"Where are we?" Greg asked.

The torch burst into flames the moment Lucky removed it from his pack. He handed it to Marvin, who accepted it gratefully before answering, "The start of the quick way."

Greg peered into the darkness of the cave. "What's in there?"

"Relax, Greghart. This is the northern entrance to Guttering Torch Caverns. There's an exit to the south no more than a quarter mile from here."

"Great, *but what's in there?*"

"No monsters, I can tell you that much. Way too dangerous for them to go wandering about."

Greg studied Marvin's face, hoping to spot evidence he was joking. "Isn't that what we're about to do?"

"Yes, but we have an eternal torch, and we'll be wandering with a purpose. Now, you'll want to stay close. One misstep and . . . well, best if you latch onto me."

Priscilla threw her arms about Marvin's waist so quickly she nearly knocked him over.

"Great. Now, the rest of you too. That's it. Okay, here we go."

The five of them shuffled through the entrance into total darkness.

"What happened to the torch?" Greg asked.

"Oh, it's burning. Give it a moment."

Greg stood motionless waiting for something to happen. Eventually he saw the faintest glimmer of light and recognized it as the flame of the eternal torch. Apparently, Guttering Torch Caverns was filled with extraordinary darkness.

"Quickly now," said Marvin, and they began shuffling through the dark, following a twisted path that only Marvin could identify. They managed only a few feet before the dull flame guttered and expired. The resulting blackness pressed against Greg's eyes. He moved his toe slightly and heard a stone fall. For several long moments it could be heard bouncing off the rock below until eventually the sound died away.

"Don't anyone move," advised Marvin.

Greg didn't think the warning was necessary. "Our torch died," he felt a need to point out.

"Yes, they'll do that. Good thing we're not using an ordinary torch or we'd be in real trouble right about now."

They waited in total silence for several more seconds during which Greg was sure he heard the faint sound of a stone falling. "Is something supposed to happen?" he asked. No sooner had the words left his mouth than the torch rekindled to its previous state, casting barely enough light to reveal Marvin's hand.

"Hurry along, then," Marvin called out, and the five of them shuffled another dozen feet before the fire flickered away again.

"This is the quick way?" asked Lucky.

"Oh yes."

Darkness had already fallen by the time the group emerged, starving and tired, from the caverns. Even so, the night sky was like a beacon of brightness compared to the gloom within.

They camped just inside the cave, figuring nothing was likely to successfully negotiate the caverns to attack them from the north. After a much-needed meal, Greg thought about practicing his chikan, but he'd been on his feet without a moment's rest since they entered the caverns. That, along with Melvin's endless banter, left him too exhausted. Who would have thought the boy could have come up with another eighty-three jokes about swinging dragon tails?

Oddly, it was Melvin who spent breakfast grumbling as if angry with the others.

"What's got into you this morning?" Lucky asked him.

Melvin scowled, but not at Lucky, at Greg. "The princess told me about the next prophecy," he said in an accusatory tone.

Greg blinked back at him. "Yeah, so?"

"So, I don't like the way you're horning in on my brother's territory again."

"I'm not horning in on Marvin's territory."

"Yeah, Melvin," his older brother said, exposing a patch of skin on the right side of his chest as he adjusted his bedrolls to cover the left. "I asked him to come along, remember?"

"I was talking about this new prophecy," said Melvin.

Marvin tried unsuccessfully a few more times to cover up his bare spots, but all he had were the two bedrolls, and his chest was just too massive. Finally he gave up and devoted his energies to trembling. "What about it?" he asked Melvin. "Greghart is the one Simon mentioned. If anything, I'm horning in on *his* territory."

"Simon never mentioned him," argued Melvin. "He said 'the Hero who slayed Ruuan.' Obviously the old coot has lost his mind."

Marvin shook his head. "How can you say that? Lucky told me Simon was spot on with his last predictions. Besides, prophecies are never wrong. You think I'd go trotting into dragons' lairs if they were?"

"Well, we'll see," said Melvin in a tone that left Greg wanting to sweep out the boy's ankles with his walking stick.

Even though Greg knew Melvin was right, the two didn't speak again that morning—not such a bad fate when Greg recalled the dozens of obnoxious jokes Melvin had shared the day before. He took the opportunity instead to talk to Marvin as they hiked. Lucky and Priscilla joined in too, eager to hear about the dragonslayer's many heroic deeds.

But while Greg thought Marvin's stories fascinating at first, about midway through the day, after listening to the dragonslayer go on and on about his accomplishments for hours, Greg was beginning to regret ever asking to hear the tales. At first he thought he was alone in his opinion, but he began to suspect otherwise when he spotted Lucky with his knapsack pulled down over his head.

Priscilla, on the other hand, managed to remain rapt with attention. Too busy staring at Marvin to bother looking where she was going, she'd tripped over a dozen roots in the last hour alone. Each time, Marvin stabbed out a bronzed arm to catch her and lift her easily back to her feet, and each time, Priscilla mumbled something about not usually being so clumsy.

"Now, a lesser man might have thought about running when he spotted the basilisk headed his way . . ." Marvin was currently boasting.

"Yeah, probably a smart thing to do," interrupted Greg. "Say, how much farther is it to the southern border?"

"What?" said Marvin, looking unaccustomed to being cut off in the middle of a story. "Oh, about a day, I guess."

Greg thought he heard Lucky groan. Marvin didn't notice. The dragonslayer cleared his throat, as if about to return to his tale, and Priscilla tripped over another root.

Greg frowned. "How many trolls do you think we'll see?"

"What's it matter?" Marvin said with a chuckle. "I'd be surprised if we found more than ten or twelve. Certainly not more than twenty."

"But isn't twenty trolls worth a bit of caution?" Priscilla asked, clearly awed by the dragonslayer's carefree attitude.

"Hah. Just like a woman."

Marvin's tone was just as condescending as his words, yet Greg wasn't sure Priscilla even noticed. Of course, the dragonslayer was just getting started.

"Don't you worry your pretty little head, maiden. You can't be expected to know anything beyond cooking and cleaning and looking good for your man. Nor should you need to. Not with the Mighty Greatheart here to protect you."

This time Greg did hear Lucky groan, and Priscilla not only appeared to notice Marvin's tone, she looked as if *she* were the dragonslayer and was just now noticing how much Marvin looked like a dragon.

"What's your strategy going to be?" Greg blurted, before the dragonslayer could dig himself deeper.

Marvin offered him a look Manny Malice often used in Mrs. Beasley's classroom. "My what?"

"How do you plan to fight the trolls?"

"Oh. I'm just going to march right in and give 'em a taste of the Mighty Greatheart, that's all. You don't need much of a plan with trolls. They aren't that smart."

"Well, marching right into a band of them doesn't sound smart either," Priscilla said with a huff. "I agree with Greg. I think we should have a plan."

The smile that had been plastered across Marvin's face all day quickly faded. "Nonsense, maiden. You just stand out of the way and let me handle things."

"Maiden?" Fortunately Priscilla took to humming after that, and Greg doubted it was coincidence that the volume of her tune increased each time Marvin opened his mouth. Shortly afterward, the two of them dropped into a silence so thick Greg considered asking Melvin to tell more annoying jokes just to break the tension. At the last second Greg came to his senses.

"Say, did I ever tell you about the dragonslayer who tried to fight two dragons with one hand tied behind his back?" Melvin offered anyway.

"Not now," both Greg and Lucky told him.

Greg strode purposefully ahead. He was still congratulating himself when a loud rustling erupted from the brush, and it suddenly occurred to him he'd left more than Melvin behind—he'd left Lucky's good fortune back there too. He froze in place as the rustling grew stronger.

The noise cut off abruptly when Lucky and Melvin strolled up the path.

"What's wrong, Greg?" Lucky asked. "That monkeydog scare you?"

"Huh?" Though no one had ever actually seen one, *monkeydogs*, Greg knew, posed little threat to humans. They preferred to stick to the sides of the trail, making impossibly loud noises for anything small enough to remain concealed by the brush. Even so, Lucky was just assuming the noise hadn't originated from something far worse.

Melvin snickered, then let out a roar and slashed boldly at the bushes with his walking stick as he stomped past. Greg frowned and followed.

That evening Greg, Lucky and Priscilla spent a short time practicing the chikan moves Nathan had taught them during Greg's last visit. Greg found it hard to maneuver inside the heavy cloak Lucky had provided, but he practiced hard anyway, knowing his skills would need to be sharp if he was to have any chance of surviving his battle with the spirelings.

Who was he kidding? It didn't matter how sharp his skills were. The spirelings' axes were sharper.

"You're not thinking of trying that on a troll, are you?" Melvin called out from the edge of the clearing. He and his brother looked on with interest, but neither joined in the fun.

Focused on his meditations, Greg ran through one of his favorite drills, spinning his stick through the routine with a fluidity only his mentor, Nathan, could best. But Melvin just laughed long and loud, and soon Marvin joined in on the ribbing. Greg ignored them both, displaying great restraint when he continued to sweep his stick through thin air instead of redirecting it toward either of the hecklers. He supposed it was all for the best. If it hadn't been for the annoyances, he'd have surely felt a lot guiltier when he was preparing for bed later and had to ask Marvin to give up the two bedrolls the dragonslayer was using to keep from freezing.

The following morning Greg got up before daybreak so he could spend the first hour in peace while the others slept. Unfortunately, Marvin was an early riser, and as soon as he noticed Greg awake, he deemed it appropriate to begin sharing more of his adventurous tales.

"*Shh,*" Greg said, "you'll wake the others."

"Great, then they'll be able to hear my tale as well." Marvin smiled broadly. "I'm sure they wouldn't want to miss out."

With that, the dragonslayer had set the tone for the rest of the morning. When Marvin wasn't sharing his tales, Melvin was telling more of his annoying jokes. The two were so irritating, Greg actually began to look forward to meeting the trolls. According to Marvin, today he would get his wish.

Shortly after noon, the group was forced to turn east along the edge of a high cliff overlooking a great river. The rock of the opposing cliff face gleamed a brilliant gold, glittering in the bright sunlight as they approached. Scattered along the wall, streams of water cascaded over the edge and plummeted into the bluest river Greg had ever seen, churning up a pure white foam that joined with the gentle waves and wound its way downstream, producing a spectacle rivaling anything Greg had ever seen, even on a postcard. If he hadn't witnessed Heaven's Canvas and Fey Field on his last visit to Myrth, he'd have thought a more spectacular spot could not exist on any world.

"What is this place?" Greg asked.

"The River Styx," Priscilla said, sounding quite happy.

"You're kidding."

"No, why?"

"It's just I've heard of a River Styx back home, too. I'm not sure, but I don't think it's a good place."

Marvin gazed out over the expanse. "Really? I think this is one of the nicest spots in the kingdom. It's certainly one of the most popular tourist attractions. Of course, most everyone prefers to view it from the other side, where it's safe."

"This cliff isn't safe?" Greg said, backing away from the edge.

"No, the cliff's fine. I was talking about the monsters."

"Huh?" Greg said, spinning to scan the bushes behind.

Melvin rolled his eyes. "He means there's no monsters on the Styx side, genius."

"Really?" Greg looked again at the beautiful golden cliffs lining the opposite side of the river. "Then why does everyone live here in the kingdom?"

"Everyone doesn't," said Marvin. "I find it a bit hot and humid in the Styx myself, especially in summer, but plenty of folks like it there." He took one last look at the view. "Anyway, the river is pretty. I'll give it that."

"It's magnificent," said Priscilla.

"Big deal," said Melvin. "It's just water. I want to see some trolls."

As exciting as that sounded, the five of them walked along the edge of the cliff for miles and still didn't spot a single troll.

"Odd," said Marvin. "I can't ever remember going far in this region without running afoul of at least one or two of the beasts."

"Lucky wasn't with you then," said Melvin. "Now that he is, we probably won't have to deal with any trolls at all."

"If only," Greg muttered to himself, but then all he had to look forward to when they finished up here was his inevitable decapitation under a spireling axe.

Eventually the going turned too treacherous and they were forced to angle back into the woods. It was there Marvin stopped suddenly and held up his sword. "Halt. What was that?"

"What was what?" Greg asked.

"That noise in the brush."

"I'm sure it was just a monkeydog," Priscilla said, plopping onto a fallen log. "The whole kingdom's loaded with them."

"No, I smelled something, too. I think we may have found our trolls."

Greg had smelled trolls before and didn't think he could overlook the scent now. "I don't smell anything," he insisted.

"*Shh*, there it is again."

"I don't hear anything either," Greg sighed. But then he *did* hear something, and a nauseating stench drifted across the breeze.

"This is it, kids," Marvin said eagerly. "You're about to see why there's never been a troll born who could stand against the Mighty Greatheart."

For a second Greg thought Marvin was going to do something foolish, but only for a second. After that he *knew* Marvin was going to do something foolish. The arrogant dragonslayer hefted his sword and shield and screamed an exuberant battle cry as he charged blindly into the woods. Admittedly, he posed a formidable presence, but Greg thought he would have looked even more threatening without the two bedrolls tied across his chest and back. "He is a brave one. I'll give him that."

But then Marvin's scream turned a great deal more hysterical and cut off abruptly with a strangled gasp.

"Something's wrong," Melvin yelled. Without another word he ran blindly after his brother.

Before any of the others could act, Rake dove off Greg's shoulders and darted between Melvin's feet. Melvin went down hard, limbs splayed amidst the fallen leaves, and Greg seized the moment to dive on top of him.

"Get off me," said Melvin. "Marvin needs help."

"Wait," Greg gasped, "we don't know what's over there."

Lucky rushed ahead and peered through the bushes. He shushed them both and waved them over. Melvin jumped to his feet, scowled at Greg, and stormed to where Lucky stood. Greg and Priscilla followed. They strained to see over the others' shoulders.

Priscilla gasped. "Oh, my . . ."

Greg's breath caught too. Not more than twenty feet away stood the edge of a clearing, though at the moment the area was anything but clear. Hundreds of trolls had banded together there to camp, and not far from the edge where Greg and the others stood, four of the trolls held Marvin off the ground, one assigned to each limb. They tugged in opposite directions and laughed as Marvin wailed in pain.

Nearby, another of the trolls stooped to pick up Marvin's sword. He smiled an ugly, disfigured grin and slashed out experimentally at one of his brethren, cleanly slicing off the creature's arm in a single swipe. The maimed troll shrieked out at first, but then looked down at the severed limb and joined with the others as they all roared with laughter.

"We've got to do something," cried Melvin.

"*Shh*," said Priscilla. "You're going to get us killed."

"But—"

"Would you shut up?" said Lucky. "What do you expect us to do? There must be a thousand trolls over there."

"*Shh*," said Greg. "Something's happening."

The crowd of trolls grew more organized and parted to allow a hulking figure to pass. An enormous troll, a full head taller than the rest, lumbered forward to survey the situation from beneath his low, sloping brow. A row of three-inch-long thorns pierced the skin of each of his cheeks, and since there was a good chance the troll had put them there willingly, Greg thought that, alone, marked him as someone the three of them shouldn't mess with.

While the other trolls were dressed in tattered clothes, little more than rags, the larger troll's outfit was more respectable. Sure, his shirt was split through the chest and shoulders, and his pants were torn through the thighs, but the way his muscles bulged it would have been impossible to imagine a cloth strong enough to stand the strain.

"Stop," he commanded as the four trolls continued to tug at Marvin's limbs.

"He talked," whispered Greg.

"Some of them do," said Lucky.

"Don't you know anything?" Melvin said with a huff.

"*Shh*," said Priscilla. "I can't hear."

"Put down," the large troll ordered.

The two trolls holding Marvin's arms released him, while the two holding his feet were slower in the uptake, causing Marvin to fall roughly on his head. The one who had talked snatched Marvin up by his rear bedroll, easily lifting him off his feet, and Marvin thrashed like a dangling turtle, as the band of trolls chortled over his predicament.

"Seen scrawny human before," the talking troll said. "Big hero in human world. Slay lots of dragons . . ."

The others studied him curiously over their heavy brows.

". . . and trolls," the large one finished.

The looks of curiosity quickly turned to rage, and when the band pressed forward, waving their gnarled clubs and axes, Greg knew things were about to take a turn for the worse.

"Stop," the large troll commanded once more. "Make example of hero. Bring pike." Two of the trolls pushed over a small tree and quickly stripped it of its branches.

"This can't be good," said Lucky as Greg struggled to hold Melvin back.

Another troll stepped forward and cut off the tree's huge ball of roots with a single swipe of his axe. Four flicks of his wrist later, he had carved a sharp point. Greg had to tighten his grip on Melvin as two more of the beasts pushed Marvin off his feet and, thankfully, used a length of heavily corded rope to tie him to the pike. They then stood the pike on end, driving the point deep into the ground, while the others laughed and jeered.

"What should we do?" cried Melvin.

"What can we?" said Lucky. "We'd need an army to get him out of there."

"That's a great idea," Greg said, his spirits suddenly lifting.

"Huh?"

"King Peter said he sent Ryder and his men out to the south to patrol the borders. They were supposed to be hunting trolls . . . and here are the trolls. If I know Ryder, his army's not far off. We've been following the western edge of the border already, so we know they must be farther to the east. All we need to do is go find them."

"But King Peter expected Ryder to take another week to get here," said Lucky. "We haven't been gone that long."

"No, but we've got your luck on our side, remember?" Greg insisted. "Ryder probably made better time than expected. We're sure to run right into him and his men."

"We can't leave," said Melvin. "We don't have time." Over his shoulder, Greg saw Marvin kick his leg to keep one of the more curious trolls from gnawing on his shin.

"But it's the only choice we have," said Priscilla.

"No, Melvin's right," Greg said. "Marvin can't wait. I don't know what I was thinking. If that many men were anywhere close, we'd have heard them."

"What else can we do?" Melvin said.

"We'll get something better than an army," said Greg. "We'll get a dragon."

"Ruuan," Priscilla said. "That's a great idea . . . oh, but how are we going to find him?"

"He didn't come looking for us," said Greg, "Let's hope when he found out we left Greatheart's place he returned to his lair."

Melvin groaned. "But Ruuan's lair is months from here. How does that help?"

"No, it's only minutes away for a dragon . . . and even less for me." Greg held up his hand for the others to see. The special ring Ruuan had given him on his last trip to Myrth glittered in the late-afternoon sun.

"Your ring," squealed Priscilla. "I forgot. You can use it to pop straight into Ruuan's lair and be back with the dragon in minutes."

From the clearing, Marvin let out a scream. One of the trolls tested his bonds by grabbing the rope and twisting it tighter, and Marvin yelled louder still.

"Let's hope that's soon enough," said Greg. He quickly said good-bye to the others, took a deep breath and recalled the magic word Ruuan had taught him six months earlier. "*Transportus*," he shouted.

Before the word had even left Greg's mouth, Priscilla rushed forward, screamed "Wait!" and threw her arms about Greg's waist. Greg felt a disturbingly familiar sense of disorientation. The forest blurred into nothingness, and when his surroundings returned, he was standing in Ruuan's white-hot lair at the center of the Infinite Spire on the opposite side of the kingdom. Priscilla's arms, he realized, were still wrapped around his waist. He breathed a sigh of relief when he confirmed the rest of her was there as well.

Unexpected Company

"Don't let go," Greg shouted. He probably didn't need to mention it. Priscilla's arms were about to cut right through him. "Ruuan's ring is protecting you from the heat, but I don't want to think what might happen if you stop holding on. Come on, let's get to the storage locker."

Priscilla nodded without relaxing her grip, and the two of them shuffled over to a crack in the wall that led to a small chamber off Ruuan's lair. Priscilla had once spent three days trapped inside this space, but she looked more than willing to return to it now, most likely because the alternative was to burst into flames. Inside, the air felt comfortably cool. Still Greg had to pry Priscilla's arms off his waist.

"Why'd you grab on to me like that?" he said. "You could have been killed."

"I wanted to ask what you were going to do if Ruuan wasn't here," said Priscilla.

"And that was worth risking your life over?"

"I didn't realize I was risking my life at the time. Besides, what *are* you going to do?"

"What do you mean?"

"Well, Ruuan isn't out there, is he?"

Greg realized he'd been too concerned over Priscilla's safety to notice even the absence of the three-hundred-foot-long dragon. "He's not?"

Priscilla shook her head slowly, and Greg could tell she understood the full meaning of her own words. Without Ruuan's help, they were trapped here, and no help would be coming for Marvin.

From beneath Greg's clothing came a deep, guttural growl. Greg felt Rake's claws tear into his stomach. He yelped as much from surprise as from the pain, and was just about to scold the shadowcat when a shuffling sounded in one of the dark recesses of the chamber.

Greg's walking stick launched itself upward, as if of its own accord. "Who's there?"

Ahead in the shadows appeared the vague outline of a man's head. The figure stepped forward until a heavily shadowed face moved under the spotlight cast from one of the many portals cut high in the stone wall. Greg's pulse approached terminal velocity.

Priscilla screamed.

Before he realized Priscilla's scream had been one of joy, Greg jumped a full foot off the ground. When he recognized the warm blue eyes ahead, he felt a welcome wave of relief. "Nathan? What are you doing here?"

The wiry man who had accompanied him on his last adventure on Myrth wore loose-fitting slacks and a light cloth shirt that seemed inappropriate for this world. He leaned against a new but weathered staff and smiled. "I might ask you the same thing, young Greghart . . . or you, Princess."

"We came to find Ruuan," Greg said.

"That would have been my guess," said Nathan, "but I'm afraid the dragon is not here."

"We can see that," said Priscilla. "Where is he?"

"He has gone on a quest."

Greg gasped, partly because of what Nathan had said, but mostly because Rake had just plunged his claws even deeper into Greg's skin and used them to pull himself out from under Greg's tunic. The shadowcat adopted a pitiful expression until Nathan reached out and scratched him behind the ears.

"I hope it's not a long quest," said Greg. "We really need Ruuan's help."

"Sorry to disappoint you," said Nathan, "but I'm afraid it's quite a long one indeed. He has gone to a special place where only dragons can go."

Greg thought about this a moment. "Sounds exactly like the kind of place I wouldn't want to be." He caught Priscilla frowning at him. "Sorry. When will he be back?" he asked Nathan.

"There's no way to know for sure. He's gone to a realm of great magic, and time has been known to do some rather peculiar things there. He could be back any moment. I cannot say. Already I've waited for days."

"Days?" said Priscilla.

"But we need him now," Greg insisted. "Marvin may not have much time."

Nathan's brow furrowed. "What is this about?"

"Marvin Greatheart was captured by a band of trolls," said Greg. "We came here for Ruuan's help to set him free."

"Marvin Greatheart, the dragonslayer?"

"Of course," said Priscilla. "How many Marvin Greathearts do you know?"

Nathan shrugged. "I just find it hard to believe the one I've heard so much about could be captured by a simple band of trolls."

"You probably shouldn't believe everything you hear," said Greg. "Besides, there were hundreds of them. Maybe thousands."

Nathan looked truly surprised. "You're kidding?"

"People from Gyrth have odd ideas about humor, I suppose," said Priscilla.

Nathan appeared to contemplate what he had been told. "How long ago did this happen?"

"Just a few minutes," said Greg, "but we need to find a way back. There's no telling what those trolls will do."

"If you've spent much time around trolls, you ought to have a pretty good idea," Nathan said pensively.

"Oh my," said Priscilla. "We need Ruuan back now."

"As I said before," Nathan told her, "there's no way of knowing when he will return. I think we dare not wait. I'll need to take care of this myself."

"You?" said Priscilla. "How can you help? The trolls are holding Marvin on the other side of the kingdom."

"I should have no trouble speeding our travel," said Nathan, "but not from here. This area belongs to Ruuan. We'll have to leave the spire, as my magic is seriously impeded in his lair."

"You're a magician?" said Priscilla.

"I knew something wasn't right about you," said Greg. "But this is good. If you can do magic, maybe we won't need Ruuan. But we still need to get moving. Who knows what may be happening to Marvin right now?"

Nathan gave him an odd look. "You did say trolls, right?"

He retrieved a light-colored cloak from the shadows. Priscilla latched onto Greg's waist, and the two of them shuffled out into the main cavern.

Nathan stepped out behind them. "Why are you walking like that?"

"So Priscilla won't burst into flames," Greg told him.

"Relax, you two. Greg's ring will protect us."

Very carefully, Priscilla released her hold on Greg. Nathan led the two of them away from the safety of Ruuan's cold storage locker and into the Passageway of Shifted Dimensions, a magical corridor that provided the only possible means for a mortal to traverse the infinite distance down to the ground from the dragon's lair.

"What about the spirelings?" said Greg.

"Won't your ring protect us from them, too?" Priscilla asked. "I mean, it did last time, right?"

Greg knew she was referring to the trip the two of them had taken with Lucky after Greg's last encounter with Ruuan, when the trio had passed right in front of two spirelings without them seeing. "I'm not sure. Ruuan may have been protecting us then, or maybe we were just plain lucky. We did have good fortune on our side."

"If you're referring to your friend Lucky," said Nathan, "I'm sure he was not the source of your success. Besides, today we will need no magic. The spirelings have abandoned their home, remember? They no longer have the amulet that makes it possible for them to live within the spire."

This made perfect sense to Greg, and he was willing to believe Nathan at first, but he lost confidence when they rounded a corner and bumped straight into a spireling, the closest of dozens that had gathered around the tiny alcove where the amulet had once been displayed.

"Humans," yelled one of the warriors, and before Greg could shout a word of warning, rough hands clamped over his mouth and dragged him to the ground. Priscilla tried to fight but landed with a grunt at his side, and finally Nathan knelt in submission near Greg's feet, apparently unwilling to take on so many of the dangerous creatures by himself.

"No, I'd say your ring *won't* protect us," the magician whispered helpfully.

"Do something," urged Greg.

Nathan shot him a look of warning, but too late. Even though both the top and bottom rows of a spireling's teeth always remain visible, even when its mouth is closed, one of the nearest warriors managed to make it look as if he'd just now bared his fangs.

"Silence. You will not speak without permission."

Greg waited in silence as he was told, suffering the gazes of dozens more of the creatures, until finally those in front moved aside so another could pass. An ancient spireling, feeble in comparison to the rest, but still a formidable-looking warrior, stepped from the crowd. He was not dressed in the same tattered pants and chain mail as the others, but wore a simple cloth robe. Unlike all of the spirelings Greg had ever seen, he carried no axe, and he wore a clear, crystalline crown above his ridged forehead. The points were arranged haphazardly around the crown, like jagged icicles protruding upward, and looked nearly as sharp as the spireling king's teeth.

The remaining warriors bowed, and Greg was immediately reminded of a similar scene minutes earlier on the southern border of the kingdom, when the huge troll with the thorn-pierced cheeks had waded through his army to confront his captive. Suddenly Greg recalled the sight of poor Marvin with his limbs being stretched to their limits. Unconsciously he squirmed backward, trying to escape the spireling king's view.

The king paused when he spotted Nathan.

"You are a magician," he stated, and Greg knew at once from the pitch of his voice that he was not a he at all, but a she. The queen's tone was confident to the point of arrogance. She was not asking to confirm a suspicion. She was declaring the fact to illustrate she couldn't be taken in.

Nathan nodded but said nothing. He looked up at the queen, but wisely remained on his knees.

"Why do you trespass in Our home?" the queen asked.

"We mean no disrespect, Your Majesty. We had business with the dragon, but he was not at home, so the passageway was our only hope of leaving the spire."

"Have you not heard?" the queen said, laughing to the others as if to indicate she was dealing with a fool. "The dragon is dead. Killed by a slayer named Greghart not two months past."

Greg tried to will himself smaller.

"We have heard rumors of the dragon's demise," said Nathan, "but we also have reason to doubt the validity of those claims."

The queen's smile faded. She studied Nathan long and hard before continuing. "And what business did you have with a dragon?"

"We, too, have trouble regarding one of Ruuan's amulets. The one formerly in the possession of King Peter Pendegrass has recently gone lost."

The queen's eyes narrowed as she examined Nathan closer still. "You know of the loss of Our amulet?"

Greg noticed that while clearly angry, she sounded a lot less sure of herself than she had a moment ago.

"There's been a new prophecy," Nathan said. "Everyone knows."

The queen frowned. Apparently some knew less than others. "We see." She paused to consult with one of her warriors, though Greg never heard either spireling speak. Afterward she regarded Nathan once more. "Do you then know the whereabouts of Our amulet?"

"Not as of yet," said Nathan, "but I believe I can remedy that if I can put some distance between myself and Ruuan's lair. As I am sure you understand, the dragon's magic interferes with my own."

The queen nodded. "Of course We understand such things, but still We are reluctant to let you simply leave unpunished. You were trespassing, after all."

"Yes, and as I said before, for that I am deeply sorry. We really had no choice."

The spireling queen was silent for a long moment. Finally she motioned, indicating Nathan was permitted to stand. "Allow Us to introduce Ourselves," she said. "We are Queen Gnarla, Ruler of the Canarazas."

Greg cringed at the mention of the word *Canarazas*, which he knew roughly translated meant *razor-teeth*. He stared up into Queen Gnarla's eyes. True, the spireling queen had just introduced herself, but it was clear from her expression this had been a matter of protocol, not friendship.

"Perhaps We can find it within Our heart to let you go," Queen Gnarla said, "if you promise to find Our amulet and return it to Us." She pulled her jagged teeth into what might have been a grin. "Of course, We shall need to hold the boy until you return."

Greg looked over his shoulder, desperately hoping to see another boy in the tunnel.

Nathan's eyes narrowed. "I must have this young man with me," he told the queen. "He plays a key role in the next prophecy."

"Really? This child? He doesn't look like someone who would play a key role in anything."

"Are you kidding?" said Priscilla. "Greg's—"

She stopped abruptly when several of the spirelings gasped and rushed forward, brandishing their double-edged axes. Queen Gnarla strode up to the spot where the princess knelt and glared down at her, then turned back to Greg and spoke as if Priscilla weren't present. "Was this one not listening when you were told not to speak unless addressed directly?"

"She's a little slow," Greg explained.

"I am not," said Priscilla, but when one of the closest spirelings knocked her flat on her back and poised his axe above her head, she reconsidered. "Perhaps I am."

Without so much as a glance in Priscilla's direction, the queen nodded to Greg, as if the matter had been settled. "Your magician friend would have Us believe a scrawny human like yourself could hold a key role in matters of prophecy. Well, We do not agree. You shall stay here as Our prisoner."

Greg gasped and recoiled out of the queen's reach, startling Rake, who wriggled out from under Greg's cloak in protest. The moment Rake spotted the spireling queen he hissed and bared his fangs, which Greg equated to trying to scare away a dragon with a lit match. But the effect was nothing if not unexpected. Queen Gnarla's eyes grew to the size of tennis balls, which is to say they widened slightly. She let out a strangled gasp and jerked backward as several of the surrounding spirelings screamed and rushed up, thrusting out their axes to protect their queen.

"Get back," Greg cried, and though he had directed the order at Rake, to his surprise the charging spirelings halted. Truth is, they seemed quite relieved to do so. He stared at the creatures, afraid to move for fear of breaking the spell he held over them.

"Rake," he whispered, "get under my tunic before you get us all killed."

Rake gave one last spine-chilling growl, then disappeared beneath the fabric of Greg's tunic. Queen Gnarla hesitated a moment, as if to ensure the shadowcat was truly gone, before she approached again.

"What is the meaning of this? Bringing that . . . that *thing* . . . into Our home?"

"Rake? He's just a shadowcat."

"Just a shadowcat." A low-pitched growl broke out among all the surrounding spirelings and didn't stop again until the queen raised a hand for silence. Greg noticed the hand was trembling. Queen Gnarla noticed him noticing. She quickly moved it behind her back. "Perhaps the magician is right," she said with an equal tremor to her voice. "Maybe you *are* essential to this prophecy. Very well, you and the magician may go . . . We shall hold the girl instead."

"No," Greg shouted. The spireling guarding Priscilla whipped around and brandished his axe. "Ah . . . I mean . . . I could really use the girl with me."

"Doesn't anyone listen to Us?" Queen Gnarla muttered to herself. "Okay, boy . . . go ahead. You may speak."

Greg stared blankly at the queen, his mouth opening and closing without a sound.

"Well?" said Queen Gnarla.

"I—I just don't think I'll be able to play my part in the prophecy without Priscilla."

"Nonsense. Prophecies are always fulfilled. After all, what would be the value of predicting the future if the future didn't turn out the way you predicted? Why, that would be like predicting nothing at all, wouldn't it?"

Nathan cleared his throat, obviously reluctant to speak without first being addressed. Queen Gnarla scowled but turned to face him anyway. "Yes, what is it?"

"The boy clearly believes the girl will be essential to his success. Whether he's right or wrong is of little importance, but I am sure you can understand how crucial his beliefs may be. Who are we to interfere with destiny?"

The queen considered this a moment. Rake shifted positions under Greg's tunic, and Queen Gnarla's gaze darted toward the movement. "Perhaps you are right," she said quickly. "We shall let the girl go as well, but—and We shall not be swayed on this—We shall send two of Our own with you, as an assurance that you will complete the task We have dealt you."

The surrounding spirelings looked quite disturbed by this statement. A shoving match ensued as they all vied to see who could stand farthest from their queen.

"Oh, and We do not recommend you test them, Magician. Theirs is an ancient power you are not likely to best."

Greg wondered if this were true. After all, as he understood it, the only magic the spirelings possessed was contained within Ruuan's amulet, an artifact they didn't even hold at the moment. Nathan may have been thinking the same thing, but if so, he gave no indication. He bowed his head slightly. "Your warriors need not fear harm, Your Majesty, from me or my friends. It has been our intention to recover your amulet for you all along."

Queen Gnarla appeared to relax slightly. "We are inclined to believe you, Magician. Still, We shall send along two of Our best, just in case. Be warned. If you have not returned Our amulet to Us within two weeks, We shall march upon your castle."

"Two weeks?" said Greg, but he said little more, what with the wind knocked from his lungs. Odd. He never even saw the guard move, aside from the way the spireling's jagged teeth pulled themselves into a smirk when Greg landed on his back on the stone.

"Did We not speak clearly?"

"Sorry," Greg gasped. At least the castle was far from the spire. If they knew they weren't going to make it back before the deadline, they would have three more weeks to beat Queen Gnarla to the castle. They just needed to hunt down the amulet and get home quickly.

But then Greg remembered Marvin Greatheart and the trolls. The southern border of the kingdom was so far away. What would the two spireling warriors think about postponing their search long enough to rescue the dragonslayer?

Unlikely Allies

"No."

The spireling's voice left no room for argument—or at least it would have, if he hadn't been talking to Priscilla.

"But our friend's in trouble," the princess insisted.

"We shall not deviate from our course. Our sole purpose is to retrieve the sacred amulet."

"Perhaps we can discuss this better outside," suggested Nathan.

"There is nothing to discuss," said the spireling, "but you are right in one thing. We should be on our way."

No one dared say a word during the remaining trip through the Passageway of Shifted Dimensions and down the long tunnel to the mouth of the Infinite Spire. The spirelings did not so much as grunt the entire way, not even when one slipped and nearly fell on the glassy smooth tunnel floor.

Even if Greg *had* been talking, he'd have quieted the moment they reached the base of the spire. He had forgotten that the valley outside was still blanketed beneath hundreds of thousands of spireling warriors.

"I don't get it," Priscilla said to the two guards. "You say you can't live in the spire, but that's where you were when we found you . . . er, when you found us."

The spirelings seemed hesitant to answer, so Nathan answered for them. "Those you saw inside possess powers the rest of the Canarazas do not."

The spirelings' faces somehow took on a more threatening look. "How do you know this?" one asked.

"There is little you could tell me about your race I do not already know. As to your mages, I hold them in the highest regard, I assure you. As I do those warriors we see here."

The spirelings seemed to calm. One even lowered his axe. "It is true. Over the past month we mages have maintained regular patrols through the passage. But the others have been camped here all week, ever since your king sent the Mighty Greghart to steal our amulet."

Greg and Priscilla exchanged wide-eyed looks.

"Fortunately they will not have to stay much longer," the guard finished.

Priscilla nodded. "So you're confident we'll find your amulet."

"That is not what I meant. Soon they will march upon your castle to exact their revenge."

"But we didn't do anything," Priscilla said.

"Except steal our amulet," said the other guard.

"We didn't steal it."

The spirelings began a low rumbling growl that gave Greg the impression of a volcano about to erupt. Nathan put a finger to his lips, and in spite of her usual inclination to speak her mind, Priscilla took the hint.

Greg held his breath as he followed the two spirelings through the mass of resting warriors. He kept expecting the others to question what three humans were doing in their midst, but to his surprise not one looked up as they passed. The air was nearly freezing, yet each spireling to the last sat peacefully on the cold ground, shoeless, wearing only pants torn high on the calves and light chain mail draped over an otherwise bare chest.

The five hiked without incident across the deep valley and up a steep incline to the top of a ridge where Greg once camped with the Army of the Crown. There Nathan brought the group to a halt.

One of the guards rushed forward and raised his axe. "Why are we stopping?"

"This is far enough," said Nathan. "Before we proceed we need to gather more information about where this amulet of yours may be found."

"How are you going to do that?" asked Priscilla.

The spireling spun toward her. "Silence."

"You be quiet. We're not around that queen of yours now. I won't be putting up with anyone ordering me to 'speak only when spoken to.' Oh, and put that axe down before you hurt someone."

Greg hadn't heard Priscilla use that tone since the time Lucky knocked her down and stuffed her into his magical backpack. Even with his razor-sharp teeth and his double-bladed axe, the spireling thought to take a quick step backward. The other guard rushed to his aid, but stopped rather abruptly when the princess spun his way.

"And that goes for you, too. We *are* helping you get back your amulet, after all."

The second spireling studied her carefully, as if sizing her up, but when the princess placed her balled fists on her hips and strengthened her glare, he lowered his axe, not to mention his huge, bulbous eyes, to the ground.

"That's better," Priscilla said with a huff. "Now, Nathan, I asked how you planned to find out more about their amulet."

Nathan stared at the princess, speechless. Then his expression turned grim. "From what you've told me about Marvin Greatheart's situation, we have little time to devote to a rescue. I don't believe we'll have the luxury of proceeding using conventional means."

Greg suddenly realized two weeks would be plenty of time with Nathan on their side. "You're going to use magic."

"No." One of the spirelings rushed forward, but stopped abruptly when he spotted Priscilla in his way. Even after sidestepping successfully around her, he faltered again when he drew too near to Greg. Rake wiggled under Greg's tunic, and at once Greg understood. Hard to believe such a fierce creature could fear any of them, yet the spireling wouldn't take a single step closer.

"You cannot use magic," the guard yelled from his current spot. "Queen Gnarla will not allow it."

"What do you mean, Queen Gnarla won't allow it?" said Greg. "When did she say that?"

"Just now," said the second spireling. "She not only will not allow it, but she has instructed us to prevent it by any means necessary."

"What are you talking about, *just now?*" Greg argued. "Queen Gnarla isn't here."

The two spirelings gasped and ducked, as if expecting to be struck down from the sky. "Queen Gnarla does not need to be with us to know what goes on here," explained the first spireling. "We of the Canarazas share a single mind. Each of us knows what the others are experiencing. We sense all the same sights and sounds and smells, and we all share each other's feelings. It is just one of the many reasons you humans are wise to fear us."

His boastful tone at the last did hold a ring of familiarity. Greg could almost believe a piece of Queen Gnarla stood before him now.

"Forgive the children," said Nathan. "They know little of your race. But your queen must realize that without magic we have no way of knowing where to look. With a simple transcendental communication spell, I believe I can greatly reduce the odds. She must know it's the fastest way she can hope to see her amulet again."

The spireling paused, staring blankly at midair, as if listening to an inaudible voice. He then looked back at Nathan. "Very well, she will permit it this once. But do not waste the opportunity." He rolled his axe handle in his palm. "If you try to use your magic after this, we are to hand you your head."

"Let's hope that won't be necessary," said Nathan.

He winked at Greg and moved to a comfortable-looking spot, where he sat cross-legged with his hands folded over his lap and his staff rested across his knees. His eyes dropped closed, and Nathan did not move or speak again for a long while. The spirelings tightened their grips on their axes and moved closer, though they did follow a rather circuitous path to distance themselves from both Greg and Priscilla along the way.

"Don't bother him," warned the princess, and the spirelings immediately backed up a step.

Greg watched the guards with a wary eye while Nathan continued his meditations. Eventually a breeze stirred. The space directly in front of Nathan shimmered, and an apparition appeared before him, blocking out the spirelings behind. Greg could see a man in a black robe, one of King Peter's magicians, but he couldn't make out the face beneath the man's hood.

"What is the meaning of this?" the magician hissed, and Greg recognized the voice at once. Mordred lowered his hood and stared intently at the spot where Nathan rested. His greasy black hair hung limply to his shoulders, and he had not shaved in recent days.

"Ah, Mordred," Nathan sighed. "It's been a long time, hasn't it?"

Mordred frowned. "Not long enough, I am thinking."

"Don't tell me you're still upset with me?"

The dark magician laughed, but there was no humor in the sound. "I am much too busy running this kingdom to be upset with you."

"Really?" said Nathan. "I thought King Peter was running the kingdom."

"Under my guidance, yes. Now why is it you're bothering me?"

"I need to know what happened to the spirelings' amulet."

The apparition shimmered, and Greg saw Mordred's eyes narrow. "And what makes you think I would know anything about that?"

"You and Hazel are the only two I know who would have the ability or the reason to take it. And though Hazel is bold, I doubt she would risk going into Ruuan's spire . . . nor, do I imagine, would she need to."

Mordred's eyes flashed. He stared defiantly back at Nathan, who smiled faintly. Greg wasn't sure, but it looked as if Nathan had somehow gained the upper hand from the exchange. Finally Mordred spoke.

"What makes you think I would risk taking it?"

"Wouldn't you?"

Mordred raised one brow. "You always were a shrewd one, Nathan. Too bad we could not have worked together."

"We can always start now. After all, I still believe we share the same goal."

Mordred seemed to consider this for a long moment. Then to Greg's surprise he replied, "Yes, I'd like to think we do. I am inclined to help . . . but I cannot. I do not know where the amulet is."

Greg felt his hopes drain away.

"Then you did not take it from the Infinite Spire?" Nathan asked.

"I didn't say that. I just said I do not know where it is."

Nathan rolled the weathered staff along his knees. "Perhaps you may know how to help us locate it more quickly."

"Perhaps. You said *us*. Is the boy with you?"

Greg felt his blood run cold. He prayed the magician wasn't referring to him.

"He is by my side," said Nathan, "and we have two spireling warriors with us as well." His voice turned grim when he added, "As you might imagine, they are quite anxious to see their amulet returned."

"I see," said Mordred, and Greg wondered if the magician knew that having two spirelings with them meant the entire Canaraza race was listening. "Perhaps I *can* help. There is a soldier in King Peter's army—I believe his name is Corporal Widget. You may know him. He was with you not long ago, when you camped outside the Infinite Spire. I'm not saying I know anything about the amulet, you understand, but if I were you, I believe I would want to speak with him above all others."

Nathan smiled faintly. "Thank you, Mordred. You've done the right thing."

"Of course. Someone has to look out for this kingdom."

Already Mordred's scowling face was beginning to fade, only to be replaced by the scowling faces of the spireling guards behind.

"This was a horrendous waste of time," one of them said before the image was fully gone.

"Yes," said the other. "We already know the thief was the Mighty Greghart."

"No," said Nathan, "we must listen to Mordred's advice. Corporal Widget will hold the answer, I can assure you."

"I don't understand," said the first. "Who is this human, and what does he have to do with the disappearance of our amulet?"

"If he was at the spire last month, then he must be a soldier under Ryder's command," said Priscilla.

"And Ryder's troops are supposed to be patrolling the southern border of the kingdom," Greg added, "somewhere near the spot we left Marvin. Looks like our course is clear. Nathan needs to take us to the southern border."

One of the spirelings rushed toward Nathan and raised his axe. "We allowed you to use magic to gather your information because Queen Gnarla permitted it, but we will not allow you to use it again."

The other stepped forward to back up his partner. "Please understand that we will escort you wherever you must go and provide whatever assistance you need, but do not try another spell, or we will teach you the full power of the Canaraza race."

"I understand," said Nathan.

"Well, I don't," Priscilla huffed. "Why can't he use his magic?"

The two spirelings looked to be arguing with each other, though neither spoke. Finally one of them addressed the princess. "Because we said so."

Priscilla took on the same look she got when Marvin Greatheart referred to her as *maiden.*

"Do not worry, Princess," Nathan said to calm her. "We won't need my magic to take us there. We can go on foot."

"What?" said Greg. He lowered his voice so the spirelings wouldn't hear. "We don't have time to hike all the way across the kingdom."

Nathan nodded. "We'll see." He hoisted his staff and strode away before Greg could argue.

Greg scrambled to catch up. "But Nathan, the border is weeks from here."

"Months, actually."

"Can't you get us there quicker?"

"Sure, with magic, but you heard the spirelings. They won't allow it."

"I don't understand," Greg said, lowering his voice again. "What can the spirelings do against your magic?"

Nathan didn't bother to lower his own voice. "You'd be surprised what they can do. Oh, and there's no point whispering. The Canarazas have exceptional hearing."

"Nathan, you don't understand. If we don't reach Marvin right away he'll be dead."

Nathan came to a sudden stop. "No, *you* don't understand, Greg. I want to save Marvin as much as you do, but he is just one man. There is much more at stake here. The spirelings have agreed not to attack the castle, for now, but we must abide by Queen Gnarla's rules. If we can retrieve her amulet for her, we can count on her to honor her agreement and stop this fight, but if she feels we have betrayed her in any way, there will be no stopping her, amulet or not. The lives of all those we love are at stake, and Marvin Greatheart knows that. His entire life has been spent in service to this kingdom. Every time he leaves his home on assignment for his king, he knows he may not return. It is a risk he chooses to accept."

Greg wasn't sure he agreed. While it was certainly true that the dragonslayer had spent his life in service to the king, he doubted it had ever occurred to Marvin he could be harmed in the process.

Nathan started walking again, and Greg had to run to catch up. "Why does Queen Gnarla even care if you use your powers?"

"By preventing me from using my magic, she looks more powerful in comparison. She wants her warriors to think she's able to control me."

"But she *is* controlling you."

"To some extent, yes. But where I come from we have an expression. *You have to choose your battles.* In this case I'm choosing to go along with her to avoid a much larger battle."

"But it's still going to take forever to get to the border and back. Queen Gnarla said she's going to head for the castle in just two weeks."

"I heard," said Nathan. "But if we can recover the spirelings' amulet, perhaps she'll give up this fight."

Greg's step faltered. "What about the prophecy?"

Nathan smiled. "I can remember a time not long ago when I would have been the one defending the prophecy while you insisted things would play out different from how they'd been foretold."

Nathan was right, but Greg also knew from his last adventure on Myrth that, as obvious as it seemed that the prophecy was wrong, it was just as likely to be true as not. He just didn't see how they could possibly walk to the southern border and back in time to fulfill it.

And one more thing he knew. Nathan was not about to tell him more. Poor Marvin. Close to two hours must have passed since they had left him struggling on that pike. But Greg could do nothing but hold his tongue for now as the group began their long trek along the ridge that, according to Priscilla, extended southwest hundreds of miles between the Smoky Mountains and the Styx border.

To Greg's right, the woods stood thick and foreboding. In other words, they looked exactly like the woods in any other part of the kingdom. But to his left, the trees dropped away to reveal an orange sun setting over a large expanse of barren desert, devoid of life—a desolate plain that somehow managed to scream of danger, even when there was really nothing there to be seen. Greg was about to ask Nathan about it when a horrifying screech rent the silence of the woods. "What was that?" he screamed instead, nearly matching the intensity of the sound.

"My guess would be a banshee," said Nathan. "Cover your ears and watch yourselves. They can be a bit dangerous."

The spirelings rushed to take the lead, and the group inched forward. They'd taken no more than a dozen steps before a woman shot from the woods directly at their party, screeching so loudly, Greg felt his head would split from the sound, even with his hands clamped viselike over his ears. Soaring out behind her as she came, her unnaturally brilliant red hair gave the impression her head was ablaze. Her complexion was a ghostly white, and from her eyes dripped tears of blood, nearly as bright as her hair.

With lightning-quick reflexes, the two guards moved to intercept her path, slashing out with their axes. But the weapons swept through her form without resistance. She thrust her face in front of the closest guard and wailed so loudly, the spireling's thick, leathery skin stretched backward.

"That's got to hurt," Greg thought he heard Nathan say, but his ears ached too much to be sure. He desperately wanted to check his hands to see if his ears were bleeding, but knew he didn't dare.

The spireling's mouth grew wide, a cavern rimmed with jagged teeth, and issued a roar of its own, causing the banshee's hair to whip out straight behind her as before. But she was up to the challenge. Again she cried out, the sound nearly a laugh. Granted, it was a laugh that shook the leaves from the closest trees and dug into Greg's skull like a knife, but it was a laugh all the same.

But the spireling grinned back at her, and the banshee's confidence was broken. With one final screech that sent shivers up Greg's spine, she turned and fled back into the woods. Greg stood afterward, quivering in the boots Lucky had provided—a real accomplishment if you stopped to consider he'd very nearly jumped out of them at first sight of the banshee.

Priscilla, too, was shaking. "Glad we're being guarded," was all she said.

The group walked no more than a couple hundred yards farther before a second roar erupted from the brush.

"What now?" Greg cried.

But when the bushes parted and a huge tigerlike creature bounded out onto the trail, baring its razor-sharp fangs, Nathan simply smiled. "Nothing to worry about. Just a bollywomp."

Greg knew better than to lower his guard. The last time he'd run across a bollywomp, he'd been attacked and nearly killed. Of course, the others had assured him the incident was a fluke, that bollywomps were gentle creatures. Perhaps that's why this one didn't put up a fight when a pair of griffins exploded from the brush and seized it around the throat. In a flash it was gone, carried off into the darkening sky amidst a chorus of panicked shrieks and the flurry of beating wings.

"Now, that's a shame," said Nathan. "Anyway, we might want to think about camping for the night. It's not safe to travel these woods after dark."

The only thing more dangerous Greg could think of would be to *camp* in these woods after dark. "What about Marvin?" he asked.

"He'll have to wait," Nathan said with a finality that couldn't be questioned.

Greg tried his best to put the dragonslayer out of his mind as he and Priscilla helped seek out a relatively secure spot to spend the night. The spirelings gathered wood for a fire, and soon the darkening sky was lit up nearly as bright as day.

One spireling disappeared for no more than thirty seconds and returned with dinner. Greg couldn't tell exactly what sort of dinner it was, just that it was large and bloody and had probably been alive moments before encountering the spireling. The thought sickened Greg, but once Nathan threw the carcass over the fire and the scent of roasted . . . well, roasted meat . . . drifted across the air, Greg's hunger won out.

"This is delicious," said Priscilla. "What is it?"

"Bollywomp," one of the spirelings told her.

She paused in midbite. "Not the bollywomp we just saw a minute ago?"

"One and the same."

"But those griffins carried it away."

"Yes," the spireling muttered between bites, "but they dropped it a mile or so south of here."

"A mile? You were only gone a few seconds."

"Yes. Sorry for the delay, but the griffins did not want to give her up."

"Her?" said Priscilla.

"Never even hit the ground," said the other guard.

Everyone looked to the first of the spirelings.

"She was soaked in blood," he said. "I didn't want the meat to get dirty. Sorry I took so long, but those griffins seemed quite intent on getting her back. We very nearly had griffin meat instead."

Priscilla tossed down her fork, grimacing, but even this small morsel never reached the ground. One of the spirelings snatched it out of midair and ate it before it made it halfway. Greg was tempted to toss his food down as well, but instead he set it aside so he'd have something to feed Rake once the two of them were alone.

After dinner Nathan moved to the campfire to meditate. He stood with his staff held vertically before him, arms outstretched in what Greg knew from his chikan training to be *sensen* position. Nathan's breathing slowed, and then suddenly he was moving, dancing about the clearing and guiding his staff through the air.

Greg watched in awe. He'd forgotten how fluid the man's movements could be. After a time he nodded to Priscilla, and the two joined Nathan in front of the fire. The spirelings looked on curiously but said nothing at first. Then one stepped forward and addressed Nathan.

"Those gyrations of yours look familiar. Shortly before the disappearance of our amulet, a small human child was discovered skulking about inside our tunnels."

Greg nearly dropped his walking stick. He hoped the spireling had as much difficulty telling humans apart as Greg did distinguishing between spirelings.

"Or so we thought," said the other guard. "But when he overpowered two of our warriors, we knew he must be none other than the Mighty Greghart himself. Apparently Greghart is some sort of magician, capable of deceiving others by transforming his appearance."

Greg felt a bead of perspiration run down his forehead in spite of the chill. He forced himself to return to his practice, and was glad when Nathan steered the conversation away from the Mighty Greghart and to the art form of chikan. Both spirelings appeared moderately impressed, but neither could understand how the skill could possibly be used to overpower two of their brethren.

"We should check the forest," said one of the spirelings, and he and his partner disappeared into the darkness before his voice had died away.

Before retiring for the night, the others gathered by the fire. Greg couldn't speak for the rest of them, but he was far too keyed up to sleep. He thought Rake might help him relax, but the shadowcat sought out Nathan instead, looking up with pleading eyes until Nathan reached out and scratched him under the chin.

"You never told us what you were doing in Ruuan's lair," Priscilla said.

"You must have been the one Ruuan was meeting," Greg suddenly realized. "But why? I wasn't even sure you knew the dragon was alive."

Nathan smiled. "I know a great many things."

"Do you know what Ruuan's quest was about?" Priscilla asked, looking up at Nathan with pleading eyes of her own.

He regarded her a long moment, possibly debating if he should scratch her under the chin as he had done with Rake. Instead he turned to Greg and nodded. "Perhaps it is time."

"Time for what?" Greg asked.

"Time you knew the truth."

Greg and Priscilla exchanged excited glances. Greg always suspected Nathan knew far more than he was willing to say. Now it looked as if he might finally give up some answers.

"Ruuan has gone to retrieve two artifacts," Nathan began, "probably the most precious artifacts to have ever been born of this world."

"What kind of artifact is born?" Greg asked.

"All in good time, Greg. All in good time. Let's see, where should I begin? Perhaps many thousands of years ago, when the world of Myrth was ruled not by men, but by dragons."

Greg shot Priscilla a smile, but she was too rapt with attention to notice. At least with Nathan she wouldn't be tripping over any roots.

"Back then people didn't go out after sunset," continued Nathan, "but stayed locked up in the castle or cowered in caves and gullies, afraid to roam the dark for fear of being snatched from the ground by invisible claws. No one risked falling victim to the thousands of magical creatures that floated soundlessly across the night skies."

A sudden scurrying high in the trees caused both Greg and Priscilla to snap their heads up and scream.

Nathan's lips turned up in a slight smile. "I said *soundlessly*."

"But Ruuan claims he's the last of the dragons," said Priscilla. "If there used to be so many, what happened to them all?"

"Ah, now that's where my story gets interesting," Nathan said, crossing his legs comfortably in front of him. "Never underestimate the ingenuity of mankind. When it became apparent that they could not stand against so many dragons, the men of that period knew they must do something to even up the odds. They began studying, learning everything not only about the dragons' magic, but about other forms of magic as well."

"What other forms?" Greg asked, only now tearing his eyes away from the noise in the trees.

"Magic has many facets," said Nathan, "but the less you know about that the better. What's important is that these men did finally learn how to defeat their foe."

"But how?" Priscilla asked. "So they learned magic. Dragons have magic too. Wouldn't the two just cancel each other out? How did they ever win against huge creatures like Ruuan?"

Nathan nodded. "Your question holds greater merit than you might think. The more these men studied, the more they realized they couldn't fight so many dragons on their own terms."

"But if men couldn't fight," said Priscilla, "what caused the dragons to go extinct?"

"Maybe it was all the smoking," Greg said.

Nathan smiled. "No, it wasn't the smoke. After all their studies, the men eventually came to realize that their best hope of winning a fight against a dragon was with another dragon."

Priscilla's brow crinkled. "Why would the dragons fight each other?"

"Because the magicians learned not to try to fight them, but to control them," Nathan said. "They pooled together all of their knowledge and all of their talent and used it to produce a very special amulet."

"The Amulet of Ruuan," surmised Greg.

Nathan shook his head. "No, that came later. The first was the Amulet of Tehrer, and it nearly caused the destruction of all of Myrth."

Priscilla gasped. Greg was shocked too, but he couldn't help wonder how much simpler his life might have been if Myrth *had* been destroyed.

"The Amulet of Tehrer was created many millennia ago," Nathan continued, "through the joint efforts of the greatest magicians of the period—men who were remarkably skilled at their craft, perhaps even more so than any we have in the kingdom today. The amulet they created worked better than anyone ever imagined. With it they were able to bend the will of dragons. For a time, magicians rode atop the beasts, pitting dragon against dragon in fearsome battles that lit up the night skies with countless blasts of fire. Within a single century nearly every dragon had expired."

"How awful," said Priscilla.

Greg nodded, thinking of Ruuan and how helpful he had been.

"That's not the worst of it," continued Nathan. "With each dragon that fell, the magicians grew stronger, and with that power came a greed for more. Then one dark day the unthinkable happened. A dragon was steered against its will over the castle, where it was forced to unleash a jet of scorching fire that burned the structure to the ground. A handful of deranged magicians had announced in their own demented way that they were unwilling to live under not only the dragons' rule, but the king's as well."

"Oh my," said Priscilla. "I never knew Daddy's castle wasn't the original. How were these men ever stopped?"

Nathan regarded her with a grim expression. "It was an easy task by no means. Much as the magicians had learned that a dragon could best be defeated by another dragon, those magicians left with their sanity knew that the stray magicians with their powerful amulet could best be defeated with the help of another amulet, equally strong as the first."

"*That's* how we got the Amulet of Ruuan, right?" said Greg.

Nathan nodded.

"But how could they make one as strong as the original if they weren't all working together?"

"They couldn't."

"Huh?" said Greg.

"Those who were left could never hope to make an amulet as powerful as the first—at least not without help."

"But who but magicians could help them?" asked Priscilla.

"No one."

Both Greg and Priscilla stared blankly at Nathan. Greg spotted a tiny flash of light and only then realized Nathan had waved his hand.

The magician leaned forward and whispered. "You must use caution when speaking around the spirelings."

"The spirelings aren't here," said Greg.

"Nor do they need to be. But at the moment they won't hear us. Now, listen. To them, the Mighty Greghart is just a faceless name from a prophecy. They cannot take action against an opponent they do not know. Fortunately they think he is a great warrior and could not possibly be a mere boy, but too much evidence to the contrary could convince them otherwise. Then they will think we are hiding their amulet from them. Our ability to keep breathing hinges on your anonymity, so be careful."

"Of course," said Greg.

"If we're going to keep them in the dark, they must not know of your role in the last prophecy. They know the Mighty Greghart was brought here from another world, so it would be wise for you not to mention that the same can be said about you."

"Sure," said Greg. "I hadn't planned to."

In spite of the gravity of his story, Nathan offered a small smile. "Yes, but I was just about to tell you Myrth isn't the only place you'll find magicians."

For a moment Greg nearly smiled himself. Then he remembered Marvin's predicament and could barely fight back his guilt. He had no right to be happy while Marvin's life was in danger. "Are you trying to say that Earth could have magicians?"

"It's hard to say. I'm sure most, if not all, were killed in the Dragon Wars."

Greg realized Nathan was serious. "Are you really saying you brought magicians from my world to fight magicians here?"

"Well, no, I didn't. But yes, men were brought from Earth, and from my planet as well."

"Of course. Gyrth has magicians too. That's how you were able to come here."

"No, I'm afraid Gyrth lost all its magic long ago," Nathan said. "I'm sure it was once a fine place to live, but it since has gone to waste."

"Gyrth has gone to waste," Greg repeated.

"Most of it, yes."

"Were you one of the magicians brought here to fight?" Priscilla asked.

Nathan actually laughed out loud. "Just how old do you think I am, Highness?"

"Oh, sorry . . . I thought with magic and all . . ."

"No, I came to this world about thirty years ago," he said, "after a boy about my age delighted me with tales of a foreign land, a place where adventure lived at every turn. I was young and impressionable and really had nothing to lose, so I came here to try my own hand at adventure.

"Ah, but that's a story for another time. For now, you need only know that by soliciting help from those of other worlds, the magicians were able to create an amulet equally strong as the first. It took another decade of bloody war, but in the end Good triumphed over Evil."

"How many dragons were left when the war ended?" Greg asked.

"A few dozen, I suspect," said Nathan. "But those that remained were not left unharmed. They were angered about the way they'd been treated, furious over having been forced to battle their own kind. And they showed it over the years by terrorizing the men of the kingdom on a regular basis. Not in an all-out war, mind you—they'd learned all too well the dangers of pushing men too far. Instead they simply took out a couple of cows here, a dozen sheep there, maybe an occasional maiden . . . anything they could to make the lives of men miserable without pushing them far enough to incur their wrath."

"Taking young women wasn't pushing too far?" Priscilla said. She shot Greg an angry glare, which he avoided, even though he was pretty sure he hadn't done anything wrong.

"Occasionally it was," said Nathan. "That's why Marvin Greatheart and all of his ancestors have enjoyed such lucrative careers. A handful of dragons have died of old age over the years, but most have fallen victim to dragonslayers such as the Greathearts."

Greg was silent for a moment, busy trying to picture how there could have been a handful of dragons. If anything, a dragon full of hands seemed more likely. "Is Ruuan really the only dragon left?"

"Afraid so," said Nathan. "Ironically the latest to go was Tehrer, the offspring of a Great Black by the same name, a dragon so terrible as to be the namesake for the first amulet. The original Tehrer was maimed badly in the final battle. He went into hiding after the new magicians regained control. I've heard he still lived into this century, until a couple of decades back, when he was killed by Marvin Greatheart's father, Norman."

"I've met Norman Greatheart," Greg said. "I think Tehrer might have been the lucky one."

"Tehrer was evil?" Priscilla said. "But why? Ruuan seems so nice."

"Yes, well, remember the Ruuan you know is not the Ruuan for which the amulet was named. Much as with Tehrer, the second amulet was named after Ruuan's father. Back then it was unheard of for a dragon to speak to a mere human, let alone help one. But Ruuan's father was wise beyond even his years. The war could not have been won without his help."

"Ruuan's father helped men win a war against dragons?" Greg said.

Nathan paused to stroke Rake's fur. The shadowcat purred and fell over on its side, prompting Nathan to scratch its belly.

"Not against dragons exactly. Remember by this time the evil magicians were controlling the dragons against their will. The dragons were just innocent pawns, a fate worse than death for such noble creatures. That's why Ruuan's father volunteered to let the good magicians control him."

"He volunteered?" Greg tried to imagine the Ruuan he knew doing the same. The dragon had been quite cooperative in helping Greg so far, but Ruuan didn't seem the type to stand for having his will bent. Greg had an idea the dragon would have a blast of fire for anyone who thought about bending so much as the tip of his tail.

"Yes," said Nathan, "and by not wasting energy resisting their orders, he allowed them to use the full power of the Amulet of Ruuan against Tehrer, surely the deciding factor that propelled them to victory."

"What a huge sacrifice," Priscilla said.

"It sure was," agreed Greg.

"I'm afraid his sacrifice went much deeper than that," said Nathan grimly. "He and Ruuan's mother both died during that final battle."

"How horrible," cried Priscilla.

"Yes. But at least their efforts brought victory to those on the side of Good."

The three of them were silent for a time as they considered the great sacrifice Ruuan's parents had made.

"You still haven't told us where *our* Ruuan went," Greg reminded Nathan.

"I'm getting there. It was at the end of the final battle. Ruuan's father had been mortally wounded and could barely hold himself airborne. Miraculously, his rider leapt between dragons and dislodged the amulet held by the magician who controlled Tehrer. The two men fell to their deaths, and Ruuan, though unable to fly, managed to guide his fall to the spot where the Amulet of Tehrer lay ready for the taking." Nathan sighed. "For the last few seconds of his life he held both treasures in his grasp, more power than anyone had ever held before."

"Wow, what happened to the amulets?" said Priscilla. "If Ruuan was dying, why didn't Tehrer go after them?"

"Tehrer was evil, as I said, but he was badly wounded. He'd fought only because the amulet was controlling him. Once free of the potent magic, he retreated high into the mountains, where he was not seen again for centuries. No, Ruuan's father, though dying, remained unchallenged. Fortunately, even in the last throes of death he retained the presence of mind to know that the two amulets must never fall into the hands of men again."

"What about boys?" Greg asked.

Nathan smiled. "No, not boys either. Ruuan's son, the dragon you know, rushed to his side, but nothing could be done to save him. It was then that his father gave Ruuan both amulets, along with instructions for their destruction."

"The amulets weren't destroyed," said Priscilla. "At least not Ruuan's. We've seen it."

Rake issued a demanding cry to Nathan, who had stopped petting his belly. "No, you've seen pieces of it," said Nathan, returning to the task at hand. Rake grinned and stretched his paws further over his head. "It's not possible to completely destroy objects of such power. The best Ruuan could do was break them apart and scatter the pieces about the land, where they weren't likely to ever be joined again."

Suddenly parts of his last trip here were beginning to make sense to Greg. "That explains why there are four identical amulets," he surmised.

Nathan nodded. "The four sections of amulet that you have seen were just quarters of a circle. Each holds enormous power, but nothing in comparison to that of all the pieces combined."

Greg gasped as he realized the significance of Nathan's words. "And I've held every one of them in my hand," he said, "just never all four at the same time."

"Actually five," said Nathan. "The four you held do form a perfect circle, but there's a fifth piece as well, an outer ring that fits snugly around the others." He glanced at the woods and held a finger to his lips. "Remember what I have told you."

He waved his hand again, and Greg heard the two spirelings shout out. Within seconds they dashed up to the fire. "What was that?"

"What was what?" asked Nathan.

"That noise."

"I didn't hear anything."

In an instant the spirelings disappeared into the woods again, apparently in search of the source of the noise they claimed to have heard. Greg took the opportunity to whisper to Priscilla.

"If you're whispering because you think the guards can't hear you, I assure you they can," Nathan said in a normal speaking voice.

Priscilla's face reddened. Greg scanned the woods to see if the spirelings were nearby.

"And I should remind you," said Nathan, "anything they hear is heard by every member of their race. I suggest if you have something private to say, and wish it to remain that way, you save it for another time."

Greg nodded. "You were telling us about Ruuan's amulet."

"Yes. The Ruuan of today was barely a century old when his father died, but even at that age he knew not to chance the amulet ever being assembled again. He took the two key pieces away from Myrth to another world, where only he would know where to find them."

"Two pieces?" said Greg. "I thought you said there were just five total. Wait, two plus four does equal six in this world, right?"

"Yes, Greg, but the Amulet of Tehrer was broken apart as well. The original pentagram was cut into six pieces. Five remain here on Myrth, each formed in the shape of a triangle, but there is a sixth piece as well, a pentagon that fits not around the outside of the others, but at their center. It is this piece Ruuan took along with the ring to a location only he would know. That way neither amulet could ever be reassembled again."

"But why?" asked Greg.

Both Priscilla and Nathan regarded him curiously.

"Why what?" Nathan asked.

"You said Ruuan went to retrieve two artifacts. If the pieces were never supposed to be found on Myrth again, why did Ruuan go after them now?"

"Ah, very good, Greg," said Nathan. "But that is where this conversation must end. It wouldn't be wise for me to tell you too much about your future."

"How is it you seem to *know* so much about my future?" Greg asked.

"Again, I cannot tell." The three stood watching each other in uncomfortable silence. "Anything else you wanted to talk about?"

Greg and Priscilla shook their heads.

"How did this food get here?" came a deep voice to Greg's right. The two spirelings had returned with astonishing stealth. One picked up the small piece of bollywomp meat Greg had set aside for Rake.

"Hey, that's mine," said Greg.

"Then what is it doing on the ground?" asked the spireling.

"I was saving it."

The spireling's eyes froze him in place. "Saving it for what?"

Greg debated whether to say or not. "If you must know, I was going to give it to Rake."

Hearing his name, the shadowcat popped his head out from under Greg's cloak and sniffed the air, his whiskers quivering in what could only be described as a cute manner. Even so, both spirelings screamed and lurched backward.

"It is loose," one shouted, reaching for his axe.

"Watch out," screamed the other.

"For goodness' sake," said Priscilla. "It's just a shadowcat."

The spirelings seemed no less upset in spite of her reassurances.

"I don't get it," said Greg. "Why are you so afraid of Rake?"

"You know why."

"Actually, I don't."

The fire cracked, and Nathan stomped out an ember that landed near his foot. "Ah, the day the spirelings slept."

"See, he knows," said one.

"So you might as well tell *me*," said Greg.

"It was nearly two months past. Our tribe had left the Infinite Spire to fulfill our part of a prophecy. We were supposed to block the cave mouth at the base of the spire, keep out the Army of the Crown. But unbeknownst to us, the humans sent one of those . . . shadowcats . . . into our midst."

"It used its powerful magic to keep us from noticing as others of its kind moved in to join it," said the second spireling. "Then, when they had us outnumbered, they worked together to cast a great spell against us. Our warriors were lulled into unconsciousness, and when we awoke again our amulet was gone."

"The spell used against us was a horror of indescribable proportions," said the first. "Two of our warriors fought the Mighty Greghart within the spire, yet the rest of us saw nothing. It was as if they had become . . . not part of us."

"The shadowcats are evil creatures," said the second. "You would be wise to stay clear of that one. I can only assume it is responsible for the disappearance of your human king's amulet as well."

"Rake didn't steal Daddy's amulet," said Priscilla. "What would a shadowcat want with a magical artifact?"

"Daddy?" said the spireling. He adopted the same glazed-over look he'd displayed on the ridge outside the Infinite Spire. "You did not tell us you were the human king's daughter. Queen Gnarla says if she had known, she would have held you for collateral until our amulet was returned."

"You don't have to coerce us into helping you," said Nathan. "We have just as much interest in returning your amulet as you do."

"How is that?" asked the second spireling.

"Long ago the amulet was given to your people because it was unlikely to ever be stolen while in your possession. It was believed that no one would likely ever find the Passageway of Shifted Dimensions, let alone fight off hundreds of thousands of Canarazas to take it from you."

"As it turned out, they didn't need to," said the spireling. He pointed at Rake. "Because of that."

"Rake didn't do anything," said Greg, pulling the shadowcat away. "And the shadowcats didn't take your amulet either."

"How do you know?"

"Because—"

"He doesn't," Nathan said quickly, "but the princess was right about the shadowcats having no use for your amulet. Remember our earlier lead? We must look to this Corporal Widget for answers. Now I suggest we get some sleep. We have a long day ahead of us."

"We spirelings do not sleep, and even if we did, we could never do so with that . . . *thing* in our midst."

"That's not what you told us earlier," said Priscilla. "If the shadowcat was the big threat you seem to think he is, it wouldn't matter what you did. He could knock you out any time he wanted."

Greg couldn't say he liked the growls that issued forth from both spirelings. Even Priscilla took a step backward.

"Calm down, everyone," said Nathan. "Sleep or not, let's get some rest. I, for one, found it a trying day. And I expect tomorrow will be no better."

Nor could it be worse, Greg thought. But then he remembered his last trip to Myrth and realized how wrong he could be.

Shortcut

The spirelings prepared a hearty breakfast of basilisk eggs and woke the others shortly before morning, so they could eat and be ready to leave at first light.

Greg was relieved to find they had all survived the dangers of the night, and only hoped the same could be said for Marvin. But soon he began to wonder if they were any safer now than they'd been the previous evening. Already the group had been attacked by a small band of goblins, three griffins, a minotaur and the ugliest ogre Greg had ever seen, though in truth, he had seen only one other, and for much of that encounter his eyes had been closed.

With each new attack the spireling guards rose to the challenge, their axes soaring with deft precision to dispatch the threat—until a moment ago, when they had run across something truly horrible.

At first Greg mistook it to be a harmless garden gnome, but when the deranged gnome opened its mouth and charged, foam slathering from the corners of its mouth, Greg suspected it was a bigger threat than it had appeared. The guards, who Greg had learned this morning were named Gnash and Gnaw, took one look and threw down their weapons, freeing up their hands to weave a powerful magic that sent bolts of electricity zapping down from a cloudless sky. Any sane monster would have fled, but the determined gnome defiantly stared them down through four near misses. It was not until Rake peeked out from Greg's cloak and shook his whiskers that the creature finally screamed and darted into the brush.

"This is ridiculous," Greg said, his breath coming in erratic gasps. "What's with all these monsters all of a sudden, anyway?"

"Welcome to the forests of Myrth," said Nathan. "They can be a bit intimidating."

"It wasn't like this when we traveled here before," Greg protested.

"Lucky was with us then," Priscilla reminded him. "Today has been a lot more normal."

"Yeah, right."

"I think you give this Lucky friend of yours too much credit," Nathan told the two of them. "Our relatively uneventful trip last time was probably no more than coincidence. Just a simple matter of good fortune."

"Brought on by Lucky," finished Priscilla. "That's exactly what I was saying."

Nathan frowned and returned his attention to the trail. The group narrowly survived two more griffin attacks before Greg shouted for everyone to stop.

"What is it?" Nathan asked.

"This is crazy. Even if we don't get ourselves killed out here, this trip is taking way too long. Who knows what's happened to Marvin by now? Or Lucky and Melvin, for that matter. And Queen Gnarla's going to march on the castle in just two weeks. We can't waste any more time. You need to use your magic."

Gnash and Gnaw both shook their heads and raised their axes to indicate the option was, well, not an option. Before Greg could object, a chilling shriek once again broke the silence. Experienced at the drill, the two spirelings rushed forward and held their axes poised for a fight.

"What this time?" Greg moaned.

"Sounded like a wyvern," said Nathan, "or maybe a wounded banshee. It's hard to tell."

A second screech split the air, shaking leaves from the surrounding trees, and all turned to witness a thirty-foot-long dragon soar over the ridge and drop from the sky with a boom.

"Nope, it's a wyvern," said Nathan.

The miniature—if that word could in any way apply here—dragon lumbered forward a step and bared its fangs at the two spirelings, but the guards' resolve did not waver. They raised their axes higher and separated, moving off the trail in opposite directions, as if to surround the beast.

Under different circumstances, very different circumstances, Greg might have described the wyvern as pretty. Iridescent streaks ran along both sides of its brilliant teal scales, from its forearms to its tail, and glittering gold ovals surrounded each of its eyes, which stared first at one spireling, then at the other. It had only two legs, not four, but with its powerful wings for balance it was able to move with astounding quickness.

Suddenly it lashed out with a foot, missing Gnash by inches—or maybe it was Gnaw. Greg had a lot of trouble telling the two apart. Had the guard not possessed the inhuman speed of a spireling, surely he'd have been shredded. Instead he lunged forward and swung his axe.

With a beat of its wings the wyvern dodged nimbly aside too. An unexpected swat of its sinewy tail sent the attacking spireling reeling backward over the ridge.

Gnaw held out a hand, and a ball of blue fire burst to life in his palm. He hurled the fire at the wyvern, but the nimble beast lunged easily aside.

From over the ridge, Gnash shot back into the fray. He dove axe-first at his opponent, the attack so quick, the wyvern barely managed to duck the blow. Gnaw took advantage of the distraction and rushed in with an offensive of his own, but again the wyvern countered with a swing of its tail that nearly decapitated both spirelings in a single swipe.

"Somebody do something," said Priscilla.

Greg weighed the stick in his hands. Luckily Nathan caught him by the shoulder and dragged him backward before he could do much else. Greg exhaled, secretly glad for the intervention, as Nathan stooped and picked up a rock.

Nathan waited until just the right moment, when the two spirelings had drawn away the wyvern's attention, to unleash his throw, and hit his mark, striking the beast squarely in the neck. For an instant the wyvern was distracted, long enough for Gnaw to raise his axe as if to throw it.

"No," Greg cried. He managed to startle Gnaw just before the spireling released the weapon, resulting in a glancing blow that caused little damage.

Gnash stepped in behind the wyvern and raised an axe of his own.

If Gnaw had been distracted by Greg's cry, it was nothing compared to the surprise Gnash must have felt when Greg rushed forward and dove at the spireling's legs. In fact, the disbelief on Gnash's face was clear from the moment Greg left his feet until the instant Gnash stepped casually aside. Greg landed with a thud. Injured and furious, the wyvern snapped its head around to look him squarely in the eye.

Uh-oh.

To Greg's surprise, instead of attacking, the creature let out an unnerving screech and leapt to the sky. The air caught beneath its leathery wings, and after one last shriek drifted down with the wind, all was silent. The wyvern had retreated.

"What did you do that for?" Priscilla screamed.

Gnash and Gnaw screamed something too, but Greg wasn't sure they were using actual words. Still, the meaning was clear.

"Sorry. I just . . . well, I thought maybe we could reason with it. Fighting all these monsters is taking forever. That wyvern could have given us a ride to the southern border."

Priscilla's mouth dropped open. "You can't ask a wyvern for a ride."

Nathan tried his best to calm the angered spirelings, but they were furious. "The princess is right," he told Greg. "Wyverns aren't like dragons. They're just animals. They survive purely on instinct, not wit. You're lucky you weren't killed."

"I guess so," said Greg, breathing heavily to try to stop his body from shaking. "It's just that it looked hurt, and I thought if I helped it, it might return the favor . . ."

Nathan glanced over at the spirelings and back again. "Don't worry. No harm done, and we're all safe now."

Priscilla shrugged to show she agreed, but the spirelings clearly needed more convincing. It was not in their nature to leave a battle unfinished. Greg cringed at the thought, recalling the prophecy and his true purpose for being here. He wanted nothing less than to have to fight an army of these creatures. Then a disturbing thought struck him.

"We may be safe from that wyvern, but without a ride we're still stuck in the wrong part of the kingdom. Poor Marvin. What do you suppose will happen to him?"

"Don't give up on him just yet," said Nathan. "I still have one trick up my sleeve."

Priscilla's eyes jumped to Nathan's arm, as if she expected to see something odd happen there. Greg noticed the two spirelings staring with similar puzzled expressions.

"What is it?" he asked Nathan.

"Just the part of my shirt that covers my arm."

"No, I mean what's your trick?"

"A special place ahead," Nathan said. He pointed along the ridge. "If I remember correctly, it should be right over that next rise."

Gnash and Gnaw both took one cautious step backward, but Priscilla stayed put. Her eyes, like those of the spirelings, remained fixed on the magician's sleeve. Nathan shook his head at the three of them, dropped his arm, and resumed his march along the path.

He led them over the next rise, scaring away two goblins and a basilisk, and then altered his course and followed a steep path descending from the ridge. They hiked east a short ways, straight toward the heart of the desolate landscape, before Nathan planted his staff in the dust at his feet.

"Well, here we are."

Greg looked about the desert. Aside from the ridge they'd just left, standing tall to the west, and an infinitely taller spire still towering high above them to the north, there was nothing here to see. "Where?"

"At the portal," said Nathan.

The others stared back at him. Nathan enlightened them by extending his arm to one side where, with a fizzle, his hand disappeared. Greg's breath disappeared right along with it, and did not return again until Nathan drew back his arm, including, Greg noticed with relief, Nathan's completely intact hand. The spirelings gasped.

"Quite a trick," said Greg, "but I thought you weren't supposed to use your magic."

"It is not *my* magic," Nathan pointed out. Gnash and Gnaw began arguing silently among themselves but soon nodded, indicating they would allow the use of the portal. "Then shall we go?"

Greg studied the spot from all angles but could see no sign of the portal. "Go where?"

"To Pillsbury, in the realm of the Styx, just a few miles from the kingdom border."

"That's great. We can be at the border in an hour or so. Maybe Marvin still has a chance."

"Let's hope so."

Gnash stepped forward. "What about our amulet? That is our true mission, or have you forgotten?"

"Not at all," said Nathan. "Our plans have not changed. Ryder Hawkins is leading a patrol of men in that area, and according to the magician Mordred, we should be able to find this Corporal Widget among them."

The spireling nodded his approval. "Very well. Then we shall follow your lead."

Nathan nodded back. Without further ceremony, he stepped into the portal. The air shimmered and swallowed him up with a smack that left the others staring with apprehension. Greg and Priscilla stepped forward and surveyed the spot closely, but Greg could see no evidence that the portal even existed. He couldn't imagine how Nathan ever knew it was there.

"Do you think it's safe?" he asked Priscilla.

"Of course. You don't see Nathan complaining, do you?"

Greg was reluctant to point out that Nathan's sudden disappearance was most certainly the reason he wasn't complaining. For all Greg knew, Nathan had just popped out of existence.

Priscilla seemed to be listening to his thoughts. "You go," she said.

After much internal debate, Greg willed himself forward and stepped through the portal as if passing through a doorway, feeling nothing unusual as he left behind the desolate plain and walked into the flower bed of a quaint little hostel on the road just outside of what he quickly decided must be Pillsbury. He decided this partly because that's where Nathan said the portal would lead, but also because he knew Pillsbury was where Brandon Alexander, the court scribe, had supposedly gone on holiday, and by all descriptions, it was Brandon who stood on the grass directly in front of him now.

"Brandon?"

"I'm sorry, have we met?"

"Not exactly. I'm Greg."

"Greghart the dragonslayer, of course. Oh this is such an honor."

Greg snapped his head around to see if the two spirelings had heard. Luckily neither had stepped through the portal yet. "Call me Greg. I insist."

Brandon extended his hand to shake, but just as Greg reached out to return the gesture, Priscilla stepped out of midair and knocked him off his feet. Brandon reacted quickly to catch him, and gave him a long hug.

"Such a friendly greeting," the scribe said, rather embarrassed. "I'm flattered."

Greg struggled to break free of the man's embrace, equally embarrassed, and cleared his throat awkwardly. "What a coincidence. I can't believe we ran into you like this."

"Yes, well, chalk one more up for your pal, Lucky." Brandon chuckled. "It's not the first time that boy has amazed me."

"Lucky's not even with us," said Priscilla.

"He's not?"

"Not everything good that happens can be attributed to your friend," Nathan reminded them. "Sometimes a coincidence is just that."

Priscilla rolled her eyes, as if Nathan were speaking foolishness.

Gnash stepped through the portal, and Brandon's eyes popped wide. Then Gnaw stepped through, and Brandon jumped back.

"It's okay," Priscilla reassured him. "They're traveling with us."

Brandon nodded, but he kept a wary eye on the two spirelings, not to mention the empty spot above the flower bed, where more spirelings could appear at any moment.

"We should get going," urged Nathan.

"Going?" said Brandon. "But you've just arrived."

Nathan quickly explained about Ryder's army and the missing amulet, and then about Marvin Greatheart and the trolls. Brandon listened to the last in horror, though it was difficult to tell if it was Nathan's tale that upset him, or that the spirelings were starting to growl between themselves.

"Hang on," Greg begged Gnash and Gnaw, "I just need a minute." He turned back to Brandon. "Maybe you can answer a question for us."

"Oh my, well, I'll certainly do what I can."

"Do you know who General Bashar is?"

Brandon thought a long moment. Suddenly his face brightened. "Of course. Yes, now I remember."

Greg's pulse quickened. "You do?"

"Absolutely. According to the prophecy, General Bashar is one of three generals who will be fighting by your side in the upcoming battle against the spirelings."

Greg's hopes deflated. He noticed the two spireling guards had turned rather angry glares on him.

"You intend to fight us?" said Gnash. He rolled his axe in his hand until it reflected the sunlight across Greg's face, flashing a warning that was hard to misinterpret.

"Kidding," Greg said. "He was just kidding." He fixed a pleading gaze into Brandon's eyes and said, "Come on, Brandon, quit messing around."

"What?" said Brandon. "Oh, right. Quite the kidder, I am." Greg remembered the man's drinking problem and thanked the Fates Brandon hadn't been drinking today.

"What more can you tell us about General Bashar?" Priscilla asked.

"Nothing," said Brandon. "Aside from what Bart told me, I've never heard of him."

Priscilla groaned. "Then we're no better off than before."

"Wait, what about the hero from the first prophecy?" Greg asked Brandon.

Brandon shot him an odd look. "What about him?"

Greg spotted a flash but didn't realize Nathan had used his magic again until Gnash and Gnaw winced and slapped their hands over their ears. Nathan leaned forward as if about to speak in confidence. He glanced again at the spirelings, who still seemed to be listening, then pretended to scratch his nose, creating a larger spark that caused both Gnash and Gnaw to squeal. They took to shaking their heads and slapping their ears while Nathan whispered to the scribe.

"You must not refer to Greg as Greghart or reveal that he had anything to do with the last prophecy," he quickly explained. "The spirelings believe the Mighty Greghart took their amulet. If they figure out Greg is Greghart, they're going to demand to know what he did with it. Now, recently you wrote about the Hero who slayed Ruuan. *S-L-A-Y*, not *S-L-E-I-G-H*."

"Of course," said Brandon. "A sleigh is a type of wagon that slides on runners."

"I know what a sleigh is," Nathan said. "It's just that in the first prophecy you wrote that Greg would sleigh the dragon. *S-L-E-I-G-H*, not *S-L-A-Y*."

"I did? I misspelled *slay* in the first prophecy?"

Nathan looked nearly as worried as Greg felt. "I don't know. Perhaps. Then you're saying you always meant it to be *S-L-A-Y*?"

Brandon laughed out loud. "Of course. The other wouldn't make sense at all, would it?"

Nathan frowned. "No, I suppose not."

Greg sidled up to the two of them. "But it was never actually written down until *you* put it on paper. You just heard Bart say it, right? There's no reason why it couldn't have been *S-L-E-I-G-H*, right?"

"Weren't you listening to that bit about the runners?" Brandon asked, his expression one of great concern.

Greg tried to match Nathan's earlier scowl. "I know what a sleigh is, too."

"Okay," said Brandon hesitantly, "then what's the problem?"

Greg gave up and returned to stand beside Priscilla. Nathan warned Brandon once more about speaking in front of Gnash and Gnaw. He waved his hand again, and the spirelings went back to acting normal, for spirelings.

"What was that?" Gnash asked.

"What?" said Nathan.

"That high-pitched noise. For a second I couldn't hear anything else."

"I, too," said Gnaw.

"Funny," said Nathan, "I didn't hear a thing."

The two spirelings stared back at him distrustfully, then turned suspicious glares on Greg.

"Don't look at me."

"I guess having such acute hearing isn't always a plus," said Nathan, smiling.

"We better go," said Greg.

Nathan nodded. "Agreed."

"Can I come too?" asked Brandon.

"Did you miss the part about the thousand trolls?" Greg asked, and even though he hadn't intended to match the condescending tone Brandon had used when he asked Greg about the sleigh, it came through anyway.

"No," Brandon assured him, "but I still want to go. I just need to grab a few things and say good-bye to Mother. It'll take but a minute."

Gnash and Gnaw clearly didn't approve, but Brandon insisted he would hurry, and Nathan convinced the spirelings it could help to have the scribe along, explaining how Brandon might recall some lesser-known details of the prophecy that could mean the difference between success or failure.

Greg might have pointed out that the prophecy said the king's army was going to be victors in the upcoming battle, so the spirelings would be crazy to help them, or that Nathan was being hypocritical—the magician had always been the first to insist people shouldn't know too much about their destinies—but Greg held his tongue. Brandon might not be much help in a fight against a thousand trolls, but Greg didn't see how it could hurt to have one more ally by his side.

"How's your mom?" Priscilla asked Brandon as they hurried down the sidewalk toward Mrs. Alexander's home.

"Mother's fine. Why she wants to live way down here in the Styx is beyond me, but . . . well, let's just say she's a bit stubborn. I've tried to get her to move back, but she won't hear of it. Says all her friends live down here now, and she doesn't want to leave them."

"How did she ever come here in the first place?" asked Priscilla.

"Came down on holiday a few years back and stayed for the weather," Brandon said. He turned down a narrow cobblestone walk toward a large building made of what looked like clay. "It's warm here all year round, you see. Claims the moist air is easier to breathe."

Greg flapped his cloak. "It is a bit warm here, isn't it? Odd. The kingdom was freezing."

Brandon reached the front door, pulled it open and called out to the empty room. "Mother. Visitors."

He slipped off the boots he was wearing and shuffled across the wood floor in his stocking feet as his mother entered the room. She studied Greg a moment before realization struck. Then she grabbed him by the sleeve and nearly pulled him off balance.

"My word, Brandy, do you know who this is?"

The scribe looked quite embarrassed at being referred to as *Brandy*. He retrieved a small pack from a cupboard, opened it and removed a wine sack, which he began to fill with water from a basin in the kitchen. "Of course, Mother. I brought him here, remember?"

"But he's—"

"Yes, Mum," he said before his mother could reveal Greg's identity, "I know."

"He's no one," said Nathan, but the old woman missed the magician's commanding tone.

"No, he's a famous drag—"

"Yep," Brandon cut her off. He threw the wine sack in the pack along with a small loaf of bread, grabbed a pair of dusty boots from the corner and hopped across the floor as he struggled to pull them on while he made his way to the door.

"Brandy, why are you acting so funny? Oh, and you," she said, noticing Priscilla for the first time. "You're King Peter's youngest daughter, aren't you?"

"Yes, ma'am," said the princess. "Please, call me Priscilla."

"Oh my," Mrs. Alexander tittered. "Brandon, did you hear? Princess Priscilla's here too."

"Yes, Mum, I know Priscilla. Remember, I work for her father."

"Royalty, right here in my home. Wait till I tell the girls." Unable to stop smiling, Mrs. Alexander introduced herself to Nathan, but then she spotted Gnash and Gnaw and her expression melted. "What are those?" she asked, grimacing.

Brandon opened a second cupboard near the front door and removed a heavy cloak. "Spirelings, Mother. They're helping the others fulfill a prophecy."

"Really?" she said, apparently working hard to overcome her revulsion. "Are they housebroken?"

With a scowl, Gnash pulled Gnaw outside. Mrs. Alexander watched them go with a raised eyebrow. "Really, Brandy, you should pick your friends more carefully."

"*Ahem.*"

"Oh, I didn't mean you, Highness," she said, her face reddening, "or you, Gregh—"

"We really need to get going," Greg said quickly, drowning out the last.

"Yes, of course," agreed Brandon. "We'll leave at once."

"Nonsense," said Mrs. Alexander. "You've barely just arrived. Sit and we'll talk."

"We don't have time," Brandon told her.

"Well, at least stay for a bite to eat. Your friends must be famished."

Greg was, but he knew they couldn't afford the delay. "We really need to go."

Once they were outside the village, following the trail leading between Pillsbury and the kingdom, Brandon thanked Greg.

"For what?" Greg asked.

"Mother can be quite demanding. She would have never let us leave so easily had you not insisted we hurry. But she's heard all the stories. She would never argue with someone of your preeminence."

"My what?"

"Oh my, they said you were modest."

Greg picked up his pace, leaving Brandon behind. He had mixed emotions about resuming the journey. Sure, Brandon's mom was a bit domineering, but her pampering reminded him of Marvin Greatheart's mother, especially when they were headed down the walk and she yelled after them from her doorway, insisting they come back for a nourishing meal. If only they could have afforded the time. But it was Mrs. Alexander's similarity to Marvin's mother that forced Greg to go on. Mrs. Greatheart's son was in trouble, and he owed it to her to reach him as soon as possible.

The weather remained unseasonably warm until they reached and crossed a rickety old bridge spanning a wide, blue river. The instant they stepped over the border into the kingdom the temperature dropped fifty degrees. Greg cinched his tunic tight and slipped his cloak back over his shoulders. "Whoa, why so cold?"

"It's winter," said Nathan.

"Of course," muttered Greg. "What was I thinking?"

"It's been forever since we left," said Priscilla. "They could be anywhere by now. Which way should we go?"

"The trolls are this way," said Gnash, pointing to the west.

"Absolutely," agreed Gnaw. He set off in that direction without waiting to see if the others would follow.

"Don't tell me you can hear them?" Greg asked, amazed.

"Of course not," said Gnash. He pointed to his nose. "We smell them."

At first Greg was astonished, but then he recalled the horrible stench surrounding the large group of trolls and was surprised he couldn't pick up the scent himself, no matter how far off the beasts might be.

They followed the familiar wide river that separated the kingdom from the Styx, traveling west for a few miles. The beautiful golden cliffs with their scattered waterfalls now sat off to Greg's left instead of his right, but Greg hardly noticed them. It was already late afternoon. He grew hungrier with every step, yet he and the others pressed on.

The ground grew more treacherous the farther they walked, until finally the group was forced to angle into the woods that lined the ridge to the north. This area seemed familiar to Greg, but it wasn't until he entered a large clearing where the grass had been trampled beneath thousands of heavy feet, that he recognized the spot where Marvin had been captured. It wasn't the trampled grass that gave it away so much as the stench.

Priscilla gulped. "They're gone."

"At least they shouldn't be hard to track," said Nathan, pointing at the wide swath of trampled bushes extending to the north. "I don't believe they're far off."

Even without magical powers of his own, Greg agreed. He wouldn't have been surprised to learn he was standing inside a troll now. He shook his head and blew his nose to expel the putrid odor.

Starving, sore and tired, they resumed their search. Not long after, Greg heard a rustling in the brush, and two men jumped from the bushes lining each side of the narrow trail.

"Halt, who goes th—" one soldier managed to shout before he landed hard on his back. The other landed more softly, as Gnash was kind enough to toss him neatly atop the first.

Gnash held both men's swords in his hand. He quickly decided the fallen humans were little threat and threw back their weapons, nearly skewering them in the process, and the two men, each clad in the royal blue uniform of the Army of the Crown, sat up looking dazed.

"W—what happened?" one asked.

"Meet Gnash," Priscilla said. "He's traveling with us."

"Princess Priscilla?" the guard said, clearly surprised to meet up with the king's daughter so far from Pendegrass Castle. "Forgive us, Highness, we didn't know it was you."

"It wasn't. I told you, it was Gnash. And please, don't call me Highness."

"Certainly, Your—er—certainly."

Nathan stepped forward and helped the man to his feet. "I assume you're part of General Hawkins's command." Nathan lent a hand to the second guard as well.

"Yes, sir," said the first soldier. "We were ordered to watch for dangers from the south. General Hawkins's troops are just up that trail about a mile from here."

"Is Marvin Greatheart with them?" Greg asked.

"Or his brother Melvin, and Lucky Day?" Priscilla added.

"The two boys are with the general, yes, but I'm afraid the dragonslayer has gotten himself into a bit of a quandary. There's more trolls up that way than I've seen in all my life, let alone together in one spot, and when last I saw them, they had the Mighty Greatheart strung up on a pike planted in the ground at the center of their camp."

Priscilla breathed a nervous sigh. "Then he's still alive."

"He was when I left. But that was hours ago. We've been expecting some relief anytime now, but . . . I'm sure the general is very busy trying to figure out how to get Greatheart back without starting a full-scale war."

"Oh dear," said Priscilla.

Nathan thanked the men for the information and herded the others past. The two guards watched for a moment, their nerves calming, but then Gnaw came zooming up from behind, and they nearly dropped their swords. They needn't have worried. Knowing from his secret bond with Gnash that the two soldiers posed no threat, Gnaw paid them little heed.

The farther Greg and the others walked, the worse the stench grew. Luckily they didn't walk far. When Ryder's men came into view, Greg was taken by the unnatural silence. Hundreds of soldiers sat scattered about the ground, some eating, others simply resting while they had the chance, but all of them wide awake. Yet, aside from the chirping of birds and the occasional rustling of a monkeydog in the brush, not a sound could be heard.

"Follow me," one said when he noticed the group's approach, and without another word he led them straight to General Hawkins. Gnash and Gnaw lagged behind, studying the area curiously. Greg wondered if they'd ever seen so many humans in one place.

Ryder Hawkins looked about ten years older than he had when Greg saw him last. The lines around his eyes deepened when he squinted at the approaching group, and then the corners of his mouth turned up slightly, no doubt the closest he could come to a smile.

"*Shh,*" he warned them. He pointed toward the trees ahead. "The trolls are camped in a clearing just on the other side of that bend. I'd have sworn there weren't that many in all of Myrth, but I can now say for a fact there are. I've actually seen them with my own eyes."

"How many?" asked Brandon.

"Twenty thousand, maybe more. We watched ten more groups join up with the others this afternoon alone. I don't know where they're coming from, but they all seem to have known to meet up here today. Spooky, if you ask me. I don't know what they have in mind, but I don't see any way it could be good."

"How did you get here so quickly?" Priscilla asked. "Dad expected you'd take at least a few more days."

"Yes, well, we made amazing time. It's as if luck were on our side."

Greg frowned. "Where is Lucky?"

"He and the little Greatheart boy are around someplace," said Ryder. "I'm afraid I've paid them little heed. I've had more pressing matters on my mind, as you can well imagine. Marvin Greatheart is being held captive, and I dare say I can't figure out how to help him. I sent in some of my scouts to look for a weakness, but, well . . . nothing. Last I looked, there was a ring of trolls around Marvin a hundred deep. Now maybe we could charge in there and reach him by force, but not without suffering tremendous losses. Even if we had the entire kingdom army to back us up, we could never drive out that many of the beasts."

"Maybe Nathan can help," said Greg.

"Yes, of course," Ryder sighed. "I'm getting too weary to think. I forgot about your magic."

Greg didn't think Gnash and Gnaw were close to hearing distance, but the pair strode purposefully forward now.

"The magician must not use his powers," Gnash said, his tone little more than a growl.

"*Shh,*" Ryder insisted, snapping his head toward the trail to the north. Unseen birds chirped ahead, the only sound to break the still air. Ryder turned back to the others, apparently satisfied they had not been discovered, but jumped when he saw the source of the voice he'd just heard. After a brief moment to gather his wits, he spoke. "Something wrong with your powers, Nathan?"

The magician sighed. "It's a long story. Let's just say it would be good if we could come up with another way."

"Forget about your dragonslayer," Gnaw said, his voice taking on a tone that was hard to disobey. "We need to find this Widget person."

"Are you talking about Corporal Widget?" Ryder asked.

Gnaw's eyes brightened. "Yes. We must speak with him right away."

"What's this about?" insisted Ryder.

"It's okay," Nathan reassured him. "We have reason to believe the corporal may know something about the spirelings' missing amulet."

"Really?" said Ryder. "Well, if so, he never mentioned it to me. Anyway, I'm afraid you can't talk to him now."

"We can and we will," growled Gnash. He raised his axe to illustrate his point, prompting Ryder to take a quick step backward.

"Relax, Gnash," said Nathan. He reached out a cautious hand to guide the weapon back to the spireling's side. "Widget isn't going anywhere. Could you just give us a minute?"

The spireling stared at Nathan as if deciding what size pieces to chop him into.

"Look, we haven't eaten all day," Nathan told him. "Why don't you and Gnaw take this opportunity to grab a quick bite? We'll talk to Corporal Widget in just a second, okay?"

Gnash reluctantly agreed, to which Greg released a pent-up breath.

"How did you end up traveling with those two?" Ryder asked Nathan after Gnash and Gnaw wandered off.

"I'll tell you all about it when we have more time," Nathan said. "For now we need to cooperate with them. They're not going to rest until they've spoken with Corporal Widget."

"That is unfortunate," whispered Ryder.

Realizing there was more to follow, Nathan quickly waved his hands through the air. An effervescent trail sparkled for several seconds and faded away to nothing. In the background, Greg heard Gnash gasp and throw his hands over his ears. Gnaw did the same. The two spirelings were still shaking their heads when Greg looked away.

"You were saying?" Nathan asked Ryder.

Greg leaned in close, until he was tilted so far, Ryder actually reached a hand out to catch him should he topple and fall.

"I'm afraid your friends are going to be disappointed," said Ryder. "Corporal Widget is not here. He transferred to General Talbout's troops when we rested at Pendegrass Castle a few weeks ago."

"General Talbout's troops," said Greg. "But they're—"

"On the opposite side of the kingdom. Yes."

Rescue

Greg glanced back at the two spirelings. Gnash was busy digging deep inside one ear with a four-inch-long claw. Gnaw winced and shook his head from time to time but mostly ignored the sound Nathan placed inside his head, apparently more interested for the moment in the turkey leg a soldier had handed him. At least, Greg wanted to believe it was a turkey leg, even if he'd never heard of a turkey growing to half that size. In any case, it was clear the two spirelings weren't eavesdropping.

"I thought you weren't supposed to use your magic," Greg said.

"I'm not," said Nathan, "but this is clearly a case where what the spirelings don't know won't hurt them. If it were up to them, we'd waste no time trying to rescue Marvin, and though I don't know a lot about events to come, I believe the dragonslayer may yet have a part to play in all of this. Gnash and Gnaw may be too shortsighted to realize it, but it is in their best interest that I do what I must to see the Mighty Greatheart safe. I need to make intelligent decisions for them, whether they involve magic or not."

"In other words, you don't care about their orders," Greg said.

"Not *their* orders. Queen Gnarla's. Now, I think it's time we go back to obeying the spirelings. We need to choose our battles, remember?"

"You know, it's weird," Greg said. "We have that same expression on Earth."

Nathan smiled. "I've noticed many similarities between our two worlds. If I had to guess, I'd say some of those who fought here during the Dragon Wars returned to the homes of their comrades in battle. Well, we'll have plenty of time to discuss the matter further once Greatheart is safely back in our midst. For now let's not mention anything to the spirelings about Corporal Widget's absence, okay?"

The others agreed. Nathan waved his hands again, winked, and raised his voice. "Widget, you say? Maybe we'd better take a closer look. Ryder, let's see if we can find a weakness in their defenses."

Gnash threw down his turkey leg, and he and Gnaw rushed forward. "We heard you say something about Widget. We will come with you."

"I won't be using my magic," Nathan assured them.

"Good. We will come anyway."

"Suit yourself," said Nathan. He offered Greg a stern look. "You kids stay here. We'll be gone only a minute."

Ryder signaled for two of his men to escort him and Nathan closer to the troll camp, and the spirelings followed the four of them up the trail to the north, where they soon disappeared around the bend.

Brandon eyed the meat Gnash had tossed on the ground and nearly picked it up before Rake beat him to it. As much as Greg would have liked to stop and grab a bite himself, he and Priscilla searched out Lucky and Melvin to see if they had any ideas how to rescue Marvin. But after scouring the entire area, they could find no sign of either boy. No one could remember seeing the pair for an hour or more.

"What should we do?" Priscilla asked.

"I guess we better tell someone," said Greg. He looked to the north, trying his best to ignore the lingering troll stench that hung cloyingly in the air, and then started up the trail, Priscilla at his heels.

"What are you kids doing here?" Ryder hissed when Greg and the princess strode into view. "Get down. Someone will see you."

Only then did Greg notice the soldiers and Nathan crouched in the bushes to the side of the trail. He and Priscilla scurried closer.

Nathan started ranting something about staying safe and doing as you're told, but Greg wasn't listening. He stretched up on tiptoes and strained to glimpse the clearing where the trolls were camped. As short as he was, he couldn't have hoped to see a thing without jumping at least three feet in the air, but then he got a fine view once he realized the tree stump he'd been leaning against was actually Gnash.

Nathan clamped a hand over Greg's mouth. "I asked you two to stay put. What do you have to say for yourselves?"

"Mm mmph."

Nathan released his grip, and Greg told him what he and Priscilla had found, or in this case, not found.

"This is exactly what I need," whispered Ryder. "It's bad enough I've got one man to rescue. Let's just hope we don't have three."

He instructed one of his soldiers to search the camp for any sign of the two boys. The man jogged off down the trail to the south and returned a few minutes later. Even though Greg knew what the verdict would be, he still felt his spirits drop when the soldier announced the two boys were no longer in camp.

"Told you so," said Priscilla.

Ryder groaned. "I knew I shouldn't have let those two out of my sight. That little Greatheart boy is no less bold than his brother. And Lucky Day . . . well, I don't need to tell you about him. He's got himself so convinced he's beyond harm, I wouldn't be surprised if he strolled right up to the trolls and asked them when they planned to turn the dragonslayer free."

Greg was about to defend Lucky, but no, Ryder was probably right. He watched the creases in Ryder's forehead deepen as the general contemplated his next move. Greg couldn't come up with anything either. As it turned out, he didn't need to. A sudden movement on the open trail ahead caught his eye. He nearly screamed when he spotted Lucky and Melvin strolling nonchalantly back toward camp.

Ryder spotted them too. "Lucky, little Greatheart, where have you been?" His voice, while little more than a whisper, somehow managed to scold as effectively as a shout. The two boys nearly bolted away, but then they must have recognized Ryder, and stepped into the brush with the others.

"We've been spying on the trolls," Melvin informed them in a tone Greg thought sounded a lot more casual than the situation deserved. He spotted Greg and frowned. "Oh, you're back. About time."

"Hi, Greg. Priscilla," said Lucky. "Where have you been?"

"Long story."

"Boys," Ryder urged.

"We think we figured out what all these trolls are doing here," Lucky told him. "They're planning to attack the king's army."

"They know we're here?" Ryder asked, peering with concern through the trees.

"No, not this army," explained Lucky. "They're going to march on Pendegrass Castle. They think that's where we're going to battle the spirelings."

Gnash turned to face them. "So you do plan to fight us?"

"There is a prophecy to that effect, yes," said Nathan, "but we do not know yet if it is true."

"Prophecies are always true," Gnaw said. "I must say I am disappointed. After your help dispatching that wyvern earlier, I had begun to count you a friend."

"I can assure you I have no interest in standing against you or your kind," said Nathan. "Perhaps the prophecy is a trick of some sort brewed up by Witch Hazel to set us against each other. It sounds like the sort of treachery she might use."

"We have heard of this Witch Hazel," Gnash told him, "and she is as you have described. But still, we do not believe a prophecy could be wrong. If it has been foretold that we will fight, well . . ." He rolled his axe over in his hands, his razor-sharp claws accidentally gouging the wood of the handle. "I am going to deeply regret having to take your heads."

"Imagine how we feel," Greg told him.

"Why would the trolls want to get involved in our battle?" Priscilla asked. "It sounds like the last place I'd want to be."

"They must intend to hit us after we fight," said Greg, "when both sides are weakened."

"Why would the spireling army be weakened after a fight with humans?" Gnash asked matter-of-factly, to which Greg felt his stomach roll.

"Yes, well, with the kind of numbers we've seen here today, they'll be able to finish off whoever is left," said Ryder. "And with both armies gone, they'll have no trouble taking over the kingdom."

"Oh dear," said Priscilla. "What are we going to do?"

"Yeah," said Melvin, turning an accusing glare Greg's way. "What are *we* going to do?"

Greg scowled back, but he was too anxious to put much effort into it.

"We'll worry about that pass when we march through it," said Ryder. "Right now we've got a rescue to pull off."

"Did your eavesdropping at least teach you guys anything that may help?" Greg asked Lucky and Melvin.

The two exchanged glances and both shook their heads. Greg struggled to come up with an idea of his own. How could they possibly get to the dragonslayer past hundreds of trolls without alerting the entire camp? Then it came to him. "Rake!" He loosened the neck of his cloak until he felt something stir beneath the cloth and a furry head popped into view. Rake's whiskers shook as he sniffed the cold winter air.

"Shadowcat," Gnaw screamed.

Gnash jumped a full six feet off the ground and carved his axe through the air on all sides before touching down again. "Where?"

Ryder nearly clamped a hand over the spireling's mouth, but wisely clamped it over Greg's instead. He signaled for one of his men to check if the trolls had heard. The man stood on tiptoes to peer through the branches. Finally he returned to a crouch and shook his head. Only then did Ryder loosen his grip.

"Keep your voice down," he instructed. "What's the meaning of this outburst?"

"I just remembered," said Greg. "The shadowcats can put people to sleep."

"Trolls aren't people," Ryder reminded him.

"Well, neither are spirelings, but the shadowcats did it to them, remember? Outside the Infinite Spire when I was here before."

Gnash looked uncomfortable listening to any discussion involving shadowcats. "Spirelings do not sleep," he insisted.

"They did that day," Greg assured him.

"Greg's right," said Lucky. "I saw it too."

"Me too," said both Melvin and Priscilla.

Gnaw scowled at the four of them, and while a scowl is never a pleasant thing, one formed out of a mouth full of jagged teeth can leave an image that sticks with a person a long time. The group dropped into silence.

"We spirelings did not sleep that day," Gnaw said. "We were possessed. Those dreadful shadowcats used some sort of evil magic on us."

"Looked like you were sleeping to me," said Melvin, who was young and still unclear about when he should and shouldn't argue with a monster.

"Maybe the shadowcats *could* help us under different circumstances," said Nathan, "but we don't have an army of them like before. We have only one. Unless you know how to go about summoning the others . . ."

"I don't," said Greg, "but I'll bet Rake does. I wonder if he'd do it if I asked him?"

If Greg could correctly interpret a spireling's expression, Gnaw looked even less pleased than before. "You're talking about bringing more of those foul beasts here? Absolutely not."

"I think we have to. Unless you know another way of getting in and out of there without being noticed."

Gnash and Gnaw began a fervent exchange without saying a word. Suddenly the two of them appeared to arrive at a decision. They jumped up and raced ahead through the trees so quickly, the others witnessed little more than a blur.

Greg jumped as high as he could to see above the brush, and for an instant spotted the blurred forms of the spirelings nearing the rim of the resting trolls. His mind continued to process the image as his head dropped below the leaves again. It was only then he realized he'd seen Marvin Greatheart still strapped to a pike in the background.

"What's happening?" Priscilla wanted to know. No matter how high she jumped, she was too short to see.

Greg didn't answer. He jumped again, this time knowing exactly where to look. In one brief instant he was able to lock in a clear image of the two spirelings lunging toward the pike, axes leading the way. Miraculously Gnash and Gnaw had already managed to thread their way through the trolls with no alarm sounded.

Greg's feet barely touched down before the blow of an axe rang out, accompanied by the loud crack of very solid wood. A booming troll voice screamed out, and suddenly the whole camp burst to life.

"Retreat!" Ryder called.

Greg must have been slow in reacting, because Nathan gripped him roughly by his cloak and hurled him out onto the trail. The magician then did the same with Priscilla, and suddenly they were all sprinting back toward camp, the thunderous roar of thousands of heavy footsteps at their backs. Greg could barely run, his muscles were so sore, but he didn't dare slow down.

"Behind us," Ryder shouted when the camp came into view.

The closest soldiers jumped to their feet, their eyes grew wide and they jumped out of the way. Behind, the noise soared nearer, until Greg feared he was about to be run down.

Only it wasn't trolls closing in, but the two spirelings. Gnash zoomed by first, carrying one end of a very large log. Gnaw rushed past an instant later, carrying the other. Between, still sandwiched between two bedrolls, Marvin Greatheart had no choice but to fly by with them, as he was still strapped to the timber the two spirelings carried.

What little of Marvin's skin Greg could see looked frighteningly gray. Greg guessed he must be unconscious. Otherwise he'd surely be putting up more of a struggle. The sight lasted only an instant. The spirelings passed in and out of the campsite and had completely disappeared by the time Greg caught his first breath.

"Trolls!" one of the soldiers finally shouted, and throughout the camp men jumped to life.

Behind, Nathan carried a cursing Priscilla under one arm. He dropped her and spun, raising his staff as a half dozen of the beasts burst from the woods. The magician anticipated their progress and swept the first off the path with a single swipe. From nowhere Gnash and Gnaw bounded into the fight. With lightning-quick reflexes, each dispensed with two of the trolls that followed.

But Nathan's back was turned when the last of the beasts raised its club. Greg screamed and charged, his walking stick held high, and while the troll chuckled over the threat, Nathan took him out from behind.

The sixth troll had barely hit the ground before Gnash turned and swept Priscilla off her feet again. Her screams did nothing to dissuade the spireling. He sprinted off so quickly, those watching disagreed as to whether he ever took her to begin with. The only reason Greg witnessed any of it was because after Gnash picked up Priscilla, Gnaw swept Greg off his feet and followed.

Greg hadn't moved this quickly since Ruuan carried him to the Greathearts' shack, and while not even the spirelings could match the dragon's speed, the trip seemed equally fast, what with the ground rushing by scant inches beneath Greg's head.

After what felt like miles, the spirelings dropped Greg and the princess on their feet, handed them each an axe and ran back toward the others. The ground felt unnaturally still, and Greg seemed to have forgotten how to use his feet. He watched the spirelings go, astounded by their speed. No more than a few seconds passed before they rushed toward him again, this time carrying Lucky and Melvin over their shoulders.

"Put me down. Put me DOWN," screamed Melvin.

Gnaw did as Melvin asked. As fast as he was, he barely managed to release the boy without getting struck by Melvin's flailing feet.

"Ha, that was a close one," Gnash said as he set Lucky down, and while Greg at first thought the spireling was talking about Gnaw's daring release of Melvin, he soon realized Gnash had been talking about the rescue.

Melvin brushed himself off. "I could have walked, you know."

"Sorry," said Gnash. "It looked to me like you were falling behind."

"Naw, I was just worried about Lucky."

"Me? If anyone was falling behind it was—"

Greg jumped when he heard a rustling from the north. To his relief, Nathan emerged from the trees at a dead run, followed by Ryder and a panting Brandon.

"Go!" Brandon screamed. "Go!"

Gnash didn't move. "We need not worry. The trolls are heading north, as that is the direction we took when we fled their campsite, hoping to throw them off our trail. The only reason we were followed is because we circled back so quickly, some of the beasts had not yet managed to react to our initial passage."

"You're kidding?" said Greg, but soon he realized no one was listening. Lucky had loosened Marvin's bonds and removed the bedroll tied to his chest, but still the dragonslayer lay unmoving in the dirt.

Nathan knelt and put an ear to Marvin's mouth. "He's alive," he announced after a long pause, "but his breath is very shallow."

Priscilla dropped to the fallen dragonslayer's side. "Oh my. He's out cold."

"Yes, literally," said Ryder. "The poor man's been strapped to that pike for over a full day now. He must be freezing."

Marvin groaned, a welcome sound, as it proved Nathan was right when he determined the dragonslayer to be alive. Priscilla hugged him, supposedly to warm him up, though Greg had his doubts. While the princess had eventually become annoyed by Marvin's boisterous attitude yesterday, her admiration for the bronzed hero before then had been clear. Greg scowled at the pathetic display. But then he witnessed Marvin's blue lips and grayish skin, and he understood Priscilla's concern.

Gnaw closed his eyes and weaved his hands together until a low blue flame erupted on his palms. Slowly he waved his hands over Marvin's muscular frame, gingerly nudging Priscilla out of the way, and warmed the man until Marvin's eyes dropped open and he began to stir.

"W—what happened?" Marvin asked groggily, and Greg knew Gnaw must have used a powerful magic to aid in the healing.

"Corporal Widget?" Gnaw asked.

"Ask him about our amulet," said Gnash.

"This is Marvin Greatheart," Nathan informed them both, "the famous dragonslayer."

A loud rumbling erupted from somewhere deep within Gnaw, the sort of noise that would have left a bear envious. The spireling picked up his axe and spun toward Nathan.

"This is your trickery, Magician. You have sought to mislead us all along."

"I assure you I have not." Nathan looked far less uneasy than Greg felt the situation deserved. Ryder and Brandon, on the other hand, mirrored Greg's concerns. They were apparently no more comfortable around agitated spireling warriors than Greg was, for they scuttled backward what they must have foolishly thought was a safe distance.

"Nathan never said it was Widget we were rescuing," said Greg. "We've been talking about rescuing Marvin ever since we left the Infinite Spire."

"Yes," said Gnaw, "but we thought you were smart enough to realize where your priorities should lie. Naturally we assumed since you were expending your energies performing a rescue, it must be Widget who needed your help."

"I don't believe my priorities are misplaced," said Nathan. "We'll still help you find your amulet, but surely you can see from all we've learned that we have more important issues at stake. The future of the entire kingdom is at peril."

"Nothing is more important than the return of our amulet," Gnaw said with a hiss.

For a moment it looked as if the argument might come to blows, but then the two spirelings grew hesitant, and finally Gnash lowered his axe. "Queen Gnarla agrees with you about the importance of the battle," he said, "to a degree. She does admit it is worthy of concern . . . just not quite as much concern as the fate of our amulet. Now, we must get back to our true purpose."

"What's all this about the spirelings' amulet?" said Ryder. "I've heard about such a thing, but I always thought you Canarazas kept it under heavy guard inside some sort of magical passageway high up in Ruuan's spire."

"Normally they do," said Nathan, "but it appears someone stole it after we fulfilled the last prophecy. Our sources tell us that your man Widget may have some knowledge of its whereabouts."

Ryder shrugged. "I've heard nothing of this. But as I said before, we weren't together long before we parted company."

"Corporal Widget is not among us?" said Gnash.

"Sorry," said Nathan, and then to Ryder added, "and if I guess correctly, even if Widget did have the amulet when he left you, I doubt he knew."

"You think someone planted it on him?" said Greg. "Like Mordred, maybe?"

Nathan regarded Greg with a neutral expression. "That is a possibility, yes."

"Then where is he?" asked Gnaw, still focused on Widget.

Priscilla, who had been rubbing the Mighty Greatheart's biceps under the pretense of warming his skin, paused in her efforts and looked up at the others. "Why would Mordred want to plant the amulet on poor Corporal Widget?"

"Because he's evil," Lucky said. "Why else?"

Gnash growled in a manner that suggested he did not appreciate being ignored.

Nathan raised a hand to appease him. "Mordred is no more evil than I am," he said, a statement that shook Greg as much as reassured him. "If I had to guess, I'd say he knew that Widget would be switching to General Talbout's division. The new prophecy says that Ryder and Talbout will be side by side in the upcoming battle. What better way to get them together than to mislead us into seeking out both?"

"But we already knew we needed them," said Lucky. "Why trick us like this?"

"Maybe Mordred just wanted to be sure we didn't count on Ryder making it back on his own," said Greg.

"Perhaps," said Nathan. "Obviously he'll get back a lot quicker with us than he would have leading home his troops."

"But don't we need his troops too?" Greg was quick to point out.

Nathan wasn't listening. "If we're going to find our corporal, it looks as though we need to head to the opposite side of the kingdom. Ryder, if we can believe the prophecy, you should probably stick with us."

Greg felt an involuntary shudder. What about the rest of the army? And while he liked the thought of Ryder joining them, he hadn't failed to notice how Nathan had implied the prophecy could yet be wrong. That might have been a good thing under the right circumstances, but from the look on the two spirelings' faces, it didn't look as if the prophecy had any chance of being wrong about Greg having to fight the Canarazas.

"I've already given my men their orders," said Ryder. "They won't wait for my return. If we got separated they were to head directly to the castle for the upcoming battle. It's imperative the king be informed of the trouble brewing."

"Dad already knows about the prophecy," said Priscilla.

"I was speaking of the trolls."

"What are you talking about?" asked Marvin, looking annoyed as he tore his arm from Priscilla's grip. His joints crackled slightly under the strain, making him greatly resemble his father, but his color was beginning to return.

"It seems your brother and Mr. Day here overheard two trolls talking," Ryder told him. "All across the kingdom the entire troll race is banding together to war against us. They've heard of the upcoming battle between kingdom soldiers and spirelings and plan to launch a major offensive against us after both sides have been weakened."

"That's incredible," said Marvin. He struggled to stand, but made it only halfway before falling back to the ground, nearly crushing Priscilla. "Two trolls talking. Who would have thought?"

The spirelings grumbled to each other for a moment before Gnash stormed up to Nathan, weighing his axe equally between his two clawed hands. "Time is passing, Magician."

Nathan removed his cloak and draped it over Marvin, who accepted it gratefully. He then regarded the axe the spireling carried. "I agree. We'll leave at once." The spireling did not seem satisfied with this response. "Is there a problem?" Nathan asked.

"My partner and I have been discussing if you truly intend to return our amulet."

Nathan nodded. "And what have you decided?"

"When we fought the wyvern on the ridge outside our home, we were very nearly defeated. Much as the trolls seek to defeat your army while it is weakened, you could have struck out against us when the wyvern was about to best us. Instead you directed your attack against the beast, allowing us the opportunity to gain the upper hand."

Nathan remained silent.

"Then later when you showed us the secret portal to the Styx, you might have tried using the shift in dimension to catch us off guard, or for that matter you might have distracted us so you could sneak off through the nearby escape route without us knowing where you went. Instead you showed us where it was and waited for us to follow. No, if you wanted to deceive us, you have had your opportunities. We believe you are an honorable man who truly wants to help."

Gnaw stepped forward and studied Nathan closely. "Plus we suspect that you are a much more powerful magician than you have let on. We would not be surprised if you could have escaped anytime you wanted."

Nathan's face remained a mask of stone. He nodded again.

"Queen Gnarla has asked us to bring you back to the spire now. She wishes to speak to you about your intentions, and about this supposed upcoming battle."

"Very well," said Nathan, after which the spirelings returned to more silent communication between themselves. Ryder eased up to Nathan's side.

"What's this about a secret portal?" he asked.

"Well, not so much a secret anymore," Nathan sighed. "Come, I'll show you."

Return

Darkness was already closing in before Greg and the others made it back to the River Styx. With each step, the air grew more frigid. Even though it wasn't safe to hike at night, they pressed on, knowing that a few miles away the warmth of the Styx awaited. Whether because of Lucky's influence on the Fates or just coincidence, they managed to reach the bridge without incident and crossed about an hour after sunset. After a brief pause to remove their cloaks, they hurried back to Mrs. Alexander's home in the dark.

"But Mother's retirement village doesn't allow overnight guests," Brandon called out to them.

"Marvin must sleep in a warm bed tonight," Nathan insisted.

Overnight-guest rules or not, Mrs. Alexander would have never said no to Greg. She seemed quite impressed by Marvin, too, fawning over him as he finished his third bowl of stew. She would have probably fed him all night if both Princess Priscilla and Greg hadn't insisted Mrs. Alexander allow Marvin to get his much-needed rest. Truth was, they could all use the rest, with the possible exception of the spirelings.

In the morning, Gnash and Gnaw woke the others early so they could eat before daybreak. Mrs. Alexander was happy to whip up what looked like oatmeal, and the spirelings were only mildly irritated that she saw fit to dole theirs and Rake's out into cat bowls.

While they ate, she resumed her pampering of the dragonslayer.

At first Marvin seemed pleased by the attention. "Thousands of the beasts," he told her, "clawing at me and gnawing on my shins, and me totally helpless, with nothing but two tiny bedrolls to protect me from the elements."

But by breakfast's end, after Mrs. Alexander practically force-fed him three heaping bowls of mystery meal, Marvin gave up complaining and turned all his efforts toward convincing Mrs. Alexander he was good as new. Still she insisted on massaging his shoulders and refilling his bowl.

Marvin finally looked to Nathan and Ryder with pleading eyes. "Tell her I'm fine."

"You've been through a terrible ordeal," Nathan told him. "It wouldn't be wise to travel until you're fully recovered."

"You call that a terrible ordeal?" Marvin cried. "Why, I've run into worse difficulties scaring up breakfast in the morning. Please, take me with you."

But Nathan shook his head, and Ryder agreed.

"Didn't you say he might play a part in the prophecy?" Priscilla reminded Nathan.

"Yes," pleaded Marvin. "Listen to the maiden. For once she's making sense."

Priscilla's face turned the same shade of red it held out on the blustery trail. "What did you say?"

"Tell them, maiden. You were speaking of the prophecy. Go on, make yourself useful. Tell them."

Greg and Lucky both took cautious steps backward. Obviously torn between alliances, Melvin hesitated at first, but then wisely backed up as well. Priscilla planted herself before the dragonslayer and somehow managed to stare him down, even though, seated, he still towered over her by a full foot.

"Oh my, I hadn't noticed that," she said.

"What?" Marvin's eyes spun about in opposite directions as he tried to examine his own face. "What are you looking at?"

"Your eyes . . . oh, and your complexion. You know, perhaps you should be lying down."

"Oh dear," said Mrs. Alexander. She, too, stepped up to peer at the dragonslayer's face, though she had to stop when he slid back his chair and jumped to his feet. Her elderly vision could reach only so far. "You know, Highness, I think you're right. That's it, no more arguments. Mighty dragonslayer or not, you need to get back to bed right this instant."

"But—" said Marvin.

"Auhp. I said no arguments, remember?"

Marvin may have been skilled at fighting dragons, but he was no match for Brandon's mom. She reached up on tiptoes to grab him by the ear and dragged him to the spare bedroom, and aside from a lot of *ows* and *buts*, the Mighty Greatheart had little to say about it.

"What if he does have a part to play in the prophecy?" Greg asked Nathan.

"He doesn't," Brandon answered.

"But Nathan said he did," Greg argued. "Just because Simon didn't mention him doesn't mean Marvin can't have something important to do. Does it Nathan?"

The magician placed a reassuring hand on Greg's shoulder. "In his current condition, I'm afraid he would only slow us down, and then we all would fail. He must stay here for now. Later, if he has a part to play, he will play it. We shouldn't be trying to second-guess the future by manipulating his fate."

Greg's attention was drawn to the doorway of the guest room, where Marvin suddenly appeared wearing one of Mrs. Alexander's robes. About fifty sizes too small, it would have barely covered his loincloth, even if he could have closed it.

"Oh, good, you're still here. Tell her I'm looking better . . . and that you need me with you. She'll believe it if *you* tell her, maiden."

Priscilla's gaze locked on Marvin and her nostrils flared. "Mrs. Alexander."

Brandon's mother's face appeared from behind Marvin's waist and pivoted upward. "Oh my. What are you doing out of bed?" She latched onto his ear again and dragged him back out of sight.

"Wait," Marvin shouted from the other room. "Take me with you."

Mrs. Alexander reappeared a few minutes later, a length of rope in her hand. "It was great meeting you all," she said happily. "I do hope you'll come back and visit when you have more time."

"Yes, we sure will," Greg told her, though secretly he wondered if he'd ever be that hungry again.

Everyone thanked her for her hospitality and said their farewells. Shouted them, actually, trying to be heard over Marvin's cries. Outside on the stone walk they could still hear the dragonslayer pleading. Then Greg heard something else, too: a repetitious puffing sound, like an old steam locomotive laboring up a steep climb. From the north ran a lean man dressed in a bright fuchsia tunic. He didn't slow until he'd covered the full distance to their party. There he stopped and stood doubled over with his hands on his knees, panting and wheezing, unable to catch his breath.

"Zappas?" said Brandon. Everyone looked to him questioningly. "He's one of King Peter's runners."

"That's right," said Priscilla. "Daddy did say he sent someone to find you."

"Brandon?" Zappas gasped. "Is it really you?" He took a deep breath and blurted out a single sentence, speaking as quickly as possible to get it all out with what little air he could muster. "King Peter wants you to return to the castle at once."

"I know," said Brandon. "These folks already told me."

Zappas took in the entire group in a single disapproving glance. "Water," he managed to say.

"What took you so long?" Priscilla asked him. She dug through her pack and handed Zappas a canteen, which he sipped from sparingly, not wanting to waste a drop. "Don't worry. It's bottomless."

The runner's mouth dropped open. He tipped the canteen straight up, spilling half over his face, and gulped uncontrollably. When his thirst was quenched, he wiped his chin ineffectually with his sleeve. "I just ran hundreds of miles in five days."

"You took the eastern trail?" said Priscilla. "Why not west through Guttering Torch Caverns?"

"No one ventures that way. The darkness is impenetrable, and one wrong step would guarantee certain death."

"Oh. In that case, you made really great time. How'd you get here so fast?"

He took a second drink from the canteen, this time more slowly. "I know a shortcut."

A scream split the air, the sound of some desolate soul being tortured within an inch of his life.

"What was that?" Zappas cried, spilling the next few gulps of water on the sidewalk.

"That, I'm afraid," said Brandon, "is our heroic dragonslayer trying to stand up to Mother. Perhaps we should go back and rescue him."

"No," said both spirelings simultaneously.

Only then did Zappas notice Gnash and Gnaw. In spite of his fatigue he jumped back with astonishing quickness. "Look out."

"Relax, soldier," said Ryder. "They're friendly. Well, sort of."

The runner looked far from convinced.

"What's wrong?" Priscilla asked.

Zappas covered his mouth with a trembling hand and spoke in a near whisper. "You must understand what it's like for us runners. We survive the forests one way: because we can outrun danger. But these spirelings . . . once I stumbled across a pair in the hills north of the Infinite Spire. I'd have never believed it possible, but they ran past me so fast I barely saw them. Who knows what might have happened if they'd spotted me."

"We saw you," said Gnash. "You just were not interesting."

"Did you want to come with us?" Priscilla asked Zappas.

The runner's eyes widened. He glanced toward the two spirelings. "You're traveling with them?"

"Of course," said Priscilla. "We're on our way back to the Infinite Spire to speak with their queen."

Zappas's eyes grew wider still. In spite of the fact he'd just run hundreds of miles, he looked as if he'd turn right around and run the whole way back if it meant distancing himself from the spirelings. "If it's all the same to you, I need to get back."

"But aren't you tired?" Priscilla asked. "Don't you want something to eat?"

"Well, yes. I suppose a decent meal would be nice."

"Why don't you stop off at Mother's?" said Brandon. "I'm sure she'd love another guest, and I'd wager Marvin Greatheart would welcome the company."

Zappas looked skeptical. "Didn't you just say that horrid screech came from the dragonslayer?"

"Oh, sure, but he's fine, believe me. And Mother's a great cook."

The others nodded in agreement, though Greg did feel a bit guilty about not saying more.

Zappas's eyes drifted over to the two spirelings and quickly back again. "Food, a bit of rest and no spirelings. Yes, I could do that."

"It's the yellow house with the bright pink trim," Brandon managed to get out before Gnaw dragged him away.

"Thanks," Zappas shouted, though the sound was nearly lost beneath a second tormented shriek from Mrs. Alexander's home. Even so, he took one last look at the spirelings and headed toward what he must have considered to be the safer of his two options.

Nathan led the group farther down the sidewalk, stepped into one of the flower beds and motioned for the others to follow. It was a beautiful area, where the mixed aromas of flowers sent Greg's head reeling, but Greg could see nothing that would distinguish it from any other spot.

"Who wants to go first?" asked Nathan.

Melvin cast his eyes about the flower bed. "Go where?"

"I will," said Priscilla. She squeezed past Melvin, stepped delicately over a mound of begonias and promptly popped out of existence.

From the way Melvin jumped back from the portal, you'd have thought he'd just spotted a swinging dragon's tail there. "Where'd she go?"

"To the kingdom," said Nathan. "You can go next."

"Not me," said Melvin, but Gnash wasn't in the mood for an argument. With a single flick of the flat of his axe, he sent the boy sailing headfirst through the portal. Melvin's scream ended abruptly the instant his body zapped out of sight.

"He was taking too long," Gnash said in answer to the many accusing stares.

As Greg stepped through the portal, he heard one last desperate plea from Mrs. Alexander's home. "Pleeeeease . . ." came Greatheart's panicked voice, but it cut off an instant later when Greg's foot met frozen sand. Greg hopped about to stay warm while he slipped his cloak over his arms and pulled it tight.

"This is amazing," said Ryder, who stepped across after him. "I've been traveling these parts for twenty years, and I never knew that passage existed."

Brandon stepped through last. He paused to snug up his bright purple cloak. "What is this place? I'm afraid I don't get away from the castle that often."

"They call this the Barren Reaches," said Nathan. "It was here that the final battles of the Dragon Wars were waged. Sadly, the area has never recovered from the magic."

"What about the Infinite Spire?" said Greg, pointing to the impossibly tall tower looming above them to the north. "It still has plenty of magic, and it's not desolate. The spirelings live there, or at least they did until recently."

"The spire is different," explained Nathan. "It will never fall victim to magic because it is a product of magic itself."

The two spirelings moved up next to Nathan. "What do you know of our spire and its magic?" Gnash asked.

"To be honest, probably more than you know yourselves."

The spireling smiled, an odd expression for a face dominated by dozens of jagged teeth. "Why is it I believe you? In any case, I hope one day to get the opportunity to discuss the subject with you further."

Nathan smiled as well. "Not half as much as I do," he said, and Greg knew at once that Nathan was just as worried as Greg about the outcome of the upcoming battle.

The distance back to the Infinite Spire from the portal seemed a tenth as long as it had in the other direction, but this probably had less to do with mileage and more to do with them not running into a single monster. Of course, Lucky wanted to take credit for their good fortune, but Nathan still insisted it was a simple matter of coincidence.

Greg wondered if the man was just too old to see the obvious, the way adults failed to hear ghosts in the attic or monsters under the bed, but it seemed unlikely Nathan would overlook something observable when he was so clear about other things that were impossible to know. In any case, Greg was just glad their fortune had improved.

When the nine travelers arrived back at the valley surrounding the base of the Infinite Spire, Queen Gnarla was quick to greet them, though Greg would have gladly traded speed for a bit of warmth.

"Where is Our amulet?" the spireling queen snapped.

"As you already know, Your Majesty, we do not yet have it," Nathan told her. "Now, I believe we have more pressing matters to discuss."

"There is no matter more pressing than the return of Our amulet. You would be wise to remember that, Magician."

Several of the surrounding spirelings moved closer and raised their axes. Queen Gnarla began pacing back and forth, talking to herself, which Greg would have thought an odd thing for anyone to do, let alone someone who could carry on a conversation without opening her mouth. Finally she stopped in front of Nathan.

"We shall discuss this other matter of yours later. For now We are giving you one last chance to seek out this soldier you call Widget. When you find him, you shall retrieve Our amulet and bring it directly to Us." The queen stopped in midthought and looked at Lucky. "Who is this boy?"

"I'm Lucky."

"Maybe not so much," said the queen. To Nathan she added, "Does he play a role in this new prophecy as well?"

"Absolutely," Greg answered before Nathan could speak. He pulled Melvin close. "And so does this boy here. Why, did you know his brother is one of the most famous dragonslayers on Myrth?"

Melvin scowled at the rough handling, but was smart enough to hold his tongue. Queen Gnarla looked to Nathan for confirmation.

The magician shrugged. "If Greg believes these two boys must help him, then I would not disagree."

"We see," said the queen, her jagged teeth drawn into a scowl. She nodded toward Ryder. "And what part does he play in this?"

"I'm General Hawkins," said Ryder. "I will be at Greg's side during the upcoming battle."

Queen Gnarla looked him up and down, clearly judging his worth as a soldier. "My condolences. How about him?" she said, nodding at Brandon. "We suppose you're going to tell Us he, too, has something to do with the prophecy?"

"Are you kidding?" said Brandon before anyone could stop him. "I'm the one who put it to parchment."

"We thought as much. You do not look like a warrior. You are a scribe, then?"

"I most certainly am," Brandon boasted, completely overlooking the contempt in the spireling queen's tone.

She smiled, though not in a pleasant way. "Your role is indeed an important one." Brandon's smile widened, while the queen's faded to nothing. "However, important as it may have been, it has already been met. Therefore you shall stay here with Us to ensure the others return."

"Er—" said Brandon.

"But I need him," Greg insisted.

Queen Gnarla stepped between him and the scribe and stared Greg down. She was shorter than he was, and theoretically female, but one look at her rippling muscles, her razor-sharp teeth and her six-inch claws, and Greg had no doubt who would win in a fight. And that was without factoring in the thousands of Canaraza warriors who stood behind their queen, prepared to die to defend her.

"Please?" Greg added meekly.

"We are still not sure what to think of you," said Queen Gnarla. "It is easy to see how the Mighty Greghart came to be named in the last prophecy, but this next . . . You seem an unlikely hero, especially given you lack the confidence to believe you can succeed without a man such as this."

"A true leader knows he is nothing without his followers," offered Nathan.

"We were not speaking to you, Magician."

"Yet I felt I must intercede—further proof that the boy's fate is strengthened by having his friends around him."

The spireling queen actually laughed out loud. "Very clever. Yet We fear his fate is as strong as it is going to get, because this man," she said, gesturing toward Brandon, "shall be staying with Us." A simple nod, and two of her warriors seized Brandon and dragged him away before he could so much as gasp.

Greg started to object but stopped when he saw Nathan shake his head.

"Due to the high praise Gnash and Gnaw hold for you," Queen Gnarla said, "and out of consideration for the fact that you are somehow tied to a prophecy, We shall continue to honor Our agreement, even if you did just lead Us on a wild goblin chase. We are giving you a second chance because We believe you did not know this Corporal Widget was not where you were led to believe, but know that if you fail this time, your fate shall be sealed. Now go. If Our amulet is not back in Our possession at the end of the two weeks, We shall wait no longer."

"But there's no wa—"

Nathan clamped a hand over Greg's mouth. "We understand, Your Majesty."

"We hope so, for you have already wasted two days, and in exactly twelve more, when the sun reaches its apex, We shall march upon your precious castle."

"Naphm, say smphm," Greg said. He eyed Nathan, waiting for the magician to argue. How could they possibly get to the northern border and back in twelve days without using magic? It was as if Queen Gnarla wanted to exact her revenge on the Army of the Crown.

But Nathan said nothing, and soon it was time to return to the trail in search of Corporal Widget.

Harpies

Greg held his tongue as he and the others prepared to leave a terrified Brandon behind and pick their way through the mass of spireling warriors camped outside the spire. There was really nothing left to say. Brandon had already spent a full quarter hour pleading, trying every possible line of reasoning, but the queen was no more open to debate than Mrs. Alexander had been with Marvin Greatheart back in Pillsbury.

"Nathan," Priscilla said as she stepped over a sleeping spireling. "What are we doing? We can't possibly reach the castle in twelve days. It took three weeks to get back last time, and that was without having to make a side trip to the northern border to get the amulet."

Gnash turned abruptly. "The amulet is not a side trip. It is our only concern."

"He's right," said Nathan. "We must do all we can to reach the northern border as quickly as possible."

"How far is it?" asked Greg.

"Depends. It is a long border. To reach the closest point, under the best of conditions . . . there is a tiny chance a person could make it in about two weeks."

Greg felt his hopes draining. "Aren't there any portals we could use?"

"None that I know of," said Nathan.

"But we don't have that much time."

"You can't change the prophecy," said Lucky. "Sure, with me along I can see us making great time and arriving at that spot you're talking about in only twelve days, and even happening to arrive there at the exact time as General Talbout, but that's just one half of the trip. We're supposed to be back to the spire with the amulet before the deadline, remember?"

"If we can get the amulet, I can use my ring to get back to the spire," said Greg. "Do you really think Queen Gnarla will cancel the fight if I make it back in time?"

"Queen Gnarla will remain true to her word," said Gnaw. "Of that you can be sure."

"What if General Talbout isn't there when we reach the border?" Greg asked Nathan. "Will we be able to reach the castle in three weeks from there?"

"Why three weeks?" asked Nathan.

"That's how long it will take Queen Gnarla to get there from the spire."

"Ha," said Gnash. "Queen Gnarla will take at most three days to reach your castle. Two if she is anxious."

"Two days?" said Greg. "Then she really will be there in two weeks. There's no way to beat her back."

"Why not turn around now and use that portal Nathan showed us to go back to the southern border?" Melvin suggested. "Then we could go back up through Guttering Torch Caverns and be back to the castle in a week or so."

"You'd have to be crazy to hike through Guttering Torch Caverns," said Nathan. "Besides, that won't get us General Talbout."

"Or our amulet," Gnaw said.

"No," said Nathan, "our only choice is to head north."

Greg couldn't say he was terribly disappointed that they wouldn't be returning to Guttering Torch Caverns. Still, the odds of success seemed low taking the northern route, even with Lucky on their side. They would have to press hard and hope for miracles.

Much like with Marvin back in Pillsbury, Brandon's screams continued relentlessly while Greg and the others hiked up to the ridge bordering the valley, and Greg could still hear Brandon's voice occasionally drifting upon the wind later, after they'd passed over the first of the mountain peaks to the north. Even so, he was fairly sure the spireling queen's opinion was not going to change.

They hiked longer than usual that evening, moving by the light of the eternal torch, until Nathan declared they must stop or risk the magical flame drawing some of Myrth's more dreaded monsters. Gnash and Gnaw sniffed the air and confirmed his decision.

Greg was glad to have his bedding back from Marvin, but the lingering stench of trolls made it hard to relax. Judging by the snoring, not everyone shared his problem. He spotted Nathan awake, meditating near the edge of the campsite, and decided to see if the man had a plan. Within seconds, Priscilla, Lucky and Melvin had joined them. Apparently the snoring Greg heard was coming from Ryder alone.

"Plan?" said Nathan. "I hate to disappoint you, but I have nothing in mind."

"Nothing?" said Greg. The spireling guards, with their overly sensitive hearing, jumped to attention, axes at the ready. Embarrassed, Greg apologized and lowered his voice. "How can we make it in time, then?"

"I don't know."

"'I don't know,' you're not telling us, or 'I don't know,' you don't know?" asked Lucky.

Nathan smiled sadly. "No, I really don't know. Look, I realize you think I hold all the answers, but in truth, I know little more about your fate than you do."

"But you do know more," said Lucky.

"Just what I've been told. A few scattered facts, that's all. Not how they fit together, and certainly not enough to formulate a plan."

Melvin's voice drifted up from behind his brother's shield of dragon scales, where he was cowering for warmth. "How could you have been told anything about our future? It hasn't even happened yet."

"Yes, well, I can see where from your point of view it may seem impossible," said Nathan, "but you must realize that your point of view is severely limited."

Melvin lowered his shield long enough for the others to observe his scowl. Greg risked suffering the same humiliation himself when he asked, "Who told you these facts about the future, Nathan?"

"Now, that I can't tell you."

"Was it Mordred? He seemed to know a lot more than he should when you did that summoning thing the other day."

"I just told you I can't say," Nathan replied. "I wish I could."

But Greg wasn't ready to give up. "Can you at least tell me if it was Mordred?"

"Very well, it wasn't Mordred. Most of what he knows about the future he's only heard from me."

"You?" said Lucky.

Greg looked to the guards, who had once again jumped to attention. The glares they offered suggested this had better be the last outburst.

"You told Mordred what you know about the future?" Priscilla asked in a shrill whisper.

"Some, yes," said Nathan.

"But Mordred is evil. He has something to do with Daddy's missing amulet, I just know it."

"He is not evil," Nathan insisted a little louder than he'd intended. He, too, glanced over at the spirelings and mouthed an apology.

"How can you be so sure?" Greg asked.

"Because at one time Mordred and I were good friends," Nathan said.

"Friends," Priscilla said. "You and Mordred?"

"Oh, yes indeed. He and Hazel were the first two friends I made when I came to this world as a young boy."

"Not the witch Hazel?"

"Well, back then she wasn't a witch. Just a girl, about the same age as you are now."

"But that would make you and Hazel about the same age," said Greg.

"That's right," admitted Nathan.

"But Hazel's an old hag," Melvin said, the concept of tact still foreign to him.

"Yes, well, admittedly she hasn't aged well since she turned to the Dark Arts."

"What do you mean?" asked Priscilla.

"A question for another time," Nathan told her. "You were asking about Mordred. He can be a bit ambitious, I'll admit, but basically he's a good man. His actions may seem questionable, but I can assure you he's done only what he thought is best for the kingdom."

"Wait, how did you get here?" Priscilla asked. "To Myrth, I mean."

"That I cannot say."

"Just what kind of actions do you think Mordred has taken?" Lucky asked in a voice that was nearly as disapproving as the one Princess Priscilla had used earlier. Obviously not wanting to be left out, Melvin repeated the question, his tone not quite as disapproving, but still quite skillful for one so young.

"I'm afraid it's a bit premature for me to answer that," Nathan said, leaving no room for argument. "Anything else you'd like to ask?"

"As if it would do any good," said Melvin, who must have felt comfortable with the irked tone he had used before, because he was sticking with it now.

"Nothing then?"

"Why would you tell Mordred things about the future when you won't tell us?" Priscilla asked.

"Good question," admitted Nathan.

Greg thought it was an excellent question, and he asked it again, just to be sure the magician wouldn't try to evade it. But Nathan surprised him by answering.

"Everything I told Mordred about the future I told him years ago, when we were kids and I didn't know any better."

"Wow, how long have you known about this prophecy?" asked Lucky.

"Since before I came to this world," admitted Nathan.

"But how is that possible?" said Greg. Then he thought about it. Was it any more impossible for Nathan to know the future before he arrived on Myrth than it was for him to know it at all?

"I was told much of what would happen in the last prophecy, and in Simon's latest, before I ever left my world," said Nathan. "In fact, it was the excitement of those stories that peaked my interest in coming here in the first place."

"But who could have told you about the prophecies back then?" asked Priscilla. "Even Simon didn't know about them yet. Who else knows about the future, Nathan?"

The magician offered a devilish smile. "Everyone knows about the future. It's just that most know only the future of those who've passed before them."

"What's that supposed to mean?" asked Melvin. Greg was glad he wasn't the only one who didn't understand.

"Ah, now you're into an area I feel we should not discuss. In fact, we really ought to get some sleep. We have a long day ahead of us, as usual."

Greg recognized that tone. Nathan was through revealing secrets. Lucky gave Greg a nudge, and the pair followed Priscilla back to their bedding. A moment later Greg heard a grunt as Melvin squirmed his way between bedrolls and pulled his shield over top of himself. Then all was quiet, aside from Ryder's snoring and the occasional scream drifting upon the wind.

For a while the stench of trolls assaulted Greg's nostrils. He fought hard to breathe through his mouth until at last he began to drift off. What seemed a moment later, he awakened to the more pleasant smell of meat cooking on an open fire, though a quick glance around the area revealed the source of the scent to be nothing more than Lucky rummaging through his magic pack. Unbelievably the others were scurrying around in the gloom just prior to dawn, and Greg was last to rise.

He sat up slowly. Rake screeched and hopped down from his chest, and only then did Greg understand how he'd finally managed to fall asleep. The shadowcat's purr was a more potent sedative than any tranquilizer sold on Earth.

They rushed to finish breakfast, knowing a few minutes saved might make the difference in them reaching their goal in time, and then set out again with the eternal torch to guide them until the sun peeked over the horizon. All day they hurried, and by nightfall Ryder announced that they had managed to cut some time off the trip.

"An hour?" Greg said. "That's all?"

Ryder shook his head. "We've only been gone a day and a half."

"At least we have Lucky with us," Melvin pointed out the next morning. "It's great to be able to travel without having to worry about running into monsters everywhere."

A terrifying screech broke the silence at that moment, proof that Fate never really cares much for boasters. Greg looked to the sky. Dozens of dark silhouettes streaked past the rising sun. A nauseating stench, like that of decaying flesh, wafted down on the wind.

"Harpies!" Ryder shouted.

Greg had seen only one other harpy in his life, on his first trip to Myrth. The creature that had shared Priscilla's cell was part human, part vulture. All parts were equally disgusting. That harpy had been too busy eating to cause Greg trouble, but these seemed to have a completely different idea of how human-to-harpy relationships should go.

"Look out!" Priscilla screamed.

One of the bird-women swooped down at Greg, her gnarled claws splayed, her sharp beak pulled into a nasty grin. Nathan's staff flashed through the air and caught the harpy midway up her torso. Her wailing shriek echoed throughout the mountains long after she plummeted to the ground.

Greg thrust out his own walking stick in time to fend off a second attack. Lucky followed his lead, striking out at a third, and Ryder wielded his sword at a fourth. Even Melvin, who didn't know the first thing about chikan, held his own, thanks to his natural agility and dragonslayer heritage.

Priscilla, however, remained glued in place, a scream frozen on her face.

"Watch out!" Greg yelled as one of the harpies soared straight at her. He raced forward, stabbed out his walking stick and barely managed to divert the attack.

Priscilla never moved. Instead she started to cry.

Greg didn't have time to ask why. For each attacker he knocked aside, another flew in to take its place. So far he'd been lucky, but each time the harpies regrouped and came back as strong as before, and if it came down to a question of which side held the most stamina, even Greg would have bet on the harpies.

A cackle from behind caused him to duck and thrust out his stick. The hard wood struck one of the harpy's extended claws and sent her cartwheeling into a shrub. Greg lingered a bit too long watching. He sensed another attack from behind, and while his mind warned him to dodge out of the way, something also told him he would be too late.

He dropped anyway, in agonizing slow motion, heard the beating of her wings, gasped at the putrid stench . . . but no impact ever came. At least not for Greg. A tormented shriek exploded just above his head, and then . . . nothing but silence.

Gnash wiped off the blade of his axe. Apparently he'd just vaulted over Greg and dispatched the harpy's nearly fatal blow with a completely fatal blow of his own. Greg didn't know what to say. "Thank you," he mumbled, but the words seemed somewhat inadequate.

The spireling swung his axe up to rest on his shoulder. "We Canarazas believe in prophecies too."

He turned then and headed down the trail as if nothing had happened. Only then did Greg take in the scene around him. With the exception of a lot of badly maimed harpies, no one was injured. Princess Priscilla stood nearby, her walking stick held loosely at her side, tears on her cheeks.

Then Greg remembered the harpy from Ruuan's lair. While Greg couldn't have been happier to know the hideous creature for only a few minutes, Priscilla had spent three days with it. The two hadn't exactly been friends, but Greg knew Priscilla had felt bad about that harpy's fate. Clearly she wasn't happy about the fate of these harpies either. He didn't know what to say to comfort her, but he knew he should try something.

"It was them or us," he finally told her.

"I know," she said, sniffling, "but who's to say our lives are any more important than theirs?"

Greg didn't have an answer, so Melvin answered for him. "Isn't it obvious? No one ever wrote a prophecy about them."

Nathan's Tale

"Two hours?" moaned Greg. "That's all?"

"We've only been gone a few days," Ryder reminded him.

"Which means we only have about a week left," Priscilla pointed out.

She was right. It should have been far quicker for the eight of them to travel this route than it had been for the king's army, but deep snow was stealing away any advantage they gained. At this rate they would never reach the northern border in time. Still Nathan refused to disobey the spirelings' orders.

"Aren't your powers a match for theirs?" Greg whispered when everyone but Gnash and Gnaw had gathered around the campfire. The two spirelings were standing a good distance away, guarding the trail, but they snapped instantly to attention and snarled.

"I could possibly overpower them, yes," Nathan said, not bothering to lower his voice, "but not without harming them, which I refuse to do." Fifty feet away, Gnash and Gnaw relaxed slightly, but still kept a wary eye on the humans.

"Oh, it's okay to kill a bunch of disgusting harpies," Priscilla said with a huff, "but not your precious spirelings."

"Well, yeah," said Melvin. "I like Gnash and Gnaw. Besides, have you ever gotten a good look at a harpy?"

"So they're not beautiful," cried Priscilla. "They still have feelings."

Annoyed over the outburst, the guards marched to the campfire, axes poised for a fight. "Why are you shouting?" Gnash shouted himself.

Melvin tossed a loose bit of bark at the fire. "The princess here is comparing you to a bunch of harpies."

"No, I would never think of insulting you like that," Priscilla snapped. Everyone stared at her blankly. Finally she screamed and jumped to her feet, and no one knew what to say when she stormed off into the dark.

After a moment, Nathan stood up too. "I better go talk to her." He disappeared into the woods, and Gnash and Gnaw quickly returned to their posts.

"Don't those two ever sleep?" Greg said to no one in particular.

"Not if you ask them," answered Ryder.

"My brother Marvin says spirelings sleep just as much as you and me," Melvin told them both, "only instead of doing it all at once they do it all day long, alternating instants of sleep with instants awake."

"You're kidding," said Greg.

"No," Lucky said, "I've heard the same thing. They're actually sleeping most of the time. They only fully wake up when they need to move really fast."

Greg studied their faces. "You're putting me on, right?"

A rustling erupted from the brush, but Greg was not alarmed, since neither spireling deemed it necessary to investigate. Nathan and Priscilla emerged from the woods. Their conversation must have gone well, because Priscilla was actually smiling.

"Look at you," Lucky said when he saw Priscilla's face. "What did he say to you?"

"Oh, nothing." Her voice could only be described as lilting. She offered Nathan a wink, glanced at Greg and giggled.

"What are you laughing about?" Greg asked.

"Not a thing," she said, then blushed and giggled again.

Greg had never felt less at ease in his life, a powerful statement when you stopped to consider the events of the past couple of weeks. "Oh, for Pete's sake, I'm going to sleep."

"I'm tired," Priscilla announced the next day.

"Me too," said Melvin. "Hey, maybe this would be easier if we made up some sort of game to pass the time."

Ahead lay a narrow rock-strewn path descending the face of a treacherously steep cliff. As if the landscape weren't bad enough, the sun beat down, unusually intense, melting the snow and leaving behind a mixture of slush and mud that was nearly impossible to negotiate. In spite of the sunshine, the air felt just as cold as always.

Lucky sighed. "How about sliding down a mountain? That sounds fun."

"You go first," Greg said with a grunt. The flat rock he picked for a stepping-stone shifted and slid downhill while he flailed madly to keep his balance. He needn't have bothered. Gnaw raced forward and caught him before he made it halfway to the ground.

"Uh, thanks," Greg mumbled.

Gnaw merely nodded and returned to his post at the back of the group. While Greg was grateful for the protection, it did little to ease his fears. Just the fact the spirelings felt they needed to guard him so closely was a constant reminder that the world of Myrth was fraught with danger, even with Lucky in their midst.

"Anyone want to hear a joke?" asked Melvin.

"No," the others shouted in unison.

"But look at Greg. He's so tense you could bounce a boulder off his chest."

Greg winced, remembering a day not long ago when the boy might have done just that.

"You *are* a bit tense, Greg," Lucky observed.

"See," said Melvin. "How about this one? Did you hear about the dragonslayer who made the same mistake twice?"

The others ignored him, but Melvin didn't seem to care.

"Trick question," he chortled, as if they were actually stumped. "There's no such thing as a dragonslayer who ever made a mistake."

"How is that funny?" asked Greg.

Melvin gave him an odd look. "Don't you get it? Maybe I told it wrong. Dragonslayers who make one mistake don't live to make another."

Greg frowned. "There's nothing funny about that."

"Oh yeah, well then why didn't the dragonslayer make the same mistake twice?"

Greg groaned. "You just asked that."

"No, this is different. Come on. Why didn't the dragonslayer make the same mistake twice?"

Greg closed his eyes, hoping the boy would go away.

"Because he got burned the last time." Melvin nearly doubled over, cackling at his own joke. Several seconds passed before he noticed no one else was laughing. "Oh, like you could do better."

"Well, we sure couldn't do worse," Greg muttered under his breath.

"Oh, yeah?" said Melvin. "Then let's hear it. Let's hear one of your *Earth* jokes."

Greg went back to pretending he wasn't listening.

"What are you, scared?" Melvin challenged.

"Oh, for Pete's sake," Greg said, realizing he would have to cooperate if he wanted any peace. He thought a moment. "Okay, how many dragonslayers does it take to change a light bulb?"

Melvin looked at him with a blank expression, as did Lucky and Priscilla.

"What's a light bulb?" Melvin asked.

"Oh, right. Okay, how about this instead? Knock, knock . . ." Again the others just stared. "Oh, forget it."

"See," Melvin huffed. "Not so easy, is it?" And with that he raised his nose and stormed ahead. Greg couldn't believe his good fortune.

Nathan scampered agilely into a very steep ravine and up the other side. Greg followed the magician's lead, although if he had followed exactly he wouldn't have landed face down in the mud. This time Gnaw wasn't paying attention. The spireling rushed forward late and, with a speed only another spireling could match, used his axe to scrape Greg clean before carrying him up the far bank. Greg gasped and spent the next ten minutes counting and recounting his limbs.

"You okay, Greg?" Lucky asked.

"I'm fine," Greg lied.

"You sure?" said Melvin, trying not to laugh. The boy had rushed back as soon as he heard Greg fall, but Greg had an idea it wasn't to lend assistance so much as to see Greg laid out in the mud.

"I said I'm fine."

Priscilla looked him up and down. "Oh dear." She slipped her backpack off her shoulder and began rummaging through it while Greg waited warily to see what she was up to. All day she'd been acting funny toward him, being extra nice for no reason, and the effect was beginning to wear on him.

"Ah, here we are." Priscilla pulled out a lace handkerchief and handed it to Greg, as if expecting him to dry off with it. Frowning, he took it by one corner and held it at arm's length.

"Well, go on," she said.

Greg shrugged and attempted to wipe his face, to which Priscilla furrowed her brow, searched her pack again and this time pulled out a large bedsheet.

"Hey, I could have used that last night," said Melvin.

"Sorry, I didn't want it get to dirty."

Greg took the bedsheet and started walking again, boots squishing, his mud-soaked clothes ten times heavier than before. While Greg dried off, Priscilla asked Nathan what Mordred was like as a kid.

"Ah," said Nathan. "You might say Mordred, Hazel and I were kindred spirits, none of us with any family, all eager to learn everything we could about magic."

"But Hazel must have been different," said Melvin. "Why else would she have turned to Dark Magic?" For an instant he slipped in the mud but, much to Greg's disappointment, caught his balance in plenty of time.

"Ah, Hazel," Nathan said. "Well, that's a hard thing to understand even today. When we met, the three of us were young and naive. We didn't care what kind of magic we learned, Light or Dark, as long as it was exciting. Oh, and believe me, it was exciting. We traveled the entire land asking people if they knew anyone with special powers. We'd follow every lead, pry out whatever secrets we could. Over the years we learned from every mage, witch and wizard we could find, first in the kingdom, and then in the Styx and even the world beyond."

It was clear from the look in Lucky's eye he was considering adopting the lifestyle for his own.

"Now, before you start filling your head with a lot of foolish notions," Nathan said, "you should know that no matter how far we traveled, we were constantly redirected to the one source we'd never bothered to pursue."

"Where?" asked Greg. He was somewhat cleaner now and paused to hand the thirty-pound bedsheet back to Priscilla. The princess grimaced and asked Melvin if he wanted it, but even Melvin looked hesitant.

"Everyone we met agreed the king's magicians were the strongest force on Myrth," said Nathan. "After twenty years of searching, we finally returned to Pendegrass Castle to ask if we might join up with King Peter's staff."

"I don't understand," said Priscilla. "Father doesn't allow his magicians to dabble in the Dark Arts. You still haven't explained what happened to Hazel."

"Yes, well, I'm getting to it."

They had reached a steep incline, and Nathan had to pause his story long enough to scurry up the bank. He barely reached the top without falling, and Greg and Melvin stared at each other to see who would go next. With a shrug, Melvin scampered up without so much as a bobble, leaving Greg sweating in spite of the cold. He made it up okay, but a slip of his toe caused him to rest his knee on the ground for just an instant. Melvin snickered and stalked away.

"You okay, Greg?" called Priscilla.

"I'm fine."

Nathan offered the princess a supporting hand. At first she just stared at it, but then she noticed Greg watching and took hold, acting quite the lady as she stepped daintily up the bank. Greg shook his head and followed Melvin. A few yards farther Greg spotted a slippery-looking puddle ahead and adjusted his step so Melvin would have to walk through it. Unfortunately the boy deftly avoided the trouble. Nathan observed the attempt and smiled. "When Hazel approached the king's magicians," he continued, "she knew nearly as much magic as many of them. This in itself caused a lot of friction that was hard for all of us to overcome, but in Hazel's case, she had even more to contend with."

"What do you mean?" asked Priscilla.

"Well, no one could have denied Hazel would have been a huge asset to the staff, but court magician had always been a man's job and a man's job only. Women weren't even supposed to be interested in magic, let alone know anything about it. As soon as Hazel's powers were discovered, everyone . . . well, they started calling her a witch."

Priscilla gasped. Greg avoided eye contact, knowing this was just the kind of thing she might blame on him.

"Hazel was shunned, at best," Nathan continued. "Oftentimes worse. Eventually the others drove her away, exiled her into the forest south of the castle."

Priscilla emitted a high-pitched noise but looked too angry to express her opinion more clearly.

"As you might imagine, she was furious," said Nathan, and it took a moment for Greg to realize he was talking about Hazel, not Priscilla. "Over the years the three of us had learned of many opportunities to advance our capabilities in the Dark Arts, but fortunately we'd had the sense to avoid them. When Hazel was exiled, something inside her snapped. She returned to all those leads we had abandoned, and soon became an expert in areas of magic better left unexplored."

"This is unbelievable," said Lucky.

"It certainly is," Priscilla huffed.

"Perhaps," said Nathan, "but true."

"You were allowed to stay at the castle, though?" Greg asked Nathan.

"Yes, but it didn't feel right. Not after all that had happened to Hazel. Mordred, as you know, stayed behind, but I left and continued the same path I'd pursued for years. The two of us communicated through apparitions for years after the split. I filled him in on everything new I learned, and he kept me up-to-date on his experiences in the king's service. It was a good arrangement for both of us. Combined we learned more than either of us could have uncovered on our own."

"But eventually you must have had some kind of falling-out," said Priscilla. "When you talked to him outside the Infinite Spire, he said you two hadn't spoken for years."

"Mordred was at the Infinite Spire?" Lucky asked.

"Not exactly," Priscilla said. "We'll tell you later."

"Without going into too much detail," said Nathan, "much I knew about the future I never shared with either Mordred or Hazel. I had reason to believe I'd need to learn more about the Dark Arts before all was through. Mordred warned me not to pursue that path—said he could no longer continue our exchanges if I did—but I tried to explain I had no choice. He demanded to know what I was keeping from him, only I knew I shouldn't tell. So we haven't spoken since . . . at least not until this trip began."

"What was it you couldn't tell him?" asked Melvin.

Nathan reached out to run a hand through Melvin's hair. "Did you really think that was going to work?"

Melvin grinned and ducked Nathan's hand. "Can't blame me for trying."

Hart-Stopping Ride

The rest of the day, Nathan barely shared a word, what with everyone continually begging him to reveal more of his inside knowledge of the future, and Priscilla continued acting strangely toward Greg, creeping him out whenever she was near. Fortunately, Greg had become quite adept at avoiding her. He talked mostly to Lucky instead. Of course, he could have talked to Melvin, tried to befriend the boy, but the idea held little appeal. He was sure he'd heard every possible dragonslayer joke, yet Melvin continued to prove him wrong, no matter how often Greg begged him to shut up.

"Can we please have a little peace and quiet, Melvin?" Lucky asked that evening by the campfire.

"That reminds me of a joke," Melvin said. "How could you tell the dragonslayer was upset about losing his fight with a dragon?"

"Melvin, please," said Greg.

"Because he was all in pieces," Melvin shouted. He smiled proudly afterward, completely ignoring the groans.

"How are we doing on our schedule?" Greg called over to Ryder, who was nearby gathering wood for the fire. The general returned to the circle and threw a log on top of the stack, sending a torrent of sparks in the air and the smell of ash into Greg's nostrils.

"Not so well, I'm afraid. We've actually lost a bit of time today. I'd say we're making about average time at best."

"You're kidding," moaned Priscilla. "But we've been pushing so hard."

Ryder offered her a sympathetic look. "Yes, well, the going's been a lot tougher in the snow. We're lucky we haven't lost more time each day."

Greg resisted the temptation to glance at Lucky, who was surely smiling. Nathan walked up to the fire to join the others.

"Please tell me you've come up with a plan," Ryder greeted him.

Nathan dropped onto a log next to Greg, rubbed his hands together and held them out near the flames. "I wish I had."

"You could still overpower the spirelings, couldn't you?" whispered Greg. Nathan scowled, but Greg was serious. "I know, I like Gnash and Gnaw too, but there's a lot at stake here."

"I will not harm the spirelings," Nathan insisted.

"Can't you overpower them without hurting them?" Lucky asked.

Nathan sighed. "Apparently you're unfamiliar with the power of a spireling mage. You've seen the potential of the spirelings when they're not using their magic. I would think you could imagine the capabilities of one willing to unleash his full power."

"But you said you learned all those different kinds of magic," argued Priscilla. "Certainly you know something you can use against them."

Nathan smiled. "I did learn much throughout the years. One thing in particular was to respect the power of a spireling mage." He observed the glare she gave him and added, "Queen Gnarla is watching our progress through their eyes. If there is a way to defeat them without her knowing, it would not be easy."

"But if it comes down to it, you'll try, right?" asked Melvin.

"You do know they're listening, don't you?" Nathan said.

Melvin's face blanched. His skin was still growing whiter as Nathan stood and ambled off into the dark.

The weather continued to warm overnight, until by morning the temperature sat far above freezing, a phenomenon Ryder assured them had not been seen in these mountains this time of year for nearly a decade. Water began to rain from everything in sight as the snow-covered wonderland began to melt.

"Lucky for us," boasted Lucky.

But the soppy mud that developed was no easier to traverse than the snow had been, and then, with just a few days left before the spirelings were due to storm the castle, the temperature dipped again, creating a coat of ice over everything in sight.

They were moving along the peaks of the Smoky Mountains, drawing near Death's Pass, when the general called the group to a halt. The going had become nearly impossible . . . that is until now, when it became completely impossible.

As Greg remembered it, Death's Pass was a tunnel that bore straight through the mountainside, providing a natural, easy-to-follow staircase of rock that ran directly from the top of the Smoky Mountains halfway to the bottom. But today they found no tunnel. The normal hole in the rock was plugged top to bottom with solid ice. Nathan walked up and thumped it with his fist. From the sound, Greg guessed the ice was only slightly harder than the rock that surrounded it.

"Great," Melvin said, "this is just what we need."

"Actually," said Ryder, "it might be."

"Huh?" Greg said. He might have expected Nathan, with his mysterious ways, to say such a thing, but Ryder usually proved pretty normal.

"I know of only three routes through these mountains," said Ryder, "around to the east, around to the west, or through Death's Pass, the usual route since it cuts straight down the center, shaving hundreds of miles off either of the other two options."

"Wait," said Greg. "If we can't use Death's Pass, are you telling us we need to go hundreds of miles farther to get to the bottom?"

"Yes," said Ryder, excitedly. "I've only seen this tunnel iced over once before, but if it's this bad here, there's a chance it might be even worse along the western ridge."

Greg started to reconsider whether Ryder was really as normal as he'd thought. "And this is a good thing?"

"It could be. I'm afraid we'll have no way of knowing until we get there."

"What are you talking about?" asked Priscilla. "Get where?"

"Remember I told you the weather warmed up in these hills once before, about ten years ago," said Ryder. "It was before I became a captain. I was part of a small scouting team sent to investigate abnormal goblin activity in the area. It had turned horribly cold, just like today, and we'd have been anxious to get back home even if we weren't out hunting goblins. Anyway, when we arrived at the pass it was completely iced over."

"Just like today, too," said Melvin.

"Right. Well, soon as we saw it, we knew we had no choice but to go around. We chose to go west, knowing the mountains would have to end within a hundred miles or so, since Bottomless Chasm runs along that side. That's when we found exactly what we'd been looking for."

"Another pass?" said Priscilla.

"No. Goblins. A huge band of them."

Greg scanned the woods to either side of the trail. "Let's hope that's not like today . . ."

"Anyway," continued Ryder, "we thought if we could just climb down to the lip of Bottomless Chasm we could follow the gap north until it met up with the trail again and not lose too much time. But as it turned out, the mountains to the west were just as icy as the pass had been."

"So what did you do?" asked Lucky.

"Yeah, and what about the goblins?" said Melvin.

"Well, we were looking for a safe route down the mountainside when the goblins came upon us," said Ryder. "Our chances looked bleak at best. We were outnumbered a hundred to one and cornered with only one chance of escape. That was to step over the cliff and take our chances on the slippery ice."

"Oh my," said Priscilla. "What happened?"

Ryder smiled. "Well, I'm here to tell the tale, aren't I?"

Greg breathed a sigh of relief. "So you found a safe route, then?"

"Safe? Not by a long shot. But we did stumble across a shortcut that shaved a full week off our trip back to the castle."

"A week? Will it get us closer to the northern border?" asked Greg.

"It would put us in a place where travel is much easier, yes."

"Then why didn't we go that way to start with?" asked Priscilla. "We've been looking for a way to save time this whole trip."

"I've never even heard of a trail to the west," said Nathan. "How could it have saved you a week when the pass would have put you halfway to the bottom in less than a day?"

The others buzzed with excitement until Ryder yelled to capture their attention. "Quiet everyone. There are two reasons I never suggested we try the western route. First, it's not exactly a trail. While Death's Pass becomes impassable when it freezes, the slope to the west becomes usable only when it's completely iced over."

Greg didn't understand how that was possible, but what did it matter? "Then we should be in luck," he said. "Everything's covered with ice up here today."

"Yeah," agreed the others excitedly.

"What was the other reason?" Nathan said, raising his voice above the rest. The chatter gradually died away until everyone was staring at him soundlessly. "You said there were two reasons why you didn't take us to the west from the start."

"You're not worried about running into more goblins, are you?" asked Greg, once again scanning the woods.

"No," said Ryder grimly. "It's not monsters I'm worried about. It's the trail. There's a pretty good chance it will get us all killed."

"What?" they all cried.

Once again Ryder had to call for their attention. He tried to explain. "When we looked down, we could see the slope was one solid sheet of ice. We knew if we stepped over the edge we might not stop again until the foot of the mountains. But the goblins had us cornered. We had nowhere to go but down."

"Sounds like fun," said Lucky, "like a giant sleigh ride."

Greg remembered his long sleigh ride out of the Infinite Spire and decided it didn't sound fun at all.

"It may sound fun," said Ryder, "but you're forgetting one thing. The foot of these mountains lies at the rim of Bottomless Chasm. When we started down that slope we had no reason to believe we'd be able to stop at the base. Chances were much better we'd keep right on falling. We fully expected to fly over the edge of the chasm and plunge to our deaths."

"If the chasm is bottomless, did you really need to worry about dying?" asked Melvin. In spite of the horror of the idea, Greg had to admit the boy's question held some merit.

"Of course they did," said Lucky. "After falling a few days, you're sure to starve to death."

"So how did you survive?" asked Priscilla.

"Yes," said Nathan, "I'm curious as well. I will certainly want to know more before I consider allowing us to choose such a dangerous option."

"We should listen to Nathan," said Greg.

"How *did* you manage to stop before the chasm, Ryder?" Lucky asked.

"We didn't."

The others gasped—all except Nathan, who frowned. "But you're with us today. How can that be?"

"We were fortunate that, try as we might, we were incapable of scrubbing even a slight bit of speed off our descent. We were also fortunate the snow had drifted at the bottom before freezing over, creating a natural ramp at the foot of the mountain."

"You're not trying to say you . . . ?"

"Jumped the chasm," Ryder finished for him. "Yes."

"But that's impossible," said Lucky. "Bottomless Chasm is hundreds of feet across."

"More like a thousand at this point," said Ryder, "but you'd be surprised how much speed you can pick up sliding down a nearly frictionless surface for thirty miles."

"This is crazy," said Greg. "You can't jump across a thousand-foot-wide chasm and live."

"Ah, but you can," said Ryder, "and I'm here as proof."

Nathan was shaking his head sternly. "Just because you were fortunate enough to survive once doesn't mean you'd survive today, or that the rest of us wouldn't be killed."

"If it's luck we need, then say no more," said Lucky. "I'm your man."

The others chattered excitedly until Nathan interrupted them with a shout. "No. We are not going to send this boy to his death just because you all think he's too lucky to get hurt."

"Don't be ridiculous. I wouldn't be going to my death," said Lucky, smiling. "I'd just be sliding down a mountain and jumping a bottomless chasm."

Nathan scowled. "I won't hear of it."

The two spirelings stepped off to one side and held a private conversation without speaking while the others argued. Soon Gnash stepped forward, a stoic look upon his face, if Greg could judge the alien creature's expressions.

"I will go first," Gnash told them.

"You?" said Lucky. "Why should you have all the fun?"

"Quiet, son," said Nathan. "Why would you volunteer to go, Gnash?"

"It only makes sense," said the spireling. "Even if the boy went first, the rest of us would have no way of knowing if he survived or not. We would find ourselves once again having to decide who should risk his life next, and so it would be for each of us in turn."

"So, what difference does it make who goes first?" said Lucky, clearly not pleased about Gnash taking away his one chance to slide down a mountain.

"Because of the connection we spirelings share. If I survive, Gnaw will know it is safe, and if not, he can advise you all to take the eastern route instead. It will not be as fast, but at least you will live through the experience."

Nathan considered the spireling's words. "You would be taking a great risk."

"Perhaps, but I am far more capable of surviving than any of you . . . except for Gnaw, of course. As spirelings we are accustomed to traveling at high speeds, and if it is possible for me to do anything to control my descent, my superior reactions could save me from harm."

"And it's possible they will not," argued Nathan. "I think I should be the one to go."

"You?" said both Gnash and Lucky.

The idea of something happening to Nathan terrified Greg. "Why should you go, Nathan?"

"I cannot be harmed, at least not if our spireling friends allow me to protect myself."

"If you mean we should let you use your magic, then the answer is no," said Gnaw. "I do not wish to see Gnash harmed, but I would rather that than to dishonor our queen."

"You spirelings ought to check your priorities," Greg said. "If your queen was worthy of the respect you seem to hold for her, she wouldn't ask Gnash to take unnecessary chances."

The spirelings' eyes bulged even wider than normal. "Keep in mind that Queen Gnarla knows what you have said," Gnaw reminded him. "You would be wise to keep your opinions to yourself."

"It is decided," said Gnash. Without another word he stormed down the path to the west. The others shrugged and reluctantly fell into line behind him. Gnaw waited until all the others had left, then followed after, guarding the rear of the party as he'd done throughout their journey.

Here and there Greg spotted breaks in the trees to his right and rushed to look over the edge, hoping to discover another pass. But each new view turned out worse than the last. While Death's Pass may have had a formidable name, it was a reasonably safe route down the mountain. Here, at each opening Greg spotted, the ground dropped away sharply for what looked like miles. If they stepped over the edge at any of these places, they'd have about as much chance of surviving as they would stepping out of a moving airplane.

Eventually Ryder called the group to a halt. "We're here," he announced.

"How can you tell?" asked Greg. "This spot doesn't look any different from any other."

"When you've stared death in the face and lived, you don't quickly forget," Ryder told him. He stood on tiptoes and pointed toward the side of the trail. "We stepped over the edge right there."

"Aren't you going over to look?" asked Lucky.

Ryder's face had gone unusually pale. For the moment he looked far from a leader of men. "Uh . . . no. Ever since . . . well, you know . . . I've been a little . . . afraid of heights."

"Afraid of heights?" said Priscilla. "But we've been hiking through the mountains all week. I haven't noticed you having any trouble."

Ryder smiled faintly. "Thanks. I guess I've hid it well."

Melvin stepped up to the cliff edge and whistled. "Where's the mountain?"

Greg moved beside him and surveyed the slope for himself . . . or at least he would have, if it had extended out in front of him the way slopes were supposed to do. Instead it cut back into the face of the cliff beneath his feet. While better than any of the other spots Greg had seen so far, it was still not something anyone would have stepped over unless intending suicide.

"We can't go down here," he said, thinking he better point out the obvious.

"As I recall, that first step was a bit tricky," said Ryder.

"Nice," said Lucky, peering over the edge himself. "Why are we standing around talking? Let's go."

"Nathan?" Greg said, looking for a voice of reason.

Nathan and Priscilla both stepped up next to the others to take a look. "Hmm," Nathan said. "Well, Gnash, I suppose there's no point stalling. You ready?"

"Ready," said Gnash. He stepped up to the edge.

"Wait," said Priscilla.

Gnash flailed his arms for balance but was able to stop in time. "What is it?"

She turned to Gnaw. "So we're just supposed to stand here and wait to see if Gnash dies?"

"If you would prefer, I can make it so you need not wait. You can share the experience with us. Then you will be better prepared when you make the trip yourself."

"You can do that?"

"I am a mage, remember?" He closed his eyes, and the smell of ozone crossed the air. Suddenly Greg felt a sensation nearly as disturbing as the thought of stepping off the cliff. His body seemed to surge with power. He could see better, hear better, smell better. But what was so disturbing was that he felt as if he were seeing, hearing and smelling from two places at once. The sensation was so disorienting that Greg tried to force the spireling's senses from his mind, but Gnaw was a powerful mage, and Greg found it easier to ignore his own senses.

He felt himself step up to the edge of the cliff and start his first step.

"Wait," Priscilla said again.

This time it was Greg who waved his arms for balance. He could hardly believe the strength that surged through his limbs. "What is it?" he said, though it was Gnash's voice he heard.

"You didn't say good-bye to Gnaw."

Greg frowned and could feel pointed teeth jutting out at every angle from his jaw. "That is because I will not truly be leaving him." And with that he turned and stepped over the cliff.

Priscilla's scream reached his ear from both close by and far away. He plummeted a full sixty yards before the slope eased out into his path. There he struck the face of the mountain for an instant, bounced away slightly, and did not touch the ice again for another sixty yards.

A short time later he contacted the face again, and then he was hugging the steep slope, already sliding out of control and picking up speed with every second. A quarter mile later the face dipped to the left, and he was thrown sideways so quickly he nearly lost his breakfast.

"What happened?" he heard Lucky ask.

"Oh, didn't I tell you?" said Ryder. "It's not a straight shot to the bottom. There are a number of twists and turns. Of course, you'll only follow the ones near the top. Once you pick up speed, you'll be falling much too quickly to hold the curves."

"Nice," Lucky said again.

Greg forced his face—Gnash's face—to point down the slope, though he was well aware he was moving too fast to alter his course even if the need were to arise. He was thrown into another curve, then another, but his Gnash self was able to handle the forces far better than Greg could have by himself.

Faster and faster the scenery rushed by, until even Greg's enhanced vision could make out nothing but a blur. He felt a stomach turn and wasn't sure if it was his own or Gnash's. He knew the spirelings were accustomed to much higher speeds than humans could fathom, and didn't want to think how fast Gnash must be moving to lose his ability to focus—especially when Greg considered that he was expected to step over the edge too, if Gnash survived the journey.

"This is not good," Greg heard Gnaw say beside him. An understatement if ever he'd heard one. "We can no longer distinguish what lies before us."

Minutes passed, an unbelievably large number of them. Greg strained along with Gnash as he fought to glimpse the way ahead, and then he soared out of a bend and saw the most horrifying sight he could imagine.

"I see the bottom," shouted Priscilla. "He made it."

"No," Greg said. "Don't you see? There's no ramp."

"But that means . . ."

"Gnash will not clear Bottomless Chasm," Gnaw said in a somber tone.

"And he'll fall forever," Melvin said, a little too much excitement in his voice.

Greg jerked himself out of Gnash's senses and rounded on Gnaw, who was standing with his eyes cast to the ground, looking just as helpless as Greg felt. "Do something."

"There is nothing I can do from here." His face adopted a far-off look. "Wait."

Greg wondered who he was talking to. Certainly he wasn't expecting Gnash to stop.

Gnaw spun to face Nathan. "Queen Gnarla says, this once, if it is possible for you to save Gnash, you may use your magic."

"You're kidding?" said Greg, though he knew even as he said it that the spireling was in no mood for humor.

Nathan wasted no time questioning the decision. In an instant he vanished.

"Where'd he go?" Priscilla asked.

"I do not know," Gnaw told her. "As you know, Gnash does not see him. Nor does he see much of anything at this point."

The sound of Gnash's name caused Greg to slip back into the spireling's senses. Amazingly he seemed to be sliding even faster than before. The edge of the chasm lay all too close ahead.

"Where's Nathan?" Greg asked.

"We do not see him," said Gnaw, "but wait." He sounded encouraged.

Greg strained to see what about the path ahead could possibly be encouraging, and then he saw it too. A wall of ice, a barely detectable white on white, lay between Gnash's position and the lip of the canyon. The slope veered right, Greg realized, the last thought he was able to get in before he hit the curve. The change in direction was so sudden he thought he would be crushed by his own weight, or rather Gnash's weight, but then he came out of the turn and realized he was sliding parallel to the edge of the canyon.

"He's going to make it," squealed Priscilla.

The others cheered.

"Where's Nathan?" Lucky asked. "Does anyone see him?"

"We see exactly what you see," Gnaw told him, "which does not include the magician. But then, Gnash is moving much too fast to focus on anything as small as a man. He was lucky to make out the base of the mountain."

"Where do you suppose he is?" asked Greg.

"I'm right here," said Nathan, suddenly stepping up from behind and placing a hand on Greg's shoulder. Greg felt proud that he jumped only a foot off the ground.

"Nathan," said Priscilla. "Where did you come from?"

"The bottom of the mountain."

"What were you doing?" asked Melvin. "Why weren't you helping Gnash?"

Greg frowned at the young boy's bluntness, but he was wondering the same thing. "What *were* you doing, Nathan?"

"You saw how difficult it was to see through Gnash's eyes. I went to see for myself if there was a ramp at the lip of the canyon like the one Ryder was telling us about."

The others just stared at him.

"There wasn't."

"But there was a curve in the slope," said Priscilla. "We all saw it."

"Not when I first got there," said Nathan.

Gnash's senses tried to creep into Greg's head again, but he shook them away. "What are you trying to say, Nathan?"

"Well, I knew of no magic I could perform that would build up a ramp the size I needed in the few seconds I was given."

"So, what did you do?" Lucky asked.

"I also knew that at the speed Gnash would be moving I couldn't expect to bring him to a stop in such a short distance without harming him. I chose instead to redirect him to the side, where he could coast to a stop at his own leisure."

"Which he is about to do at any time," Gnaw noted, and for a very brief instant Greg allowed himself to feel what Gnash was feeling. Already the trees to his right were zipping past at a more reasonable speed, but to his left the land dropped away into nothing, and Greg couldn't say he liked the view.

"But how did you redirect him?" Priscilla asked Nathan.

The magician tapped his staff on the ground absently, looking as if he wanted to avoid the question. "It was all very complicated. Let's just say it involved moving an adjoining hill over a furlong or so and leave it at that."

"You moved a mountain?" said Greg.

"Nice," said Lucky.

Nathan waved away the thought. "Not a mountain, just a hill. It wasn't more than a furlong across."

"You moved a mountain," Greg repeated.

But Priscilla didn't seem satisfied. "Gnaw finally let you use your magic. It seems to me, if you could move a mountain you could have built a ramp to get us over the canyon. Now we'll never make it to the border in time."

Nathan frowned. "Moving a mountain is easier than reshaping one."

But Priscilla didn't look convinced. She stood with her arms crossed and her brow furrowed, looking at the man as if he'd disappointed her rather than just saved Gnash's life.

"Besides," said Nathan, "there was also the matter of the wyverns."

Greg looked at him quizzically. "What wyverns?"

"Oh, um, nothing." Nathan took a step to the side and peered over the edge of the mountain. "Now, who wants to go next?"

Expanding Forces

Greg could find no words to describe his own slide down the mountain. Actually, he could find no words at all. He'd screamed himself hoarse the entire way, or at least until he lost consciousness about two minutes into the trip.

The trouble all started as Greg took his first step over the edge, when the shadowcat popped out from under his cloak and started flailing its limbs in a desperate attempt to return to the top of the mountain. Between Rake, the sting of the frigid wind, and the stars that burst in front of Greg's eyes when his skull hit the ice, Greg saw very little during those two minutes he was awake. He wished he had seen less. And while he had already experienced the trip once through Gnash, he should have realized that living through it with a spireling's senses would be nothing compared to barely surviving it with his own.

Oddly enough, he'd traveled just as fast before on several occasions, each time he flew with Ruuan, but none of those trips seemed as terrifying—with the possible exception of the time Ruuan carried Greg up to his lair in his mouth. Greg supposed it was the dragon's magic that made those trips seem smooth in comparison. Or maybe it was because he was safely stowed on the dragon's back—or at least in its mouth—and not actually touching the ground as it rushed by. Still, Greg remembered touching the ground very little on the mountain either. He woke up briefly when the curve Nathan had *built* tossed him roughly to one side, but fainted immediately again once he witnessed the view from the lip of Bottomless Chasm.

"That was so much fun," Lucky said once it was all over. They were miles away, resting in a clearing with darkness closing in, but he still couldn't stop talking about his adventurous slide down the mountain.

Greg was starting to be able to talk too, but for now was sticking to single syllables. "Are . . . you . . . nuts?"

"Tell me you didn't think that was the most incredible ride of your life," Lucky said, laughing.

"No . . . speed . . . ice . . . thought I would . . . crash . . . die," said Greg.

"What's wrong with you?" asked Melvin. "You're not making sense."

"Yeah, Greg, you look horrible," Priscilla said, dabbing his face with a handkerchief in a way that made him feel even less comfortable. His cheeks and forehead were covered with scratches, a result of Rake's attempts to return to the top of the cliff.

"Maybe you should leave him alone for a while," suggested Nathan. "You may have noticed his trip did not go nearly as smoothly as ours." He glanced over at Greg. "How *did* you manage to start spinning that fast, anyway?"

Earlier the magician had melted some snow to dampen a small swath of cloth, which he used now to dab Ryder's brow. The general had not been scratched, but he'd suffered quite an ordeal of his own, having been forced to relive the events that had once led to his daring leap across Bottomless Chasm.

Once Ryder's fear of heights was out in the open, it was there to stay. It had taken all of them to shove him off the mountain, and by the time he reached the bottom, the general had been nearly delirious with fear. Nathan had needed to help Ryder walk ever since, and now here he was, shaking too badly to hold the cloth for himself.

Greg hated seeing Ryder this way, but he'd witnessed the view from the lip of the canyon himself and couldn't imagine what it must have felt like to soar over tha. gap, not knowing if he would reach the other side.

Melvin, on the other hand, didn't seem to notice Ryder at all. He was focused solely on Greg. "Don't tell me you were scared of a little slide down a mountain." He snickered. "What kind of hero are you?"

Priscilla scowled at the boy. "Now, don't make fun. I thought it was scary too."

"Yeah, but you're a girl."

Had Greg been feeling better, he might have enjoyed watching Priscilla bowl Melvin over. She was doing a fair job of rubbing his face in the snow when Nathan pulled her back.

Melvin jumped to his feet and spun toward Priscilla, eyes wide with terror. "Grrrofffommee," he mumbled, snow spurting from his mouth.

"I suggest we get some sleep," said Nathan. "We still have a long trip ahead of us."

"Yeah, a lot longer than it should have been," accused Melvin. He dug a finger inside his cheek and withdrew a twig. "Gnaw gave you free rein on your magic. I still don't see why you didn't build a ramp to jump the canyon."

"I thought I explained that earlier."

"Not really," said Priscilla. "All you said was some nonsense about wyverns. What did you mean by that anyway?"

Nathan's expression turned grim. "You'll know all you want about wyverns soon enough . . . sooner than you care to, I'm sure. Now, let's set up camp."

Greg still held a vivid picture of his last encounter with a wyvern, and the idea of meeting wyverns, in the plural, kept him wound tight as a dragon's grip in spite of Rake's best efforts to calm him. He looked about the clearing. "Wouldn't it be better to camp in the forest? You know, where we'll be sheltered from the . . . elements."

"No, this will be better," Nathan said. "From here we'll be able to see the . . . I mean, *any* . . . attacks coming."

Not feeling reassured, Greg lay awake for over an hour, jumping alert every time a frog croaked or an owl hooted. It looked as if the only rest he would get this day was the few minutes he'd spent passed out during his slide down the mountain. Then a horrible cry sounded from the north. It took Greg a moment to realize Gnash was screaming.

Instantly the camp became a flurry of activity.

"What's going on?" Melvin asked.

Greg jumped to his feet. He heard something moving toward him and raised his walking stick, but before he could swing, Gnaw zoomed past, knocking him over from the wind. The second spireling may have been miles off patrolling the woods south of the field, but he had no trouble hearing Gnash's call. And even if he hadn't heard, his unusual bond to others of his race would have told him Gnash was in trouble.

Priscilla and Lucky ran up from behind. Lucky helped Greg to his feet, and they all stared in the direction Gnaw had disappeared.

"See anything?" Lucky asked.

"No." Greg strained so hard his eyes hurt, but the area ahead held only darkness. The surrounding forest, normally alive with noises, had fallen deathly quiet. "Wait, what's that?"

Several dark forms emerged from the woods at the northern edge of the meadow. Greg, Lucky and Priscilla all raised their walking sticks.

Melvin stepped up behind them. "What's wrong with you three?" he said, causing them all to jump. "It's just Nathan and Ryder. And the spirelings. And two others. I can't see from here."

They waited for the group to move closer. Even under the bright moonlight, Greg had trouble making out the features of the strangers until they were less than ten feet away.

"Bart?" he said, finally recognizing one of the men as the traveling bard he'd met on his last visit to Myrth.

Bart opened his mouth to speak, but before he could utter a sound, Nathan flung his arms forward and a bright light flashed. When Greg's eyes once again adjusted to the gloom, Ryder and the two spirelings were frozen in midstride.

"You must not refer to Greg as Greghart in front of the spirelings," Nathan told the newcomers. "This is most important. Whether you are just speaking, or singing one of your ballads, Bart, you must avoid revealing any link between Greg and the first prophecy."

"I don't know," said Bart. "Every song I've written this year refers to Greghart. I can't just change them all now."

"But you must," said Nathan.

Greg allowed his walking stick to droop. "You can just change any Gregharts in your new songs to Gregs," he told Bart. "Apparently I don't fit the spirelings' image of a mighty dragonslayer, so they'll never make the connection."

"Yes," Bart decided. "I suppose that could work."

"You mustn't use the Hero who slayed Ruuan in connection with Greg either," said Nathan. "Remember, there are hundreds of thousands of spirelings listening. One slip-up could be disastrous for us all."

"I understand," said Bart. "I will be most careful."

"What can you tell us about the second prophecy?" asked Greg.

Bart relayed what he knew, which was exactly what they knew.

"That's it?" said Greg. "That's all you can tell us?"

"I didn't come up with the prophecy, Greg. I'm a songwriter, remember?"

"Who're you?" Melvin asked the second stranger.

"Name's Daniel," the man replied. "King Peter sent me to find Bart and bring him home."

"You're a tracker," said Greg.

The man beamed proudly. "Yes. I caught up with the bard just as the sun started to set. We're heading back to Pendegrass Castle now, so King Peter can learn all he needs for the upcoming battle."

"A little late for that," said Melvin. "The battle will be decided within the week."

"Oh? Then why are you here instead of there?"

"We're trying to find General Talbout and his troops," Greg said.

"Oh, are they out here too?" Daniel dropped to his knees and began scanning the ground in the darkness.

"No, they're clear on the northern end of the kingdom," Nathan told him. He moved into line beside Ryder and the spirelings. "Now, we really shouldn't leave our friends like that too long. Stand beside me, and get back into step."

Bart and Daniel did as they were told. When Nathan waved his arms again, everyone resumed walking as if nothing had happened. The spirelings stopped and stared at Bart curiously. Bart stared back.

Suddenly Greg remembered he and Bart had been in the middle of introductions when Nathan froze the spirelings. He acted quickly to help the bard. "Greg, remember?"

"Oh, of course," said Bart. "It's good to see you again. And look, it's Princess Priscilla too, and Lucky Day."

"*Ahem.*"

"And little Melvin Greatheart. Well, I'll be."

"What are you doing out here, Bart?" asked Priscilla.

"I have to be somewhere."

"But no one even lives out here," said Melvin. "Who do you sing to?"

"You'd be surprised. These woods are full of scattered cabins and hostels."

"Really?" Lucky said, looking about the meadow. "Of all the spots we've seen in this area, I'd think this would be an ideal place to build a cabin."

Bart laughed. "Sure, if you like being attacked by wyverns."

Greg shot a glance at Nathan. "Wyverns?"

"Oh, yes," said Bart. "Whole area's loaded with them. But they especially love this field. Anyway, we were just talking about turning in."

"You'd sleep in a field where you knew wyverns liked to fly at night?" Greg asked.

"Why not? You've got two spirelings and, now I find, Lucky Day with you. I don't expect any problems."

"Well, I think we should be wary just the same," said Nathan, and Greg had an idea the man knew what he was talking about.

Greg thought he'd better ask Daniel who he was, so the spirelings wouldn't think it odd everyone already knew. At first Daniel regarded him with a look that suggested the Mighty Greghart was a disappointment, but then he caught on and told them again.

Afterward, the spirelings returned to their posts in the woods adjoining the meadow, and Greg and the others anxiously returned to their bedrolls. All except Melvin, who had only the shield of dragon scales to cover him and a muddy sheet to place between himself and the ground. They lay quietly for a time, but not one of them seemed capable of falling asleep.

Ryder sat up and propped his back against Lucky's pack. How about one of your songs to soothe our nerves, Bart?"

"Oh, I don't know," said the bard. He watched Gnash near the southern edge of the field and then glanced over at Nathan. After a brief, unspoken exchange, Nathan nodded his approval. Bart grinned and picked up his lute. "Well, I do have one I wrote about the upcoming battle."

Greg cringed. He'd heard Bart's songs before and had never found them particularly soothing. Yet in spite of Greg's silent wishes, Bart began to play.

> *Across this land, a tall spire stands,*
> *And Canarazas gather.*
> *Woke up one dawn, their magic gone,*
> *Its loss no laughing matter.*
> *The massive clan formed up a band,*
> *To march upon the castle.*
> *Upon fine lawn they'd send their pawns*
> *To hack and chop and wrassle.*

"Here we go," muttered Greg.

> *Those for the king would feel the sting*
> *Of blades so deftly wielded.*
> *Skulls crushed, skin sliced, limbs chopped and diced*
> *And bones so cleanly yielded . . .*

"Okay, well, I think we get the drift," Greg interrupted.

"But I'm just getting started," said Bart, his hand still poised over the strings of his lute. He looked at the others to see if they, too, wanted him to stop.

"It's late," said Greg. "Nathan had a point. We really should be resting."

Priscilla studied Greg's expression. "Maybe Greg's right. We're all kind of anxious."

"But if you just let me finish," said Bart, "we do win in the end, you know."

"Yes, of course," Priscilla said, "and I'm sure it's a wonderful song, but . . . maybe after the battle would be better."

"But it won't be the same then. Anyone can write a song about a battle that's already been fought."

"I'd like to hear it," said Melvin, but Bart didn't hear, and Melvin wasn't likely to say more after Priscilla kicked him.

"We know we're missing a great treat," she said, "but Greg's right. We really should get some sleep."

Bart lowered his lute. "I understand."

He stowed away the instrument while Greg offered Priscilla a secret look of thanks. She smiled and winked at him as if they shared a special bond, but Greg was pretty sure the bond he was offering was not the same one she was accepting.

While the princess settled into her own plush bedding, Greg became more unsettled in his. Priscilla smiled over at him. He hid his head under Rake. By the time Greg finally drifted off, dawn was nearly upon them. He was able to enjoy only about ten minutes of uninterrupted slumber before his nightmare began.

He was on a train winding through the mountains, climbing higher and higher toward a great peak. At first the engine was barely able to pull the hill, but then it crested the top and began to pick up speed.

Soon the scenery melted into nothing more than a blur. Greg tried hard to focus on the track ahead, but the rails faded from view. In their place loomed a large swath of ice. To Greg's horror the train picked up speed. Within seconds it could barely grip the slope. It swerved, first to one side, then the other, teetered further and further, until finally it tilted too far.

Greg was thrown hard to the side. He felt his stomach lurch and clamped his hands over his ears. The horrid screech of metal on ice was deafening. He couldn't be more frightened, or so he thought, until suddenly he realized he was no longer dreaming, and still the deafening screech roared on.

Surprises from the Sky

"Wyverns!" Ryder was up and drawing his sword as if he'd spent the entire night preparing for battle. Nathan, too, was already poised in sensen position awaiting the fight, not a surprise, given the man's record for knowing the future and all his talk of wyverns.

Greg jumped to his feet as another deafening screech split the air. "Get down," said Nathan.

As fast as he'd risen, Greg dropped, barely avoiding the huge talon that swooped down from the darkness to tear off his head.

"Watch out," both spirelings advised, and Nathan scrambled to dodge a second attacker.

From the ground Greg watched the second wyvern sweep through their campsite. The creature moved so swiftly, Greg could almost convince himself it was never really there, but that was probably largely due to his wishing so strongly it wasn't.

"They're coming back around," warned Gnash. He and Gnaw were both standing with axes poised for a fight, their eyes fixed to the north.

Greg couldn't see a thing, but he knew better than to doubt the spirelings. Then he did spot something. Bart was stepping forward, lute in hand, and beginning to play. "What are you doing? You'll get yourself killed."

"The music will subdue the creatures," said Bart. "You'll see."

"Here they come," Gnaw warned, his voice rising in pitch to nearly human levels.

Greg crawled to his knees. Through the moonlight, he could see Nathan facing the attack with his head not searching the sky but lowered in meditation, the muscles in his neck dancing lightly beneath his skin. When the first wyvern burst through the darkness, Nathan's staff flew up to meet it, striking cleanly and filling the woods with the loud crack of what Greg hoped to be wyvern bones breaking. But no. Nathan stared at the splintered wood in his hands as a second wyvern swooped down from the sky.

"Watch out!" Greg screamed, though the wyvern's piercing screech offered a far clearer warning. Before he knew what he was doing he was up and running, racing to Nathan's rescue.

If Nathan had waited on Greg, he'd have surely lost his head. Luckily he sensed the attack and spun even before the roar. He ducked and struck out, tearing at the creature's flesh with the splintered end of his staff, a skillful display of chikan that couldn't have been more impressive, except maybe if the magician hadn't been launched across the campsite from the impact.

"Nathan!" Priscilla ran toward him.

Greg started that way too, but stopped when he remembered Bart standing helpless in the clearing.

Fortunately the two spirelings knew better than to drop their defenses to check on a fallen comrade. On the other side of the campsite, Ryder and Daniel joined in the fight, and the next time the wyverns attacked they were met not by a staff, but by two axes, a hunting knife and a sword.

But the four defenders fared little better than Nathan had. Greg dove to the ground again as a flurry of weapons sailed across the clearing, so close he was scratched in the shoulder by one of Gnash's claws. It seems the spireling had never fully released his grip on his axe.

Greg clamped a hand over his bleeding shoulder. To his left, both Gnaw and Ryder were down. To his right, Daniel was on his feet but mumbling to himself and walking in circles. Ahead, Nathan lay unmoving, his head resting in Priscilla's lap. Lucky and Melvin were checking on Gnash, who was stirring somewhat but moving slowly, even by human terms.

And then there was Bart, still standing defenseless in the open, playing his lute.

Greg's heart played an ambitious tune of its own. He may not have had the spirelings' ability to see through the darkness, but he was sure another attack was near. Alone in the clearing, he jumped to his feet and held up his feeble walking stick. If Nathan, Daniel, Ryder and the two spirelings had been bested, what chance did he stand on his own?

A series of deafening screeches announced the next attack. The sounds pressed in from the west and from the east. The wyverns must be hunting in pairs, and Greg wasn't sure which way to swing. He tried to sense their presence but swept his stick through nothing but air. To his surprise the noise cut off with a horrifying thud.

For a moment Greg thought the two wyverns must have collided. He strained to see, hoping to find both creatures laid out in front of him. That's when the screeching took up again. Ahead were not two wyverns but three: one badly shaken and having trouble regaining its feet, the other two locked in battle. The fight was fierce but short. Within seconds the third wyvern had chased off the other two, and the original attackers were fleeing with their tails between their legs.

Greg raised his walking stick. One wyvern may be only half as bad as two, but that was still worse than most things he could imagine. Then he noticed the bright gold ovals outlining the wyvern's eyes, and the iridescent scales streaking down each of its brilliant teal sides. He had seen this wyvern before. It was the same one he'd encountered outside the Infinite Spire when their trip began.

Suddenly Greg understood. When it looked as if this wyvern were about to lose its battle against the spirelings, Greg had stepped in to save its life. Now the wyvern was repaying the favor. Who says wyverns were just mindless beasts? Maybe a ride wasn't out of the question. Blinded by enthusiasm, he lowered his walking stick and waved to capture the creature's attention.

The wyvern, having been about to offer an unfavorable critique of Bart's ballad, spun its long neck Greg's way. Its eyes flashed with an excitement equal to Greg's own.

Greg froze, questioning his decision.

Another screech broke out, so close, Greg dove for cover. At the same instant, the teal wyvern took to the air, its talons passing straight through the spot Greg's head had occupied a moment before. Greg jumped to his feet and spun to fend off this new threat, but then realized the latest screech had not come from a wyvern, but from Rake. The tiny shadowcat stood with his back arched and his blue-black fur raised in warning. The wyvern, already hundreds of yards away and soaring noiselessly through the moonlit darkness, didn't likely notice.

"Rake, you saved my life." Then Greg remembered the excitement he'd felt moments before, and he watched his hopes disappear along with the fleeing wyvern.

Priscilla quit fussing over Nathan and ran over to check on Greg. "What's wrong?"

"That was our last chance," Greg said, dropping his head. "I thought that wyvern was protecting me. I was going to ask it to give us a ride to the border."

"Give us a ride? We told you before you can't reason with a wyvern. You're as crazy as Bart, standing there like wyvern bait, playing that silly lute of his."

Melvin came striding up. "Quite a competition, if you ask me."

Lucky joined them, holding his hand over a bad scrape. Melvin, who'd survived the battle without a scratch, paused to tell the older boy how lucky he was he hadn't been more seriously hurt, to which Lucky smiled in spite of the pain.

Daniel stumbled up as well, mumbling something about stewed cabbages and party hats, after which Ryder asked him to lie down so he could check the tracker over.

Nathan limped over, nursing one shoulder. "That wyvern wasn't protecting you, Greg. It was staking a claim, showing those others this was its territory. In the future I suggest you keep that in mind."

"You knew those wyverns were going to attack," said Greg.

Nathan inspected the scrape on Lucky's arm. "I knew, yes. But don't expect me to tell you anything more. I truly don't know how we can meet General Talbout in time. I don't mind telling you, as of this moment, the extent of my knowledge of future events has been exhausted . . . except for one point, which I will only share if—I mean *after* the prophecy has been fulfilled."

"But how can the prophecy possibly be fulfilled?" Greg asked. "That wyvern was our last hope to get back before the spirelings storm the castle."

"No," corrected Melvin, "the slide down the mountain was our last hope. The wyvern was just a good chance to get ourselves killed."

"Like the slide down the mountain wasn't," Greg grumbled.

"Greg, you're bleeding," said Bart.

Nathan stepped up to inspect the reddening slash in Greg's cloak. He offered a reassuring nod and placed a palm over Greg's shoulder, turning so the spirelings couldn't see. Greg felt a cool sensation spread outward from the wound, and soon the pain subsided.

"It's not serious," Nathan told him, winking, "but you should keep it wrapped up good and tight anyway."

"Uh-huh," Greg muttered, "I sure will."

He wanted to ask why Nathan hadn't healed him last time he was here, when his shoulder had been scratched by a bollywomp. After all, Greg had nearly been killed. But he knew he didn't dare ask in front of the spirelings, or even behind.

Gnaw limped up and asked if anyone was hurt.

"We'll be fine," Nathan assured him. "How's Gnash?"

"He will be okay. No limbs were severed. After seeing that shadowcat, I doubt those wyverns will be returning anytime soon. I suggest you take advantage of the opportunity to get some rest. We will want to be on the trail again at sunrise."

Greg doubted the wyverns shared the same fear of Rake as the spirelings, and after the attack, the last thing he wanted to do was close his eyes again, but Nathan assured him it would be all right, and Greg had an idea the man knew what he was talking about.

Rake tried to comfort Greg, but even the shadowcat had trouble sleeping—not because of the recent attack but because of a comment Gnaw made at dinner about not really hating shadowcats. In fact, he said, before the incident outside the Infinite Spire, he thought they were quite tasty.

Shortly after the group set out the next morning, Daniel pointed at the ground and started jumping with excitement. "What are those?"

Greg saw nothing aside from Gnash's footprints leading off to the north through the snow. "What are what?"

"Right there in front of your face. Look."

"You mean Gnash's tracks?" Lucky asked.

"Those aren't spireling tracks," said Daniel. "They're much deeper. Spirelings weigh twenty, thirty pounds at most. Whatever made those tracks must weigh close to ten times that."

Gnaw strode forward and, in lieu of a lot of unnecessary words, stepped on Daniel's foot, to which Daniel screamed appropriately.

"You are mistaken," Gnaw told him needlessly. "We spirelings are built much more solidly than humans. Normally we leave shallow tracks because our feet are not on the ground long enough to sink in, but recently we have been forced to drag along so you humans can keep up."

"You're kidding?" Daniel gasped.

"Spirelings do not kid."

By the time darkness fell that night, the group was one day closer to their destination, no more, no less, as was the case with each day that followed. Hopes were waning, even with Bart continually offering to boost everyone's spirits with a song and Melvin sharing more of his jokes. Finally the day came for Queen Gnarla to leave for the castle.

"It's time," Greg announced once the sun reached its peak. "We missed our deadline. You can use your magic now, Nathan. We have nothing to lose."

"We do. Queen Gnarla has not yet reached the castle."

But two days later Gnash announced that the spireling army had indeed arrived.

"Nathan," Priscilla insisted. "It's now or never."

But Nathan was being most stubborn.

"What are they doing?" Priscilla asked. She was barely moping along now, resigned to the fact that no amount of hurrying was going to help.

Gnaw regarded her with what Greg thought might have been sympathy. "They have not moved on the castle yet, if that is what you are asking. The attack will not come until noon. For now they are busy sharpening their axes."

"Can't you do something?" Greg asked. "They can share your thoughts, right? Why don't you ask them for more time?"

"Believe me, we have tried," Gnash told him. "Gnaw and I do not want our races to fight any more than you do. We know you all will be suffering for the actions of only one of your kind, which is not right, and we believe you have done your best to help us, even if it has not been enough."

"But still there is nothing we can do," said Gnaw. He lowered his voice. "We will let you know when the battle begins."

"Nathan," Greg urged. "You've got to do something. It's the only way." The words had barely left his mouth before he was knocked off his feet by a powerful wind. Fortunately Melvin was there to break his fall.

A booming voice drifted down from high above the treetops. **"I CAN THINK OF ONE OTHER."**

The Hero Who Slayed Ruuan

Greg strained his neck upward to regard the immense dragon's head hovering high above him, but his view was blocked by the even larger dragon body holding it up. Still it was hard to mistake the voice.

"Ruuan!"

"YOU WERE EXPECTING SOMEONE ELSE?"

"No. We weren't even expecting you."

Priscilla ran up and tried to hug the dragon's toe, but she was about eight feet too short, and it would have been hard to get a decent hold even if she could reach.

Ryder seemed unsurprised to see the dragon. He collapsed onto a comfortable-looking stump and took up a conversation with Bart and Daniel. A few steps away Gnash and Gnaw were busy talking too, oblivious of the dragon's presence.

Melvin squirmed out from under Greg and jumped to his feet. "What do you think you're doing?"

"Oh, sorry," said Greg. "Ruuan caught me off guard."

"What are you talking about?"

Greg observed Melvin's blank expression and suddenly realized Ruuan must be using his magic again to selectively reveal his presence. "Oh . . . nothing. Sorry."

Nathan bent his neck backward to look up at the dragon. "I must say, Ruuan, your timing couldn't be better."

Greg glanced at Melvin, who seemed unaware even of Nathan speaking to the dragon.

Ruuan settled onto the trail, knocking down some of the closest trees, as this section was barely fifty feet wide and therefore a tight fit.

Bart jumped back from a falling tree. "Whoa . . . You don't see that often."

"I CAME AS SOON AS I COULD. I HOPE YOU WEREN'T WORRIED."

"Did you get the amulets?" Greg asked.

Ruuan dropped his head to offer a disapproving glare, causing Greg's knees to give out. Luckily Melvin was still there to break his fall.

"Cut it out," said Melvin.

"Sorry."

"WHAT DO YOU KNOW OF MY REASONS FOR LEAVING?" Ruuan asked.

"I told the boy what he needed to know, nothing more," Nathan assured the dragon.

Ruuan glared at Greg doubtfully, and Greg found the fact the dragon trusted him to carry out the last prophecy but was wary of him now spoke strongly of the importance of the artifacts Ruuan had recovered. Ruuan's head swung around to face Nathan again, nearly plowing down Melvin, who couldn't see it coming.

"HAVE YOU MANAGED TO RECOVER THE SPIRELINGS' AMULET?"

"Did you say something, Nathan?" asked Ryder.

Nathan shook his head and didn't speak again until after the captain turned away. "Still working on it," he told Ruuan.

Ruuan nodded, causing Greg's stomach to pitch. **"YOU'LL BE HAPPY TO KNOW I ACCOMPLISHED MY GOAL. WHEN WILL WE BE MEETING THE WITCH?"**

"*We* won't," Nathan said. His eyes sought out Greg briefly, then turned away again.

Greg didn't know what the two of them were talking about, but he didn't like any conversation that included the witch, especially after the way Nathan just looked at him.

"I UNDERSTAND," said the dragon. He curled his long neck around and dug between his scales. When his head spun back around, his forked tongue shot forward. Lying on each of the tips was a glittering object. Nathan snatched them away before Greg could focus.

"VERY WELL," Ruuan said with a sigh. **"DID I HEAR SOMEONE SAY THAT YOU NEEDED A WAY TO THE CASTLE?"**

"The battle is still an hour or so off," said Nathan. "It is imperative we first find General Talbout. He's supposed to be on the trail somewhere along the northern border."

"THAT SHOULD BE NO PROBLEM. WHAT ABOUT THEM?" Ruuan asked, indicating the others with a single roll of his eyes. Even with the dragon's deceptive magic, it was hard to believe they could miss such a motion.

"You don't need to hide yourself from Melvin," said Greg. "He already knows you're not dead."

No sooner had the words left Greg's mouth than Melvin screamed. "*Dragon!*" He backed up so quickly he tripped over his own feet and landed bottom-first in the snow, then scuttled backward a good distance (though after his countless swinging-dragon's-tail jokes, he should have known to cover a few hundred more feet). There he remained, eyes wide, making no attempt to rise. Greg had to suppress a chuckle. Of course Melvin had been startled, but Greg had to wonder if after all his talk the boy had ever been this close to a dragon in his life.

"Something wrong with the Greatheart boy?" asked Ryder.

"Yeah, Melvin," said Bart, "you okay?"

"He's just resting," said Nathan, "as should you. We'll be leaving soon." He turned back to Ruuan. "General Hawkins can be trusted too. I have trusted him with my life on many an occasion, and he's never let me down."

Now it was Ryder who screamed. He adopted the same look he'd used when the others were about to hurl him off the mountain, and drew his sword, though Greg did notice he'd backed himself against a tree and looked prepared to dart behind it if the dragon so much as looked his way.

Bart glanced at Ryder curiously but continued talking as though nothing were wrong.

"I DO NOT THINK IT WISE TO TELL THE BARD."

"Agreed," said Nathan. "The man holds a strong voice in this kingdom. His music is known throughout the land. He couldn't possibly be the same performer if he had to hide this knowledge from the world."

"STILL HE WILL PROBABLY FIND OUT IN TIME."

"Yes, well, I'll discuss it with him in depth when we're not in such a hurry. It's not a subject I want to rush. The same goes for the tracker."

"What about them?" Lucky asked, pointing at Gnash and Gnaw.

"Now those two I'm not sure of," said Nathan.

"I UNDERSTAND YOUR CONCERN," said Ruuan. **"IF I REVEAL MYSELF TO THEM, I'LL BE LETTING THE ENTIRE CANARAZA RACE SEE ME. AND WITH HUNDREDS OF THOUSANDS KNOWING OF MY EXISTENCE, IT JUST WOULDN'T SEEM LIKE MUCH OF A SECRET ANYMORE."**

"But surely the spirelings know you're not dead," said Priscilla. "They live with you in the Infinite Spire."

"YES, BUT YOU MUST UNDERSTAND, WE'VE ALWAYS HAD AN UNSPOKEN AGREEMENT. THEY GUARD THE PASSAGEWAY OF SHIFTED DIMENSIONS, MAKE SURE NO ONE EVER COMES INTO MY LAIR AND STAY OUT OF MY AFFAIRS . . . AND I, IN TURN, DO NOT INCINERATE THEM."

"Wait a minute," said Greg. "You still have to go in and out to eat, and I've heard you come down the tunnel. There's no way the spirelings could miss a pin drop, let alone a noise like that."

"THEY CAN IF I USE MY MAGIC TO CONCEAL MY PRESENCE," said Ruuan, **"AND I'VE BEEN VERY CAREFUL SINCE OUR LAST MEETING. I DON'T WISH TO JEOPARDIZE ANY PROPHECIES."**

"But you can't keep that up forever, can you?" asked Priscilla.

"FOREVER, NO. BUT I SHOULDN'T NEED TO. I'M MUCH OLDER THAN I LOOK. I PROBABLY WON'T LIVE MORE THAN ANOTHER CENTURY OR TWO."

"That's still a long time to go skulking about, hiding from the spirelings," said Lucky.

Ruuan's eyes flared. **"WE DRAGONS DO NOT SKULK. BESIDES, A COUPLE OF CENTURIES IS HARDLY A DROP IN THE BUCKET."**

"Still, wouldn't it be better if you let the spirelings in on the secret?" suggested Ryder, who was just now stepping away from the safety of his tree. Even though the general could see the others carrying on a normal conversation, he looked uncertain about the situation himself. All eyes turned toward him, including Ruuan's, which explained why he took a quick step back and stood with most of his weight resting on his rear foot, his toes pointed down the path away from the dragon.

"Did you say something, Ryder?" asked Bart.

"BUT WHAT OF THE LAST PROPHECY?" said Ruuan, ignoring them both.

"What about it?" said Lucky. "According to Priscilla, everything Simon predicted occurred just as written. Why shouldn't the spirelings know the truth?"

"HOW DO YOU MEAN?"

Priscilla told Ruuan what she'd read, explaining how Brandon had actually written that Greg would *sleigh* the dragon, not *slay* him, and how technically nothing happened inside Ruuan's lair that violated the prophecy as written.

"HMMM," said Ruuan, reaching up to scratch his chin with a six-foot-long talon. "THIS IS AN INTERESTING DEV-ELOPMENT. ALL THIS TIME I THOUGHT WE WERE STRETCHING THE TRUTH TO SUIT OUR OWN NEEDS, WHEN REALLY OUR INTERPRETATION WAS CORRECT."

"So you'll reveal yourself to Gnash and Gnaw then?" said Greg.

He barely had time to get the words out before Gnash and Gnaw were both screaming hysterically and forming balls of red energy in their fists.

"The dragon lives!" Gnash screamed, jumping as high as his short legs would carry him.

"It's true!" shouted Gnaw. He, too, started jumping up and down, not so much from excitement as because the fireball in his hand was starting to burn. He threw it aside and blew on his palm.

"Calm down," Nathan told them. "I can explain everything."

"What you told Queen Gnarla was true," Gnaw interrupted. "The dragon is not dead. How did you know?"

"As I said, I can explain everything." And explain he did. He told the two spirelings all he knew of the last prophecy, except, of course, for the one minor detail about Greg being the Mighty Greghart.

Bart took a seat at the base of a tree next to Daniel, where the two stared blankly at the others, blissfully ignorant of the events around them.

"SO YOUR QUEEN KNOWS, THEN?" Ruuan asked the two spirelings.

Gnash nodded. "She knows."

"And she understands why you have been hiding from us," said Gnaw. "She wants me to assure you that your secret is safe with us."

"You can hardly call it a secret anymore," said Lucky. "About half a million spirelings know about it now."

"Yes," said Gnash, "but do not worry. We will not tell anyone."

"What are we doing?" Priscilla interrupted. "Have you all forgotten? Everyone at home is about to be attacked."

"There is no cause for alarm," said Gnash. "Queen Gnarla has not yet rallied her troops."

"She does not intend to march until noon," Gnaw added, but then he lifted his chin, and everyone followed his gaze upward, where the midday sun was climbing high in the sky.

"We need to go," urged Greg.

"What about our amulet?" Gnash insisted.

Lucky smiled. "No problem. Ruuan can fly to the northern border and back in minutes."

"AND I WILL," said Ruuan. **"EVERYONE CLIMB ABOARD."**

After Nathan, Lucky and Greg teamed up to pry Ryder's arms off the tree he'd stepped behind, they hiked off the trail a couple hundred feet, looking for a spot on Ruuan's tail short enough for them to board. The others followed.

"Why are we walking in circles?" Bart wanted to know.

"Yes, why?" asked Daniel, who, even after climbing in and out of an enormous track in the snow, still remained unaware of the dragon he was about to board.

Melvin seemed to warm up to Ruuan far quicker than Ryder did, perhaps because he'd grown up in a family where his brother and father had spent their entire lives slaying dragons. Or maybe it was because he'd once witnessed Greg riding on Ruuan's back and thought if Greg could do it, then so could he. Either way, it was not long before he sat perched between Ruuan's shoulders with a huge smile plastered across his face, bragging about how he wasn't the least bit scared and how he'd ridden on the backs of more dragons than Greg could count.

Ryder sat next to him, and though the general had not plastered the same smile across his face that Melvin managed, his face had grown so pale it could have passed for plaster.

"Relax," Melvin said, when the dragon first took to the air. "This should be fun."

"You look rather peaked, General," said Bart. "Maybe you should lie down a moment. I'm sure the others won't mind. I don't know why we've stopped, but it looks as though they don't seem intent on moving just yet."

Greg found it hard to believe that even with magic the bard could be riding atop a dragon, thousands of feet above the ground, and not notice anything unusual. With magic like that, Greg was even more glad Ruuan was on their side. But Bart was right about one thing. The general looked awful.

"You need to calm down," Melvin told Ryder. "Hey, I know. I'll tell some of my jokes." Greg, Priscilla and Lucky all groaned, but Melvin grinned as if he hadn't heard. "How does a dragonslayer prepare for battle?"

Ryder didn't seem to hear. His gaze remained fixed on the ground, or at least, where the ground used to be.

"He gets fired up," shouted Melvin.

The joke did nothing to improve Ryder's mood. In fact, the only one who seemed to enjoy it was Ruuan. The dragon started to chuckle, which Greg wouldn't have minded so much, except when Ruuan laughed his ribs shook, sending the ten passengers lurching in all directions. Even though he was fairly certain Ruuan's magic would keep him from falling, Greg could barely fight back his panic. Unbelievably, Ryder turned a paler shade of white. Melvin had to struggle to keep his balance, but the near disaster did little to put him off.

"You hear about the dragonslayer who lost his temper?" he said, and this time the question was directed as much to Ruuan as it was to Ryder. "They say he got steamed."

"**HA**," said Ruuan, and Greg was thrown so hard to the left he wondered if his theory about the dragon's magic protecting him could be trusted. **"THAT WAS A GOOD ONE."**

"Cut it out," Priscilla shouted.

"Yeah, Melvin," said Lucky. "You're going to get us all killed."

Bart smiled happily and picked up his lute. "Anyone want to hear a song?"

"No!" everyone shouted at once. All except Daniel, who smiled happily and took a seat near the bard's feet.

Greg heard a peculiar whining noise. He checked on Rake, then realized the sound was coming from Ryder. The general had given up staring down, as Ruuan was now flying so high it would have been impossible to see the ground. Yet somehow the dragon knew their position. Ruuan stifled his chuckles long enough to announce they'd reached the northern border.

Gnash strode forward, looking less than comfortable walking atop a dragon soaring thousands of feet in the air. Ironic, since he and Gnaw had spent their whole lives living within an infinitely tall spire. "Why aren't we stopping?"

"THE KING'S ARMY IS NOT HERE," Ruuan answered. **"I COVERED THE ENTIRE BORDER FROM EAST TO WEST AND SAW NO SIGN OF THEM. ARE YOU SURE THIS IS WHERE THEY WERE HEADED?"**

"King Peter did say they might be on their way back," Greg reminded them. "Do you know what route they might have taken,

Ryder? Ryder?" He decided from the look on Ryder's face that the general couldn't have answered even if he wanted to.

"It's okay," Lucky tried to reassure him. "Ruuan's trying to help us."

"It's not the dragon that has me frightened," Ryder finally revealed. "Remember, I'm afraid of heights."

"Oh dear," said Priscilla. "You must be terrified."

"Yes, well, it hasn't been one of my best weeks."

"I think I can help," said Melvin. He was silent for a moment, a sober expression across his face, before he shared his carefully chosen words of wisdom. "Tell me, why didn't the dragonslayer come home for dinner?"

Everyone moaned, including the spirelings, but Melvin was not put off. "He had a hot fling with an old flame."

Again Ruuan began to shake, and each passenger scrambled to grab hold of a horn to keep from being thrown off.

But Melvin wasn't finished. "I hear she was a real knockout."

Ruuan laughed so hard, for an instant he actually lost control of his wings. Greg felt his stomach rise as the dragon dropped a full hundred feet.

"STOP, YOU'RE KILLING ME."

"Yeah, Melvin, stop," shouted Lucky. "You're going to kill us all."

Greg tightened his grip, knowing that if Lucky was starting to worry, there must truly be something to worry about.

"Yes, you really should be quiet, son," advised Nathan. "Ruuan is trying to concentrate. He needs to stay focused if he's going to find General Talbout and his troops."

"I DON'T SEE THEM ANYWHERE," Ruuan announced. **"I'LL MOVE SOUTH A FEW DOZEN MILES AND MAKE ANOTHER PASS."**

The dragon turned, and Greg watched as the Infinite Spire glided soundlessly by. The landmark was hundreds of miles away, he knew, yet it towered so high above everything else, it would have been impossible to miss. Within seconds the dragon had swept through another pass.

"NO SIGN OF THEM," Ruuan announced.

"We're running out of time," groaned Priscilla.

"There is no point abandoning our search before we recover the amulet," Gnash warned. "Its return is the only thing that will stop the battle."

Though the spirelings surely held little power over the dragon at this height, Ruuan turned and began another sweep. Gnash's heavily toothed jaw pulled itself into a grin, but the expression faded as soon as Melvin resumed telling his inane dragonslayer jokes. In spite of everyone's objections the boy just wouldn't stop.

"You're all so tense. The least I can do is try to lighten the mood," he insisted.

Greg just hoped Ruuan's laughing didn't cause the dragon to lighten his load. With each pass of the surrounding countryside, Ruuan's chortling grew more forceful and the passengers grew increasingly frightened. Everyone, that is, except Melvin, who'd managed to gain a firm handhold on one of Ruuan's horns and was relentless in his efforts.

Greg noticed that with each sweep the dragon completed, the Infinite Spire grew wider. He tried to drown out Melvin's voice by asking Ruuan how much distance they had covered.

"WE'RE ABOUT TWO HUNDRED MILES SOUTH OF THE BORDER. I IMAGINE EVEN YOU HUMANS WILL BE ABLE TO SEE PENDEGRASS CASTLE WITHIN THE NEXT TRIP OR TWO."

"That's incredible," said Ryder. It was the first he'd spoken since reminding Priscilla of his fear of heights and, given the lack of color in his face, a remarkable achievement.

Ruuan banked again, this time sweeping from east to west across the distant face of Myrth. As the countryside streaked below, Greg spotted Pendegrass Castle nestled among the trees.

"Hey, what do you call a dragonslayer with slow reactions?" Melvin started again.

The others begged him to be quiet, but Ruuan seemed excited to hear the joke. **"GO ON, LITTLE ONE. WHAT *DO* YOU CALL A DRAGONSLAYER WITH SLOW REACTIONS?"**

"Claude."

It took a moment for the punch line to sink in, but when it did, Ruuan nearly doubled over with laughter—no mean feat when you happen to be a three-hundred-foot-long dragon in midflight. Priscilla screamed. Greg might have too, if he could have found his voice. Melvin, on the other hand, looked pleased over his effect on the dragon.

"What do you call a dragonslayer with even slower reactions?" he asked.

"Cut it out, Melvin," warned Lucky.

"Patty."

The dragon burst out laughing, spraying fire over the landscape. Fortunately they were flying so high, the flames died away before reaching the ground.

"I think that should be the end of your jokes," Nathan advised the boy rather sternly, though given the circumstances, Greg thought he might have wanted to say it more sternly still.

"Wait. Just one more," chuckled Melvin. "What do you call a dragonslayer who dives into a lake to dodge a blast of dragon fire?"

Both Gnash and Gnaw released their grips on the dragon's scales to stride purposely forward and present their double-bladed axes. "We agree with the magician."

Melvin opened his mouth to speak, but hesitated when he saw the looks on the two spirelings' faces. "Stu?" he muttered anyway.

Ruuan practically exploded with laughter. His wings folded, and Greg felt the reassuring support of the dragon's back drop out from under him. The spirelings gave up trying to intimidate Melvin and dove for the spikes lining the dragon's back.

"STOP," Ruuan shouted, though Greg found it hard to hear past the rushing wind and the pounding of his heart in his ears.

As the dragon fought to regain control, even Melvin screamed. Ruuan would never be able to pull out of the dive in time. Only Bart and Daniel remained calm. The bard strummed a chord on his lute and began to tune it.

Greg knew they were surely doomed, but then the dragon flapped with all his might, grunting under the exertion, and arced out of the dive, banking hard to one side to avoid a tree. In a moment they were rising again, and Ruuan was exhaling in relief. Still the dragon couldn't help releasing a few last chuckles over Melvin's joke.

"BOY, YOU SLAY ME. IN ALL MY YEARS I CAN'T REMEMBER WHEN I'VE LAUGHED SO HARD."

"What did you say?" asked Greg.

"I SAID, IN ALL MY YEARS I CAN'T REMEMBER WHEN I'VE LAUGHED SO HARD."

"No, before that."

"UM," said Ruuan, trying to remember, **"I'M NOT SURE."**

"You said he slayed you."

The dragon wound his sinewy neck back to offer Greg an intimidating glare. **"IS THAT SUPPOSED TO BE FUNNY?"**

"No, it's not a joke."

Ruuan's glare strengthened. The others screamed and urged him to keep his eyes on the trees.

"I'M NOT SURE WHAT YOU'RE IMPLYING, SMALL ONE, BUT I DON'T THINK I LIKE IT."

"No, don't you get it?" shouted Greg. "Melvin just slayed you."

"IT'S JUST A FIGURE OF SPEECH . . . AND YOU DON'T HAVE TO LOOK SO HAPPY ABOUT IT."

"You don't understand. All this time we thought I'd be the one bringing the Army of the Crown to victory because we thought Simon was talking about the hero from the last prophecy."

Both spirelings emitted an odd noise and stared at Greg questioningly.

"We all assumed that the hero from the last prophecy and the hero from the upcoming battle were the same person," Greg continued. "But Simon never said that. The first prophecy said I was going to sleigh the dragon, *S-L-E-I-G-H*, which I did. But this one's different. It talks about the Hero who slayed Ruuan, *S-L-A-Y*."

"Which never happened," finished Lucky.

"Until now," Greg corrected him.

"UH, I HATE TO INTERRUPT," said Ruuan, **"BUT I SEE SEVERAL HUNDRED HUMANS APPROACHING THE CASTLE FROM THE WOODS BELOW. DO YOU WANT ME TO SWOOP DOWN FOR A CLOSER LOOK?"**

"By all means," said Nathan, grinning widely, and Greg had to wonder if he'd known Melvin was the true hero all along.

Everyone started buzzing with excitement—but Gnash and Gnaw were not looking down like the others. They were staring intently at Greg.

Ruuan steered toward the ground as he was asked, and for the moment Greg's unease over being the focus of the spirelings' attention was replaced with the much greater horror of feeling like a passenger on a jet as it drops from the sky. In spite of all contrary images that sped through Greg's mind, Ruuan landed safely in a wide spot on the trail just east of the area where General Talbout's troops were allegedly marching.

The spirelings rushed toward Greg as Ryder led Bart and Daniel away down Ruuan's tail.

"Finally," said Bart. "I thought we'd never get moving again."

"*You* are the Mighty Greghart?" Gnaw said, his voice so feeble as to be barely audible.

Greg couldn't determine the spireling's expression. It was somewhere between anger and awe. He regarded the axe in Gnaw's hand. "Um, yes?"

Melvin made a rude noise, but said nothing.

"Where is our amulet?" Gnash demanded, though with obvious uncertainty.

"I don't know, I swear."

"Do not deny taking it. You were seen by . . ." Gnaw shuddered, "two of our kind."

"I did take it," Greg said, to which the spirelings' expressions darkened, "because I was told I needed it for the first prophecy. But I put it back when I was through. Think about it. Would I have spent all this time and effort hunting out Widget if I knew where it was?"

"The boy is telling the truth," said Nathan. The others, even Melvin, nodded.

The spirelings continued to stare at Greg in a way that made him uncomfortable, not that there existed any other way. "Very well. Queen Gnarla says to continue hunting out this Widget person." Still they stared.

"Okay . . ." said Greg. He was quick to disembark via Ruuan's tail. The others followed.

"MY MAGIC SHOULD HAVE KEPT ANYONE FROM SEEING US," said Ruuan. **"HUMANS HAVE NEVER BEEN AS OPEN-MINDED AS SPIRELINGS."** He bent his neck until his head was even with Nathan's—or at least the bottom of their chins were even. Ruuan's forehead, of course, was even with a spot about ten feet higher.

"I'LL BE LEAVING NOW," he told the magician. **"THE CASTLE IS JUST A SHORT WAYS AHEAD, SO YOU NO LONGER NEED MY HELP, AND I DON'T THINK I COULD BEAR TO WATCH THE EVENTS TO COME."**

"It's the only way, I assure you," said Nathan.

A tear dropped from Ruuan's eye, drenching Melvin, who was unlucky enough to be walking under the dragon's head at that moment. Lucky, who was walking next to him, escaped without so much as a splatter.

"I WILL HAVE TO TRUST YOU, OL' FRIEND. MAY THE FIRE IN YOUR LUNGS BURN HOT AND PURE. I HOPE TO SEE YOU AGAIN SOON." And with that the dragon took to the sky, knocking everyone to the ground with the rush of air pushed beneath his wings. On the bright side, at least it helped dry out Melvin's tunic before the poor boy caught his death of cold.

"What was that about?" Greg asked Nathan.

"You'll know soon enough," Nathan told him.

Anxious to be rid of the dragon and redeem himself as a leader of men, Ryder quickly took charge of the group. "Follow me," he ordered.

"What happened?" asked Daniel. "I seem to have fallen. Where are we? What happened to the chasm?"

"No time to explain," said Nathan. "We need to find General Talbout's troops. They're supposed to be marching close by."

Daniel dropped to all fours and began studying the ground. "If they passed this way, I'll know in a second."

"Of course they passed this way," said Melvin. "Don't you see the huge swath cut through the snow?"

"Come," said Ryder, "we already know where they are." He led them west at a pace Greg had trouble matching, but one that allowed them to overtake the soldiers within a few minutes.

"Halt! Who goes there?" Two uniformed men stepped onto the trail before them, their swords drawn and no-nonsense looks in their eyes. "Oh, General Hawkins, sir," said one, saluting. "We didn't realize you were patrolling these parts."

"We need to see General Talbout right away," Ryder said.

The soldier did not question the general. "Yes, sir."

After signaling for his partner to stay put, he led Ryder and the others past several hundred marching soldiers until finally they caught up with General Talbout traveling midway up the pack. He was an old man, with the kind of face Greg normally associated with musty scents and faded photographs, but he was spry as any half his age.

"Hawkeye," he shouted when he spotted Ryder. Though he came to an abrupt halt, his men kept walking, eyes glued forward. Ryder's face reddened. "Sorry, I mean, *General* Hawkeye."

"Uh, it's Hawkins, sir."

Greg had never heard Ryder use such a meek tone. Even when he was hysterical over dropping off the cliff or the thought of riding Ruuan, he had argued with conviction.

General Talbout roared with laughter. "You served under me for ten years, Hawkeye. Do you really think I don't remember your name?"

"Uh, no, sir. Of course not, sir."

"You're no longer under my command, son. We're both generals now. You don't need to call me sir anymore."

"No, sir," mumbled Ryder. "I mean, no, I know."

General Talbout laughed so loudly, Greg was reminded of Ruuan just before he lost control and nearly dropped from the sky. "Look, I'm pretty sure you're not following me across the kingdom to discuss how we should or shouldn't address one another. What is it you wanted?"

"We're looking for Corporal Widget, si—er—we're looking for Corporal Widget."

The general's smile disappeared in an instant. "What's this about?" he asked, his tone no longer playful.

Nathan stepped forward. "Perhaps I can explain."

"Nathaniel Caine." General Talbout's smile returned, but with far less enthusiasm than before. "How long has it been, my boy?"

"I'm afraid we don't have time for pleasantries, General," said Nathan. He quickly explained about the spirelings' amulet and how he believed Corporal Widget either had it or knew who did.

The general's expression turned grim again. "I'm afraid Corporal Widget can't help you."

"But he must," Priscilla said. "The spirelings are going to attack my family if we don't give back their amulet now."

"I am truly sorry, Highness," said General Talbout. "I understand your concern, but as I said, Corporal Widget cannot help. I wish he could, but believe me, he has the best of reasons."

"What reason?" the spirelings demanded.

"I'm afraid the young man has recently passed away."

Greg's New Task

"We were not more than a week out from the castle when we ran into the largest band of trolls I've ever seen."

Greg noticed Priscilla had a hard time standing still while General Talbout told his story, even though both Gnash and Gnaw assured her that Queen Gnarla had not yet begun to rally her troops.

"It was a fierce battle," the general explained, "and many of my men were lost, but in the end we were the victors, and not more than a handful of the beasts escaped alive." General Talbout's face was as stoic as any Greg had ever seen, but still Greg thought he saw moistness in the old man's eyes. "Corporal Widget was one of the first to fall—one of far too many, I might add."

"What about our amulet?" said Gnash. "Sorry," he said upon observing the general's expression, "but it is most important that we discover its whereabouts quickly."

The general shook off his sadness and regarded the spirelings grimly. "I'm afraid I don't know anything about that."

"Sir, pardon me, sir," came a voice from behind. Greg looked to where two columns of soldiers extended into the woods as far as the eye could see. General Talbout had called the troops to a halt soon after Nathan asked him about Corporal Widget, and the men had been standing at attention ever since.

"Who said that?" asked General Talbout.

One of the men stepped out of line. "Sir, Sergeant Hosselmeyer, sir."

"At ease, sergeant. Did you have something to say?"

"Yes, sir. It's about the amulet, sir."

The others looked hopeful.

"Go on," General Talbout prompted.

"Corporal Widget started boasting about an amulet soon after we left Pendegrass Castle. I asked him where he got it, but I don't think he knew. I think it just showed up in his bedroll."

"I see," said the general. "Do you know what happened to it, sergeant?"

"No, sir. I have not seen it since . . . well, since the battle. Corporal Sanderson checked the bod—checked Corporal Widget to see if he had any last effects, and he did not report finding it."

"Where is Corporal Sanderson now?"

"Toward the rear of the troops, sir."

"Tell him to come here immediately."

"Sir, yes, sir."

The sergeant bellowed for Corporal Sanderson, much the same way Greg often let his mother know she had a phone call. He could almost understand now why she hated it so much.

But as the sergeant stepped back into line, the soldiers to the east hollered in response, and then Greg heard more cries from still farther off as word carried down the line. After a while the calls died away, and a minute later, a rotund soldier came jogging up the path from the east, his belly bouncing noticeably beneath his tunic with every stride.

He stopped in front of the general, panting. "Sir, you . . . wanted to . . . see me, sir."

General Talbout ordered him at ease and asked if he remembered seeing the amulet.

"Many times," said the soldier, "but not the day Corporal Widget was killed. Or any time since."

"Very well. You may return to your position."

The large man's eyes grew slightly wider, but he did not complain. Instead he turned and puffed back down the trail in the direction from which he had come.

"This is terrible," said Priscilla.

Gnash stepped forward. "More than you know, princess. But I do not think we should waste time discussing it. Queen Gnarla is not pleased. She asked me to let you know she is assembling her troops for the attack."

"Nathan, let's go," Priscilla insisted.

General Talbout had instructed his troops to head straight for the castle, and they'd already marched away at double speed, but for some reason Nathan was lagging behind.

"You go ahead, Princess. I need to talk to Greg alone a moment."

Greg glanced at the magician cautiously. It was bad enough they were really going to battle the spirelings. What other horrific news did Nathan have in store for him?

Priscilla hopped about as if she couldn't decide whether to stay and argue or let them be and run along ahead. In the end she disappeared down the trail after the last of General Talbout's troops.

"What's going on?" Greg asked, not sure he wanted to hear the answer.

"I need to speak to you before the battle begins," said Nathan. "I may not get another chance."

Greg felt his mouth go dry. He replied with a nod.

"I told you days ago that I'd shared with you nearly all I know about the future. These past days have been difficult because I've had no way of knowing how much I should reveal. My intuition tells me it's time I shared the last of my knowledge."

Still Greg said nothing. He found himself staring at Nathan so intently he had to force himself to blink.

"Relax, Greg," Nathan said, forcing a smile. "You're safe, for the next few seconds anyway." He dug under his cloak and withdrew the two objects Ruuan had given him. Even at a distance they made Greg's skin tingle. One was ring-shaped, about the size of a bracelet. Nathan inspected it briefly and returned it to its hiding place. The other he held out to Greg. It was pentagon shaped, about half the size of the ring.

"You were very clever to figure out Melvin would be the true hero of the upcoming battle, but that does not mean you don't have your role to fill. I want you to take this."

"Me? But isn't that the missing piece of the Amulet of Tehrer you told us about? Why would you want me to have it?"

"You must take it to the witch."

Greg's mouth dropped open. "Witch Hazel? Are you crazy?"

For a brief moment Nathan's smile looked more genuine. "Perhaps. But it may be the only chance Myrth has."

Greg gulped. "What do you mean?"

"Take the amulet first. Then I'll tell you what I know."

Greg reluctantly took the pentagon from Nathan. The metal felt unnaturally cold and left his whole arm feeling as if he'd just struck his funny bone. He quickly moved it to a pocket in his tunic, where it caused his skin to prickle right through the cloth.

"Now, we must get moving," said Nathan. "We don't want to be late."

"Wait, you didn't tell me—"

Nathan spun Greg around and pushed him off balance so that he had to begin walking or land face-first in the snow. "I don't know where the spirelings' amulet is," the magician said as they walked, "but I have an idea where it will end up."

"Hazel's?" said Greg.

"Ah, you've been paying attention."

Actually, thought Greg, it was a lucky guess. "What makes you think Hazel will get it?"

"Because she's got the other three, of course."

"How do you know tha—? Oh, never mind. How did she get them?"

"Well, she got the first several years ago, from me."

Greg stopped abruptly, but Nathan pushed him forward again. "Why would you give one of the sections to a witch?"

Nathan took the lead and motioned for Greg to hurry. "She wasn't always a witch, remember? She was my friend. Besides, I thought it important I didn't have all three."

"You had three of the four pieces?" Greg asked. He quickened his stride, but still found it difficult to keep up.

"Three of the *five* pieces, yes," said Nathan.

"But how did you get them?"

"I told you that Hazel, Mordred and I scoured the countryside looking for anyone and anything magical we could find. Unfortunately we learned much more than children so young should know. We had obtained great knowledge and power without having to pay the price of experience, and we were too naive to know the dangers we were unleashing.

"I'd always been a bit of a prankster," he continued, "and I guess Hazel and Mordred followed my lead. All across the country we met generous people who were kind enough to help us, and we repaid them with trickery. Occasionally they'd give us magical artifacts of their own free will, thinking they were helping us. Other times we used what power we had to steal what wasn't rightfully ours. I'd managed to get my hands on three of the amulet sections before I turned eighteen, years before I learned what they were. But fortunately I did grow older, more responsible, and I began to understand much of the danger inherent in magic."

"But you didn't have the amulets when I came here last time," said Greg. "What happened?"

"Snake," said Nathan.

"How's that?"

"Snake!" Nathan's staff shot out inches in front of Greg's foot and speared the coiled reptile before it could strike. "You need to watch yourself," said Nathan. "It wouldn't do for you to get yourself killed now."

Greg exhaled deeply. "I'll try to be more careful."

"Anyway," said Nathan, picking up the pace again. "I had the three sections for years without knowing much about them, until one day I ran into Ruuan."

"I'll bet that hurt," Greg said, scouring the trail ahead for more snakes.

"What? No, I mean I *met* Ruuan, in the woods. I learned he held the fourth section in his spire, or at least the spirelings did. The other three he thought were distributed safely throughout Myrth, so he was quite shocked to discover I'd found them all. Lucky for me we had a history together, or he might have scorched me and taken the pieces back for a second try at distributing them."

"You had a history together?"

Nathan nodded. "A story for another time."

"So, Ruuan let you keep the amulets?"

"Not exactly. He explained what I told you and the princess about the significance of the five pieces. Believe it or not, none of the others who held them before me knew the sections were part of a larger whole. Once Ruuan told me the entire history, I knew I must give them back. But Ruuan didn't want that kind of responsibility either. He entrusted me to scatter the pieces I'd found out into the world."

"So you gave them to your friends?"

"I asked each to hide one. From what Ruuan told me, I knew it wouldn't be wise for me to know the whereabouts of all three. So I gave one to Mordred, which he in turn gave to King Peter upon taking up service to the crown. The second I gave to Hazel. She may have kept hers, or she may have passed it to someone else and gone back for it after her exile. I don't know. The third I kept for a while but later gave to Norman Greatheart, who helped me out of a tight spot. He used it throughout the remainder of his career, and then passed it on to his son Marvin when he retired."

"So, what makes you think Hazel has three sections now?"

"Because it's not especially easy to remove a magical artifact from its rightful owner. Hazel and Mordred are the only two people I know who have the power and the know-how to take them."

Greg's next stride covered no less than eight feet. The stick he had been about to step on looked an awful lot like a snake. He picked it up and weighed it in his hands, considering its worth as a weapon. Nathan did not slow his pace.

"Come, Greg, we must hurry."

"But if either Hazel or Mordred could have taken the amulets," Greg said as he ran to catch up, "then Hazel might not have them. Mordred might."

"He probably did at one time," Nathan said. "But if so, he's surely given them to Hazel by now."

"I knew he was evil."

"No. Everything Mordred's done, he's done to help the kingdom."

Greg heard voices drifting on the wind. The others must be close. "By what stretch of the imagination is giving Hazel the amulets helping the kingdom?"

"When we were boys, I told Mordred about Simon's two prophecies," said Nathan. "Not the details, mind you, just the gist of things."

"You never did tell me how you knew about Simon's prophecies before Simon did."

"And I don't plan to. Mordred knew Hazel would hold four pieces of the amulet by the time the upcoming battle was through. If I were to guess, I'd say he didn't trust Fate to deliver them to her, so for the good of the kingdom he delivered them himself. He also knew Hazel had already recovered the one originally given to her, and the two belonging to King Peter and Marvin Greatheart would have been simple for him to retrieve, but the fourth was a different matter. He knew a soldier from the Army of the Crown would end up with the spirelings' amulet because I told him. But even I didn't know how it would be taken, so neither did he.

"After your encounter with Ruuan in the last prophecy, you mentioned smelling ozone in the Passageway of Shifted Dimensions. My guess is that Mordred was there too, just as he had been throughout our journey, lending a hand to the prophecy whenever he felt it needed his intervention to come true."

"But I kept smelling ozone that whole trip," Greg said, "every time something horrible was about to happen."

"Just as described in the prophecy, yes. I know it sounds like Mordred did a terrible thing, but who's to say? If he hadn't taken advantage of the spirelings' evacuation of the spire to sneak in and retrieve that amulet for himself, who knows where we might be today?"

"Probably back on Earth where I belong," said Greg angrily.

"Yes, well I was referring to the rest of us," said Nathan. "After all, it wouldn't do for one of Simon's prophecies to go astray."

Again Greg heard voices ahead, but he could see nothing through the trees. "Do you think Hazel has the spirelings' amulet?"

"If not yet, then soon."

"So if she has all four pieces, how are we going to get them back?"

"We aren't. You are. You're going to trade her the pentagon I gave you for the other four."

"The pentagon? But you said that's the most powerful piece of Tehrer's amulet."

Nathan grabbed Greg's arm and helped him hop over a narrow gully, nearly pulling Greg's shoulder out of the socket. "Correct. That's why she'll be willing to trade four for one."

"But why trade at all? Without the last piece she'll never have the full power of Ruuan's amulet. Why not just let her keep what she has and hide the other pieces again so she'll be sure never to find them?"

Nathan shook his head. "The spirelings feel they have dishonored the dragon by losing the amulet he gave them. They are a proud race, and they will not return to a normal existence until they get it back. Make no mistake about it. They will do anything to retrieve it, including attacking the castle if they think it will help."

"But that's crazy," said Greg. "Would they really fight the entire Army of the Crown over an amulet we don't even have?"

"Why don't you ask them yourself?" Nathan said.

"Huh?" replied Greg.

Nathan stopped and motioned toward an opening in the woods ahead.

Greg's stomach had attempted many unusual gyrations over the last few weeks, but nothing compared to the way it flipped over now. Ahead, the woods opened onto the highly manicured lawn of Pendegrass Castle, only today it was impossible to see even a single blade of grass. Every square inch was covered by spireling warriors, each standing with a double-bladed axe poised at his or her side, no doubt awaiting Queen Gnarla's command to attack.

The Battle of the Spirelings

"Wait!" Greg shouted.

The two closest spirelings turned at the noise, and their faces broke into wide, toothy grins.

"Gnash?" said Greg. "Gnaw?"

One of the spirelings laughed. "I am Nibble," she said, her voice much more feminine than her appearance. "And this is Nip. Queen Gnarla is anxiously awaiting your arrival. We will take you to her."

Only then did Greg notice that Nibble and Nip were not the only two who had turned and recognized him. Every toothy face in the crowd had spun his way, and the entire yard was abuzz with excitement. Spirelings everywhere were shouldering each other out of the way just to catch a glimpse of him, an odd enough behavior in its own right, but even odder when you considered that every spireling present could have viewed him just as well from the other side of the kingdom as long as just one of their kind got a good look.

"Make way, make way," Nibble shouted as they pressed through the crowd.

"The Mighty Greghart coming through," Nip called excitedly beside her.

Nathan had to struggle to move along with them, since the entire length of the yard spirelings tended to crowd in behind Greg as he passed, nudging the magician out of the way. About halfway across the lawn a low chant was started.

"Greghart! Greghart!" the spirelings screamed, and where normally it might have taken a few minutes for the chant to riffle through the crowd, here even those farthest away knew it had been started with the very first call. By the third "Greghart!" the noise was so deafening, Greg thought he would be crushed by the sound. The whole world had gone mad.

When he reached the front of the lines, just steps from the castle wall, and spotted the others standing next to a very nervous-looking Brandon Alexander, Greg couldn't have been happier. Well, that's not true at all. He would have been happier just about anywhere else, doing just about any*thing* else, but at least he was happier now than he'd been a moment ago.

Queen Gnarla stalked into view, accompanied by King Peter, Queen Pauline and Princess Penelope. The spireling queen stopped in front of Greg and called for silence. Her face had changed so much since Greg last saw her that he didn't recognize her at first. Okay, he probably wouldn't have recognized her anyway, since all spirelings looked alike to him, but still something about her was different. And then he realized what it was. She was regarding him not with contempt but with admiration.

"Congratulations, Greghart," said King Peter. "I'd ask how you were doing, but from what Queen Gnarla has been telling me, things are going quite well."

"You're kidding, right?"

"Bring The Book," Queen Gnarla called to no one in particular.

Within moments the spirelings to Greg's right pulled back so another of their kind could pass. He was taller than most of the others, and dressed in finer chain mail. Even the jagged cuffs of his pants seemed slightly straighter. With him he carried some sort of object, which he took directly to Queen Gnarla. He bowed and held out his hands, and Greg could then see that he held a bound volume. Something about it seemed oddly familiar.

"My journal."

"Then it is true," said Queen Gnarla, taking the book. "You *are* the Mighty Greghart."

Greg wasn't sure how to respond. "Uh . . . I don't know how mighty, but yes, I'm Greg Hart."

The queen smiled, and throughout the crowd, spirelings chuckled at his remark. "Such modesty. How refreshing."

"Where did you find my journal?" Greg asked.

"The Book was found inside the Passageway of Shifted Dimensions, near the Forbidden Door."

"Forbidden Door?"

"The one leading to the dragon's chambers," Queen Gnarla clarified.

"Of course," said Greg. "I must've dropped it when I left Ruuan's lair."

Queen Gnarla's expression changed. "There is but one thing we do not understand."

Greg nodded. "Just One?"

"When We found The Book and read the history recorded within, We knew We had found an artifact of great import. The hero described on those pages was someone even the bravest among Our warriors could admire. He had single-handedly faced the most dangerous creatures of Myrth and won, and even some We had never heard of—bizarre creatures from a strange world We can only imagine. This human has quickly become an inspiration to Us . . . but still, We do not understand."

"*You* don't understand?" Greg said.

Queen Gnarla glanced at the men scattered throughout the yard, and then at Greg. She moved her lips, but no sound emerged.

"Did you say something?" Greg asked.

Again she spoke so quietly, Greg could barely hear. Greg stared back blankly.

"My, you humans have dreadful hearing. We said, the last adventure described in The Book described the destruction of Ruuan. Yet We have seen the dragon with Our own eyes. How can that be?"

Greg hesitated before answering. He couldn't believe a race of warriors like the spirelings could possibly have come to admire any human, let alone someone like himself. But it was more than just admiration. It was almost as if they worshiped the hero from his journal. What would Queen Gnarla do if she found out the stories described on those pages were nothing more than a fabrication of Greg's imagination?

He was afraid to tell her the truth, but he was even more afraid to lie to her. Confused, he looked to Nathan for support. The magician smiled with his warm blue eyes and nodded, indicating Greg should trust his own judgment. Greg turned back to Queen Gnarla and spoke barely above a whisper.

"I wrote about that last fight before I ever went inside the dragon's lair."

"Quiet," Queen Gnarla warned. "It is supposed to be a secret."

Greg frowned. "To be honest, I never expected to survive my meeting with Ruuan. I wanted to record the battle, but I—I guess I just didn't want to write the story the way I imagined it would go. I wanted whoever read my journal to think that the Mighty Greghart had remained a hero to the end."

"We see," said Queen Gnarla, and it looked to Greg as if she was trying to decide if she approved. "What about the other stories in The Book? You didn't write those before they happened, did you?"

"Absolutely not," interrupted Nathan, stepping up from behind the queen. "I can attest to the fact that not one of the events described on those pages occurred *after* they were written."

Greg held his breath while the queen considered Nathan's words. Technically Nathan hadn't lied to her. None of the events in Greg's journal happened at all. He didn't like the idea of deceiving the queen, but he had an idea the omission was the only thing standing between him and hundreds of thousands of swinging axes.

A muffled noise drifted around from behind the queen. Greg leaned to his left and observed Nathan with his hands clamped over Melvin's mouth. An odd blue glow appeared beneath Nathan's palm. When Nathan pulled his hand away, Melvin's own moved up to take its place, and the boy took to fighting with his own mouth.

"We see," said the queen, oblivious of the events behind her. Greg was just glad she and the other spirelings considered him such a great hero. With their gazes fixed on Greg, not one noticed Melvin's struggle, but if just one had seen, then all would have seen, and then surely Queen Gnarla would have demanded to know what the boy was trying to say.

"Eez ndda hrro!" Melvin insisted. No one bothered to listen.

"We can't say We approve of your falsifying a historical record," said the queen, "but We can understand how you would not expect to survive your encounter with the dragon. And yet here you are, alive in one piece without so much as a scorch."

"Yes," Greg chuckled nervously. "I was quite lucky."

"Nonsense," Queen Gnarla said. "We have read The Book. The dragon was the lucky one."

"If you say so."

"Ah, there is that modesty again."

"Queen Gnarla, if I may interrupt," said Nathan.

"You already have," said the queen, clearly annoyed.

"We must discuss the upcoming battle. It would not be wise to forget the trolls amassing to the south."

"Not south," she told him. "East. Two of Us have been marking their progress. They are just a couple of miles away now, near the edge of the Weird Weald."

"But how?" asked Priscilla. "They should still be a week from here."

Greg nearly fainted when a large grizzly stepped up from behind King Peter. Then he realized it was not a bear at all but Marvin Greatheart, dressed in a full-length fur coat. The runner Zappas appeared at his side. "I'm afraid we may have had something to do with that."

"Marvin? Zappas?" said Greg. "How'd you get here?"

"If you mean, how did we escape Mrs. Alexander," Zappas said, "we waited until she retired for the evening and then slipped out while she slept."

"But we left you less than two weeks ago," said Priscilla. "How did you make it back so soon?"

"Zappas knew a shortcut," said Marvin. "Oh, sorry . . . apparently now the trolls know it too."

"Then we must act quickly to prepare for their arrival," said Nathan. "They're expecting to find us locked in battle. I suggest we give them what they want."

Greg felt a fever rush through his entire body. "Nathan . . . are you listening to yourself?"

"You *wish* to fight Us?" said Queen Gnarla. Two of her strongest-looking warriors stepped up from behind and raised their axes.

"No, I only want to make it appear as though we're fighting," said Nathan. "When the trolls attack they'll be expecting us to be weakened, but if we're not, together we can fight them and win. They might be defeated by either the Canarazas or the entire Army of the Crown alone, but at what cost? Together we can run them out quickly with a minimum of losses."

Queen Gnarla did not look convinced. "What about our amulet?"

"We have a plan for its recovery," said Nathan, "but we must deal with these trolls first, or we cannot hope to succeed."

Queen Gnarla studied him long and hard before replying.

"Very well." She turned toward Greg and flashed a grin full of pointed teeth. "We will enjoy fighting side by side with a warrior of the Mighty Greghart's caliber."

Greg felt a knot in the pit of his stomach. Ever since he got here he'd been dreading the thought of fighting the spirelings. Now that he realized he'd be fighting with them instead of against them, he was dreading it no less. The spirelings thought him some sort of superhero, and he hated to disappoint them. Plus he had seen the trolls.

For a moment Queen Gnarla looked deep in thought. Within seconds one of her warriors rushed forward and handed her a small vial filled with a swirling blue liquid. She turned and regarded Greg with pride in her bulbous eyes. "I know you need no help from Us in the battle to come, but We would like to give you this just the same."

"What is it?" asked Greg.

"A spell. Normally it would be reserved for one of Our leaders, who would swallow it just prior to stepping into battle. With it, your abilities will be increased tenfold. You will be stronger, quicker and more agile than you have ever felt before. We can only imagine for someone with your extraordinary abilities, that with it you will prove unstoppable."

"Oh, I don't know . . ." said Greg.

"We understand," said the queen. "Of course you do not need it. According to the magician, the prophecy says you will fight with just the strength of ten men, and We are sure you could do that without Our help. But still, We would like to do this for you."

Greg thought about what the queen was offering. With this gift he might hope to survive the day. Then a disturbing thought struck him. "But it's not me who's supposed to fight with the strength of ten men. It's Melvin."

"Zzme," Melvin said, prying at his jaws with both hands.

Queen Gnarla looked at the boy. "This human child with the bad puns is Melvin, correct? We heard you announce your slaying theory earlier, but We naturally assumed you were joking. Are you saying now that you were serious?"

Melvin made a muffled noise, the best he could manage without opening his mouth. Nathan waved his hand over the boy's face, and Melvin responded with a fitful bout of coughs and sputters.

"Did you say something, child?" Queen Gnarla asked.

"Greghart's right," Melvin nearly spat. "I was the one who slayed the dragon. I should get the spell."

Greg explained his theory again. Queen Gnarla had heard it before, of course, when Greg told it in front of Gnash and Gnaw, but now it held new meaning, as the Mighty Greghart himself was insisting it was true.

"We see," said the queen. "Very well. You shall have your spell, young dragonslayer."

Melvin glanced sideways at Greg and lifted his nose into the air. Greg frowned. Sure, Melvin was the one who should get the spell, but still . . . it was a hard thing to give up. The little brat could at least appreciate the sacrifice.

"And you shall have a spell of your own, as well," Queen Gnarla told Greg, and no sooner had she said it before one of her warriors rushed up and handed her a second vial. She was about to take it from him when her hand stopped in midreach. "They are coming."

"Who?" said Greg.

"The trolls. They are pouring from the Weird Weald as We speak, spilling out onto Pendegrass Highway just about a mile from here. We must hurry."

She asked Greg and Melvin to stand before her while she waved the two vials above their heads and chanted. Her fists began to glow a fluorescent red. Smoke emerged from between her fingers. When her hands opened, the vials were empty.

"I don't feel any different," said Melvin.

"Are you sure it worked?" Greg asked.

Priscilla stepped up beside him and gave him a brief hug. "You be careful, Greg Hart."

"Wait, I'm not sure the spell wor—"

"Come along, Priscilla," said King Peter. "I want you inside with your mother."

"But I want to talk to Greg a moment," she said, tugging on Greg's arm to lead him away from the others.

Greg tried to pull away but was no match for her grip. This was supposed to be the strength of ten men? "Didn't you hear? I said I don't think the spell worked."

"Yes, yes, but I need to talk to you about something important. Nathan told me what you said about me."

"The spell *is* important. Wait, what did Nathan say I said?"

Priscilla blushed. "You know."

"No, I don't. What did he say?"

Priscilla stepped up and adjusted the collar of Greg's cloak, staring into his eyes in a way that disturbed him nearly as much as the thought of the trolls approaching. "Just that you think I'm pretty," she told him.

"He said *what?*"

"It's okay. You don't have to be embarrassed."

"I'm not embarrassed."

"Really? Then why is your face all red?"

Greg slapped his hands over his face. "It's not. And I never said that." He pulled away and made a point of messing up his collar again.

"Men," Priscilla said, stomping her feet. "Fine. Go out and fight your trolls. I don't care anyway."

"You don't?"

"They're coming," someone shouted.

"Positions everyone," ordered Queen Gnarla.

The king's soldiers began moving about the yard, scattering themselves among the warriors. Some drew their swords and prepared to act as if they were locked in battle, while others lay sprawled out in the grass, as if they'd already fallen.

"No, no, everyone," Queen Gnarla called out. "Trolls may be imbeciles, but even they will never believe this. We need more human soldiers on the ground."

"Priscilla," urged King Peter, "you need to go now." He started to take his daughter's hand, but she pulled away and crossed her arms over her chest.

"I'm not ready."

Greg felt someone tugging on his arm.

"Greg, what's the matter with you?" It was Lucky's voice. The boy was holding up the magic sword he'd been carrying in his knapsack. "Come on, take it. They're almost here."

Ryder stepped from the crowd with General Talbout at his side. "We figure we should stick close to you," he told Greg. "After all, the prophecy says we'll be fighting at your side."

"Hey, that's supposed to be *my* side," said Melvin.

"It's okay, Melvin," said Greg. "We can all stick together."

Priscilla gave up her pouting, rushed forward and hugged them both. "You two be careful."

"We will," said Greg. "But you shouldn't be out here. Get inside the castle like your father told you."

Priscilla's nostrils flared. "Why? Because I'm a girl?"

"No, because I don't want you to get hurt." Her mouth dropped open, and she stared with that same look she'd been using on him all week. "And you're a princess," he added quickly. "You owe it to the people to stay out of harm's way."

"I see," she said, looking as if she didn't know how to feel.

"Yes, come along, dear," said King Peter. "Your mother is waiting."

Reluctantly Priscilla allowed her father to drag her away. Greg watched her go, and as uncomfortable as she'd made him feel the past few days, he still hoped he would live long enough to see her again.

"You okay?" It was Nathan's voice this time. The magician laid a hand on Greg's shoulder to try to comfort him, though it was a small hand for such a large task.

"Why did you tell Priscilla I thought she was pretty?"

"Don't you?"

"What—? That's not important. I never said it."

"I don't think you realize how long never is," Nathan told him.

"But now she thinks I like her."

"Again, don't you?"

"Well, sure, but I don't want her knowing it."

Nathan smiled and steered the boy to face the forest to the east, where the trampled weeds everyone referred to as Pendegrass Highway met up with the immaculately groomed castle yard.

"I wish that was the worst thing you had to worry about. Now, get ready. The battle will begin in just a moment."

"But why does there even need to be a battle?" Greg asked. "The trolls are only going to attack because they think we've been weakened. If they saw the Army of the Crown and the spirelings all waiting to fight, I'm sure they'd go away."

Nathan chuckled, though there was no humor behind the sound. "You don't know trolls very well, do you?"

"But they can't possibly win."

"Winning is not overly important to a troll," Nathan told him. "The fact they were timing their attack after we fought the spirelings was, frankly, nothing if not surprising. Trolls are always willing to battle, no matter what the circumstances, and now that they're here, they'd never consider leaving without a fight. For that matter, it would be hard to get the spirelings to leave at this point. Their entire identity has been built upon their prowess in battle. Many have waited their entire lives for an opportunity like this."

"But can't we reason with them?" Greg pleaded.

Nathan shook his head sadly. "You're not in Ruuan's lair this time, Greg. You were able to reason with the dragon because you both wanted the same thing: peace. These two sides want nothing but to fight, and they shall have their war no matter what you do or say about it."

"Action, everyone," shouted Queen Gnarla, and Nathan's words were cut off when the entire yard full of spirelings and soldiers suddenly engaged in mock battle.

Throughout the lawn swords clanged on axes. Spirelings moved about the grounds so quickly, Greg could barely focus on their blurred forms. The noise was deafening, yet Greg could still hear Queen Gnarla's voice ring out above the din.

"You humans need to fall sooner," she advised, and Greg was suddenly very glad this was only a staged battle.

Fortunately the trolls didn't notice the warriors holding back. Or maybe they did notice and just didn't care, anxious to at least start up a fight if they couldn't join one.

The first of the beasts reached the edge of the yard and dove straight into the fray. The closest spireling altered the course of his axe at the last instant, missing a bewildered soldier by scant inches, and struck the troll down. Two more trolls rushed to take its place, and the spireling dispatched them just as quickly. But when ten more rushed in to take their place, the spireling finally fell.

Greg found himself backing away from the carnage as thousands more trolls pushed forward, slashing out with their axes at those unfortunate to be nearest the eastern edge of the yard.

Nathan stopped him with a hand to his shoulder. "No, Greg. You have every right to be scared, but you must face this. The entire fate of the kingdom rests on your shoulders today."

Greg felt tears build in his eyes. He didn't want to be responsible for this. He watched in horror as thousands upon thousands more trolls poured from the highway. The fighting raged mainly along the southeastern quarter of the yard, as those spirelings and soldiers not engaged in battle were blocked by their comrades from reaching the front. But the band of fighting slowly grew wider, seeping across the grounds like spreading wildfire, and fate of the kingdom or not, Greg never wanted to flee more.

"This isn't right," said Melvin.

Greg had been so caught up in his own horror, he didn't notice the boy still standing by his side.

Nathan looked concerned over Melvin's statement. "What is it, son?"

"According to the prophecy, we're supposed to be out here fighting with the strength of ten men. Remember, we're supposed to make the difference that leads our side to victory."

"You keep saying *we*," Greg noted.

"Well, we both have the strength of ten men, don't we? Let's go use it."

"Be patient," said Nathan. "The battle will come to you."

Truer words had never been spoken. In the few seconds Greg had taken his eyes off the battle, the trolls had managed to push their way to the center of the yard. The line of fighting was spreading at an alarming pace.

"Don't worry, Greghart, Melvin," said Ryder behind the two boys. "General Talbout and I are right here with you, just as it says in the prophecy."

Greg appreciated the thought, but he'd have felt better supported if the third general from the prophecy, General Bashar, were here too. The fact that no General Bashar even existed was proof that the prophecy was wrong, and that meant there was no guarantee Greg would even survive the battle, let alone make any difference in its outcome.

"They're getting close," warned Nathan. "Take this time to acquire your center. Remember, from sensen comes peace, and only from peace can you overcome violence."

"Yeah, Greg," said Lucky, "we can't forget what Nathan has taught us."

"Lucky?" Greg said. "What are you doing out here? You're not mentioned in the prophecy. There's no reason for you to risk your life."

"Are you kidding? Without General Bashar here, you're going to need all the luck you can get. Besides, I stuck with you when you went looking for Ruuan's lair. I figure I ought to stick with you now."

"Here they come," said Melvin, and accompanied by Lucky or not, Greg felt his panic rise. He tried to meditate like Nathan advised, but it was hard to concentrate with so many thousands screaming all around him.

"Got any more of those dragonslayer jokes, Melvin?" Lucky asked, forcing a nervous chuckle, and Greg had to admit, even Melvin's grating humor would be a welcome distraction from the approaching horrors.

But if Melvin did tell one of his jokes, Greg never heard. The first of the trolls broke through the crowd and made a beeline for Greg, and even though trolls move with a slow, lumbering gait, Greg felt as if he were standing in the path of a speeding locomotive.

His chikan training took over in an instant. His sword sprang upward, so light he barely noticed the weight in his hands. The troll swept a heavy wooden club through a slashing arc that should have cut Greg in half, but amazingly Greg's sword met the strike and diverted it away.

Whether a trait of the magic sword or of the spell Queen Gnarla had bestowed upon him, Greg barely noticed the blow. With a quick flick of his wrist, he slapped the troll across the forehead with the flat of his blade. The troll's eyes rolled up into its head, and it dropped like a felled tree. Greg stood dumbfounded, gawking at the fallen beast.

"Watch out!" Lucky screamed, and Greg looked up just in time to see a second troll's club rounding toward his head.

Greg barely saw the blow coming, yet he managed to dodge out of the way as if the club had been wielded with a tenth the speed. And then he knew it was indeed Queen Gnarla's magic helping him. His reactions, agility and strength had all been improved tenfold. He never felt so capable in his life.

Lucky called out again, and Greg spun, lashing out with his sword to knock away not one, but two crushing blows. In spite of his fear, he smiled. The prophecy was right. He actually could make a difference in this battle.

A nearby soldier screamed, this time not in warning but in pain.

Greg snapped out of his thoughts and watched the man fall. All around him men and spirelings were being hurt or worse. He had to do something. To his left he saw a soldier fighting desperately, pinned between two trolls. The man didn't stand a chance without help. Greg lunged forward and batted one of the beasts in the head, again with the flat of his blade.

The troll dropped as if the blow had been dealt by one of its brethren rather than a mere boy, but Greg didn't take the time to watch. He dispatched the second attacker as swiftly as the first.

The soldier stood, mouth agape, as he watched the troll fall. He grinned and raised his sword high into the air. "Fear not, men. We have the Mighty Greghart by our side."

Throughout the crowd, men took up cheering Greg's name.

In spite of the danger all around him, Greg took a moment to search out Melvin. For once the boy was not wasting time being jealous. His brother Marvin fought nearby, thrashing about like a wounded grizzly in his enormous fur coat, but his skills paled in comparison to his brother's. Melvin fought with a skill far exceeding Greg's own heightened abilities, rushing through the crowd, dispatching troll after troll with a speed rivaling that of the spirelings. In his wake Ryder and General Talbout followed, finishing off any trolls that were stunned or injured, and Greg knew they were fighting by Melvin's side not because Melvin needed their help, but because he was the Hero who slayed Ruuan, and they wanted to make sure the prophecy played out as predicted.

And Melvin truly was a hero, Greg realized. The boy may not have possessed the experience slaying dragons that his brother Marvin had, but he certainly possessed the skill and the courage. He was born to be a hero, and today he would prove that he was ready to fulfill his destiny.

Suddenly Rake dug his claws into Greg's chest and shrieked. Greg shrieked too. He spun, expecting the shadowcat had been warning him of an attack, but not a single troll was within reach. Too many of their comrades lay in the grass surrounding Greg's feet for any to get close.

But then Greg spotted four trolls joined together to trap a soldier with his back against the castle wall. Even with heightened reactions it took Greg a moment to recognize the man did not wear the royal-blue uniform of the Army of the Crown. At first Greg thought this might be the infamous General Bashar who was supposed to fight at Greg's side—or at least at Melvin's side—but then Greg recognized the rich magenta fabric of the man's robe.

"King Peter."

With a speed and power he couldn't believe he possessed, Greg used the back of one of the nearby trolls to launch himself up and over the rest. He landed at a dead run outside the circle of fallen trolls and raced toward King Peter so quickly, he passed two spirelings along the way. One of the trolls held its club out like a baseball bat. Greg was still a full twenty paces away when the beast began its swing. He watched the blow in slow motion, willed himself to run even faster, and surprisingly he did.

The troll's club swept through the air three feet from King Peter's head . . . two . . . one . . .

Greg dove forward, sword point extended, and thrust his blade deep into the troll's side. He felt a crunch of bone as his sword lodged itself to the hilt. The troll's club jerked back, and the troll fell hard, nearly tearing the sword from Greg's grip.

Greg didn't dare let go for fear of being catapulted into the Enchanted Forest. He shook his head to clear it and found himself lying atop the fallen beast, his nostrils assaulted by a familiar rotten stench. Quickly he rolled away.

Nathan and two spirelings came to King Peter's aid to overpower the three remaining attackers, but Greg was too dazed to notice. He gripped the hilt of his sword and pulled, trying unsuccessfully to ignore the sickening vibration of metal against bone as the blade slipped free.

Bile rose in Greg's throat. When he took down the previous trolls he'd used the flat of his blade, and though each of the beasts had fallen quickly, he was willing to believe they'd just been knocked unconscious. But this troll was undoubtedly dead—and Greg had killed him. Sure, trolls were horrible mindless beasts who reeked badly and hated humans, but Greg felt horror-stricken. He finally understood why Priscilla had been so upset when they fought the harpies at the base of the Smoky Mountains. Surely King Peter was alive only because of Greg's quick actions, but still Greg felt ashamed of what he'd done.

"Get up, Greg," King Peter shouted, and even though Greg knew more trolls were certainly attacking, he couldn't convince himself to stand. Come to think of it, perhaps that was why he couldn't convince himself to stand. Instead he knelt on all fours, cringing as the deafening cries of battle closed in around him.

But then Greg heard something that caused him to raise his head and squint through his tears at the gruesome scene around him.

"General Bashar, sir," came the booming voice of one of the trolls.

Three of the beasts were thrown aside as a fourth sought to pass. Nearly half again as large as the others, this troll wore clothes that were slightly finer than the tattered rags worn by the others, but not until Greg spotted the three-inch-long thorns piercing both cheeks did he recognized this as the leader he'd seen in the clearing near the River Styx.

The troll general spotted Greg and lumbered forward with a gait so determined, it might have been called a stride. Reluctant as he was to stand, Greg scrambled to his feet and swung his sword up in front of him, easing into the familiar sensen stance Nathan had ingrained in him so many evenings on the trail.

Several of the king's soldiers rushed to Greg's protection, but the troll swept its arm to clear a path, and the men were thrown backward to a one. Three spirelings rushed forward as well, and even though they were quick enough to dodge the huge troll's next blow, they were no more effective at slowing its progress than the soldiers had been.

So, this was the General Bashar of Simon's prophecy. When Brandon wrote that the general would be fighting at Greg's side, he didn't mean Greg would be receiving aid at all. If anything, Greg would be receiving blows from the general's club.

Greg marked the troll's stride and wondered how to time his swing, given his newfound speed. He pictured himself striking too early and missing the troll completely, spinning his back to the beast just as it dealt a crushing blow. He didn't have time to worry long. Bashar was just steps away and closing fast. The troll raised his club and slashed down like a falling tree.

Greg struck out just as Nathan taught him, parrying the blow with his sword. The jolt rang through his shoulders and down his spine, clear to his toes. General Bashar had magic of his own.

Greg fought back his panic. He might possess the strength of ten men, but what good did it do if Bashar had the strength of ten trolls?

"Watch out!" screamed Melvin, and Greg watched in amazement as the boy launched himself onto the troll's back.

Bashar's eyes widened in disbelief. He tried to pull his attacker away, but he was too muscle-bound to reach above his shoulders. Melvin circled his arms about the troll's throat. He could barely clasp his two hands together around the beast's neck, which rivaled a tree trunk in girth, but he had Queen Gnarla's spell to help him. General Bashar's eyes widened further still, and he swatted at Melvin with his club.

Melvin saw the strike coming and ducked, leaving Bashar's own head to stop the blow. The troll screamed hard enough to shake the castle walls. He thrashed about like a bucking bronco to toss the small boy loose, but Melvin gripped with the strength of ten men, his legs flapping out behind him.

"Hold on, Melvin," Greg screamed, and in spite of the horror he felt when his sword point pierced the last troll, he tried to stab this one too.

Even with the distraction of Melvin squeezing his neck, General Bashar saw the strike coming and parried it with his club. Greg was knocked off balance and nearly crushed by one of the troll's feet as it stomped about the yard.

Ryder and General Talbout had been sticking close to Melvin's side throughout the battle. They weren't about to follow the boy's lead now, but they did at least lash out at the troll with their swords, and though neither blade connected, they provided enough of a distraction for Greg to scramble out of harm's way. Now all three generals were fighting not only at Melvin's side, but at Greg's side as well, and if the battle ended right this instant, it wouldn't matter whether Greg or Melvin was the true hero. The prophecy would be fulfilled.

But the battle wasn't ending. Bashar lashed out with his free hand and knocked Ryder backward. The kingdom soldier crashed hard into General Talbout, and the two of them disappeared into the crowd of fighting spirelings, soldiers and trolls.

General Bashar grinned madly, took two determined steps toward Greg, and raised his club. Greg tried to back away but tripped over a fallen spireling and fell. Bashar closed the remaining distance between them. He launched a blow that could have easily shattered a boulder.

In a flash, Nathan bounded out of the crowd and struck the troll in the hand with his staff. General Bashar groaned and dropped the weapon, which still nearly crushed Greg as it fell.

Before Greg could bring himself to move, Lucky dove into the ruckus, risking his life to drag the club away. The troll stabbed out one leg but, whether a matter of good fortune or not, missed Lucky by no more than an inch. Greg watched in horror, unable to move, as the troll general hovered high above him.

Melvin screamed. He gritted his teeth and tightened his grip on the troll's neck. General Bashar tried to scream as well but couldn't find the air. He fought with a desperation found only in the face of death, and even with his spell-enhanced strength, Melvin finally lost his grip and fell.

General Bashar howled and clasped his hands over his throat, drawing Greg's attention to a glint of metal that slipped free and slid down the troll's massive chest to the ground. *The missing section of amulet!* Greg realized too late. General Bashar was already bending to retrieve it.

Nathan leapt forward with his staff again and landed a solid blow to the troll's ear.

Greg didn't waste the opportunity. He lunged for the amulet.

No sooner had his fingers clasped around the shape before Greg felt his world lurch. As if someone had flipped a switch, the deafening roar of battle disappeared and the light of day was extinguished. Greg was left in a murky darkness surrounded by unpleasant odors he'd smelled only once before. He didn't know how it had happened, but proof that it did was lying just beyond the edge of recognition behind the shadows.

Somehow he'd just hopped across the kingdom to the center of the Shrieking Scrub, and now here he was, alone on the rotted wood floor of Witch Hazel's tiny shack.

Trading Harts

"So, you managed to survive," came a familiar voice from the darkness.

Greg squinted but could see nobody responsible for the sound. Then a small patch of black shifted, darker than the surrounding gloom, and a man's face was revealed by a small bit of light cast by a nearby candle. "Mordred," Greg gasped.

"Quiet," the dark magician told him. "It is most certainly not what you think."

"So," came a grating voice from behind. Greg felt his blood run cold. "You've brought me my amulet. Give it to me."

Greg spun to find Hazel looking deceptively feeble, one arm stretched outward, her wrinkled palm turned up to receive her prize. He tightened his grip on the amulet General Bashar had dropped, but felt his arm reach forward against his will.

"No," Mordred commanded, and Greg's arm stopped in midreach. "That is not the agreement we made."

Greg couldn't move. He glanced helplessly between the two of them. As terrifying as the battle had been, he wished he could return there, where the threats, though more abundant, were at least predictable. Here he didn't know what to expect. Mordred seemed to be helping, but to what end?

"Fool," Hazel hissed. "I made that agreement only to bring the boy to the Shrieking Scrub. You hold no power here in my home." Sparks shot from her fingertips, and a bolt of energy launched toward the magician. The magic engulfed Mordred in an eerie blue glow that pulsated for a few seconds and dissipated.

Mordred frowned. "Ah, Hazel. My magic may be weaker here, but it is still far stronger than you know. Remember, you invited me into your home. Besides, my spell of protection was cast before I ever entered your domain. I think you will find it quite sufficient to protect me from your treachery."

Hazel shrieked, the sound incredibly loud as it echoed about her eerie quarters. A large black crow cawed from the back of a nearby chair and took to the air, disappearing into the shadows. "Then I'll kill the boy." Again she raised her hands. The air crackled at her fingertips.

Greg shot a pleading glance at Mordred.

"Fine," said the magician. "Kill him. But it won't give you what you seek."

Rake popped his head out from under Greg's tunic to see what was happening, screeched and disappeared again. Greg wished he could disappear as well. Then he looked again at Hazel and took back the wish.

"Hmmph," Hazel said. "We'll see." And an icy blue bolt of electricity shot from her splayed fingertips.

Greg leapt to the side, barely dodging the blow.

Hazel's face darkened with rage. "What manner of magic is this?" she screamed, and sent another bolt soaring Greg's way.

Again he barely dodged the blow, but Queen Gnarla's magic provided the speed he needed.

Mordred, too, looked surprised by Greg's ability to avoid the strikes. "Leave him be." Slowly he raised his hand, and Greg was able to see the faintest glitter of metal through the gloom. "He does not have what you're after."

Greg felt his heart drop. He eased open the fingers of his clenched fist, only to discover the spirelings' amulet was no longer there. He patted his tunic and found the precious amulet Nathan had given him in the forest near Pendegrass Castle was gone too.

Mordred waved his hand, and the spirelings' amulet appeared in Hazel's palm. He then held out his own palm, where the pentagon-shaped center of the Amulet of Tehrer lay ready for the taking.

"So, you have it," Hazel shrieked. "Give it to me."

"You must first fulfill your end of our bargain. Give us the amulets you hold, and I will release this one to you."

"No," Hazel spat. "Why should I trust you? If I give up my amulets you will take them and run, just as this wretched boy did before."

Mordred shook his head, his face disappearing and reappearing as his black hood moved from side to side in the darkness. "As I understand, the boy did not break his agreement with you then. You asked him to trade two amulets he carried for two that you held, and that is what he did. It was you who tried to take all four for yourself."

"Trivialities. You seek to deceive me."

"No," insisted Mordred. "Unlike you, I still stand for what is good and right. You need not worry about me breaking our bargain. Just take what I have offered, and do with it what you can. It is the best you will manage."

Hazel's face filled with rage. She looked between Greg and Mordred, clearly uncertain what to do.

"Be patient, Hazel," Mordred told her. "Destiny may allow you to one day rule this kingdom, but that day is not today. Now, give us what you know is ours, and the boy and I will be gone from your home."

The witch's face knotted with frustration, but Greg could tell she knew she had no choice. She shuffled toward Mordred, who stopped her with his commanding tone.

"Not to me. Give them to the boy."

Hazel scowled and turned to Greg. It was all he could do to keep from darting away as she crept forward and reached out a withered hand. In it she held three tiny pie-shaped amulets. Greg reached out to her the way he might if feeding a shark, and Hazel dropped the treasures into his palm.

"So much for the three we brought you," said Mordred. "What about the last?"

"That one's mine!" said Hazel. "Nathan gave it to me."

"Maybe so," said Mordred calmly, "but it was part of our bargain."

"I will see you die for this," she hissed, but still she waved her hand, and a fourth amulet appeared upon her palm. Slowly she leaned toward Greg.

He wondered if she would clamp her bony fingers around his wrist if he dared reach for the gift, but she did not. He snatched up the fourth amulet and quickly hid it beneath his cloak with the others. He now possessed all four inner sections of Ruuan's amulet, and his skin prickled so much under his tunic, he wondered if Rake had mistaken him for his next meal.

"Now give me mine," Hazel shouted. "You promised. You promised."

Mordred hung his head sadly. "Ah, Hazel, you poor thing. You need not worry about me breaking my word to you. The piece I promised is yours."

The magician waved a nearly invisible hand through the darkness, and Greg once again felt the tingle of metal in his hand. Actually this was more of a jolt. Greg was so shocked he literally threw the amulet at Hazel. In a flash his world once again shifted, a sudden blinding light struck his eyes and a deafening roar met his ears. The damp smell of things best left unimagined was replaced by the pungent odor of trolls, also best left unimagined, and Greg found himself once again on the lawn outside Pendegrass Castle amidst a raging battle.

"Greghart, there you are." Ryder came running toward him. "We couldn't figure out what happened to you."

Greg quickly took in the scene around him. General Hawkins's troops must have followed Marvin's secret route too, because they were spilling onto the grounds from the east. Surrounded and beaten, the trolls that remained were retreating into the Enchanted Forest, where a chorus of horrible shrieks indicated that the foe waiting there might be worse than the one they faced in the yard.

Nearby, Melvin stood next to King Peter, who had a long tear in the fabric of his robe but appeared otherwise unharmed. General Talbout had not been as fortunate. He lay on the ground, blood rushing from his side even as Lucky pressed his fingers over the wound.

Nathan crouched over him and busily recited some sort of incantation. A blue energy formed in the magician's palms, and Lucky moved his hands out of the way so Nathan could cover the wound with his healing magic.

"Will he be okay?" Greg asked.

Nathan did not respond but concentrated instead on his spell.

General Talbout looked up at Greg under heavily lidded eyes and nearly smiled. "No, I'm afraid he won't." He started to chuckle, but the sound cut off with a gasp. "Don't worry. I'm an old man, and I've been a soldier all my life. I always hoped I would die in battle." His eyes dropped closed, and he coughed violently, blood spraying from his mouth. But then his eyelids rose again. "I'm just glad I got to see this one before I went." He made as if to shift to a more comfortable position, grimaced and fell backward.

Nathan stopped hovering his hands over the wound and pressed on the general's chest to discourage his movements. From the looks of it, General Talbout wouldn't have had the strength to rise anyway. Still the man sought out Greg with his eyes.

"I've never seen men fight as heroically as you and the young dragonslayer fought here today. Perhaps the prophecies were a bit misleading, but there can be no doubt the world of Myrth has never known two greater heroes." His eyes dropped closed then, and he fell silent, and Greg felt a terrible emptiness inside.

"Is he . . . ?" he asked Nathan.

"Dead?" Nathan responded. "No, just a bit melodramatic. He's going to be fine."

The general's eyes popped open again. "I am?"

"Of course," said Nathan. "You're feeling weak because you've lost a lot of blood, but the wound has already healed. You'll be as good as new in a couple of days."

Ryder bent over the man and smiled. "You kidding? He hasn't been good as new for as long as I've known him."

The others laughed, and King Peter stepped forward, taking in both Greg and Melvin in a single glance. "I think General Talbout spoke for all of us when he commended you boys on your daring efforts here today. You two have acted above and beyond anything we could have expected."

Melvin puffed out his chest and grinned, but Greg felt too overwhelmed to appreciate the king's words.

"But tell us, Greghart," King Peter said. "Where did you disappear to? We were all so worried."

Greg looked to Nathan, wondering if the magician already knew what had happened.

Nathan was just rising from General Talbout's side when he caught Greg's eye. He gave no indication whether he knew or not, but he did nod as if wanting Greg to speak.

"I went to Witch Hazel's shack," Greg said, his voice quavering as he recalled the ordeal.

"You're kidding?" said Lucky.

"Does that sound like something I would kid about?"

"Go on," King Peter said. "Tell us what happened. How did you get there?"

"Wait, wait." Bart climbed over the body of a fallen troll and approached the others. He never missed an opportunity to gather lyrics for another song. "Okay, I'm ready," he said, grinning widely. "Go on."

Greg looked again toward Nathan, but the man's face revealed nothing of what he might be thinking. "I'm not sure how I got there. I think it may have had something to do with Mordred."

"My head magician, Mordred?" said King Peter.

Nathan looked on with interest, and Greg thought for once it was possible the man didn't know in advance what had happened.

"Yes," Greg said. "He was in Hazel's shack when I got there. He seemed to be expecting me. I think he may have cast some sort of spell on the amulet, because it took me away as soon as I touched it."

Nathan raised one eyebrow, as if contemplating the possibility.

Bart began snapping his fingers, talking to himself. "*Whisked away to the witch's shack, Greg found a magician, dressed in black . . .*"

"Quiet," said Ryder. "Greghart's trying to talk. What happened with Hazel, Greghart? How did you get away?"

"Well, I think Mordred had something to do with that, too."

Greg explained everything that happened inside Hazel's shack, afraid of what Nathan would say about Hazel ending up with the most powerful section of the Amulet of Tehrer.

But Nathan did not look upset. "That's exactly what I wanted you to do, remember?"

Of course. Greg had been so terrified, he'd completely forgotten Nathan asked him to trade the key piece of Tehrer's amulet for the others. He was glad he hadn't disappointed anyone, but still he was concerned. It didn't seem wise for Hazel to possess such a powerful object.

"What if she finds the other pieces?" he asked Nathan.

Nathan's expression was grim, yet hopeful. "Much like with Ruuan's amulet, those pieces have been scattered throughout the kingdom. It is not likely she will ever find them all."

"She found the pieces to Ruuan's amulet," Greg pointed out.

Nathan smiled faintly. "Yes, I suppose she did. Well, in any event, you're forgetting that we hold Ruuan's entire amulet now. It could mean a battle far worse than we have seen here today, but it is a battle we won years ago, and if need be, we have strong hopes of winning it again."

General Talbout sat up. Already his color was beginning to return. "You're talking about the Dragon Wars, aren't you? I've heard of them, but I always thought they were nothing more than myth."

"If only that were true," sighed Nathan.

General Talbout's expression turned sad. "A lot of brave men died in those wars, didn't they?"

"Very many indeed," Nathan said. He stood and turned away, avoiding their eyes.

Greg watched him go, thinking of all the questions he wanted to ask. Did Nathan know more about the future? Would Hazel ever find all six pieces of Tehrer's amulet? Would Myrth be faced with another battle of Good versus Evil like nothing they'd witnessed since the Dragon Wars? Most importantly, was Greg prophesied to return? He wanted to ask all of these things, but he never got the chance.

"Greg!" a girl's voice shouted, and Greg barely had time to turn before Priscilla banged into him, nearly bowling him over. She hugged him more fiercely than Melvin had squeezed General Bashar's neck during the recent battle. "I was so worried."

Embarrassed, Greg struggled to break free. "I'm okay," he insisted. "Really, I am."

"Do you have our amulet?" a commanding voice called out from behind.

Greg spun to face Queen Gnarla, whose expression was hard to interpret, even for a spireling.

"Oh, right," he stammered. He reached into his tunic and pulled out the one amulet tied to a leather cord instead of a chain, the one worn by General Bashar of the troll's army. "Here," he said, extending his hand toward the queen.

Her eyes brightened, and her face broke into what Greg knew must be a grin, though it looked much like the same ferocious expression she used whenever she was angry. As one, every spireling that remained standing after the day's battle cheered to the Mighty Greghart for the safe return of their amulet. Queen Gnarla thanked him and took her prize, but Nathan stepped forward and forced the queen to meet his eye.

"What do you want, Magician?"

"This one section of amulet was originally given to you to guard, and it is being returned to you now for that purpose. But if the time comes when Ruuan's amulet must be rejoined, you must be willing to give it up freely for the good of the greater whole."

"We do not appreciate you telling Us what We must or must not do," said Queen Gnarla. "But We do understand the significance of the artifact Ruuan has given Us. If the dragon asks for it back, he has every right to receive it."

"It may not be the dragon who asks," Nathan told her.

She stared into his eyes a long moment before responding. "If and when the return of the amulet is requested, We shall determine the need. Should the future of Myrth be in peril, you can count on Us to do what is right."

"That is all I ask," Nathan said, bowing.

Queen Gnarla waited until he raised his head again. "Good. Because that is all We are offering."

Without another word she turned and took up the march for home. Every spireling standing bent to pick up a fallen comrade and fell into step behind her. Within seconds all evidence of the Canarazas was gone.

But plenty of soldiers remained strewn across the lawn to remind Greg of the horrors they'd faced here. And even more trolls. Greg shuddered as he remembered the feel of his sword piercing that first troll's body. He struggled to push back his shame. He was no hero. He was a murderer. Others rejoiced over the victory, but Greg could not find it within himself to join them. Hero or not, he wanted nothing more than to curl up into a tiny ball and cry.

Second Chances

"Come," said King Peter. "You've been through a great ordeal."

"Wait," shouted Bart. "There's still so much I don't know about the confrontation in Hazel's shack."

"Not now," Nathan told him.

"But if you take Greghart away, you're going to send him back home, and then I won't be able to learn anything more."

"It'll be all right," said Nathan. "I'll help you with the details later."

"Excellent. I'll be waiting right here."

Nathan led Greg through the crowd toward the castle gate, with Priscilla and Lucky a half step behind. Melvin tagged along too, though he did look reluctant to leave all the attention.

"Nathan?" Greg asked once they were safely inside.

"I know nothing more of the future, if that's what you're about to ask," Nathan told him. "No, that is not entirely true. I do know you will return here at least once more, but I don't know why, nor can I say when. As far as I know, Simon will make no more prophecies concerning you, but just because I don't know of them doesn't mean they won't exist."

"But you never told us how you knew so much about the future to begin with," said Priscilla.

Nathan smiled. "I only knew what Greg told me," he said. "That's why I'm so sure he will return. He has yet to tell me all the things I have known."

"*I* told you?" said Greg.

"That doesn't make sense," said Lucky.

"Yeah, you're talking crazy," Melvin added helpfully.

"I'm sure one day you will understand," said Nathan. "If it makes you feel better, I don't know all the answers myself. Now, isn't it about time we got Greg home?"

"There's no rush," said Priscilla, hugging Greg's arm as if afraid to let go. "He's going back to the same moment no matter when we send him home."

"Oh, no," said Greg. "I can't go back there."

"What do you mean?" asked Lucky.

Greg explained about Manny Malice and his trouble at school, and how just before the king's magicians plucked him off the Earth he had hit the huge boy with an errant sweep of his knapsack.

"He'll kill me if I go back. Believe me, you don't hit a guy like Manny Malice and expect to walk away in one piece."

Melvin laughed. "I can't believe after all you've been through, you'd be afraid of some kid at school."

Melvin was right, Greg realized. Still, he hated the thought of returning. "You don't know Manny. I think even your brother would think twice before picking a fight with him."

Melvin nodded, though he looked as though he was sure Greg had lost his mind.

"By the way," said Greg, "you did a great job today. I'm glad you were out there with me."

Melvin smiled and offered Greg his hand. "Me too."

Greg smiled back and shook Melvin's hand, although afterward he wasn't sure if Melvin meant he was glad Greg was out there with him or just that he was glad to be out there himself.

"Can we send Greg back earlier?" Priscilla asked her father.

King Peter scratched his head and looked somewhat embarrassed. "I don't know," he admitted. "Let's ask the magicians."

They made their way to the small antechamber off the main ballroom, where all of the king's magicians patiently waited to perform their final responsibility in this latest prophecy.

"Mordred, you're back," said King Peter. The magician nodded to acknowledge the obvious but said nothing. "Greghart here tells us you were quite helpful during his encounter with the witch."

"I only did what I thought was best for the kingdom," Mordred told him.

"Well, it sounds like you made the right choices," King Peter said. "I thank you, and the kingdom thanks you."

"Yes, good work," Nathan said, stepping up from the shadows. "I knew things would work out well if we joined together on this one."

Mordred regarded him coolly. "I do not recall us joining together."

"What do you mean?" said Nathan. "You told me where to find the spirelings' amulet, and I brought Greg to it so you could get him to Hazel's shack. We make a good team."

"Don't fool yourself," Mordred said. "I only did what needed to be done to protect this kingdom."

King Peter moaned. "When are you two going to stop your feuding? Mordred, Nathan is the same good man you spent half your life with. I don't know why he's continued to research the Dark Arts, but I trust he has his reasons. And he's right. This prophecy would never have been fulfilled without the two of you working together. You both did a great job. Now, there may come a day when you need to work together again, so I won't have any more of this nonsense. I want you to make up this instant."

"Okay with me," said Nathan, smiling as he reached out a hand.

Mordred stared a moment before he reached out and shook it quickly. "Fine. If the need arises I will work together with you again. Now can we get this boy out of here and get things back to normal?"

"Not until I say good-bye," came a woman's voice from behind.

Queen Pauline entered the room and glided over to hug Greg. Princess Penelope was there too. She thanked Greg with her eyes by not looking at him with disgust. Her expression, Greg noticed, was not much different from her sister's. Now that Priscilla was sure he was all right, she was apparently back to being mad at him for not admitting he thought she was pretty.

"Brandon was just telling me how heroic you were," the queen told him.

"Brandon was out there?" Greg asked.

"Yeah," said Melvin, chuckling. "I guess after Queen Gnarla made fun of him being a scribe he wanted to show everyone he could be a soldier if he wanted."

"But I don't remember seeing him."

"Well, you had to look close. I spotted him once, hiding behind a fallen troll. Anyway, I guess they were lucky he didn't get more involved in the fighting."

"Yes, well, I heard it was very gruesome out there today," Queen Pauline said. "I don't think you should be making fun of Brandon if he was a bit scared."

"Sorry, ma'am," muttered Melvin, looking hurt by the scolding.

"And you. I heard you were quite the hero."

Melvin's face brightened. "Brandon said that?"

"Everyone's saying it."

The queen thanked the boy for his role in the prophecy, and the others buzzed excitedly about how things had worked out, until Greg brought them all back to reality by reminding them how many soldiers and spirelings had lost their lives today.

"We have not forgotten those men," said the queen, "but you must understand. When you were here last time you were quite fortunate to resolve your problems without bloodshed, but as much as we'd like it to be otherwise, all our problems cannot be solved without a fight. This kingdom, as beautiful as it is, comes to us with a price. At times it can be a very harsh place, as we must struggle to protect it. Yes, a lot of men died here today, but far fewer than would have died had you not come to help us. We mourn those we lost, but at the same time we celebrate all the lives you have saved. I wish you didn't need to, but someday you will understand."

"I hate to interrupt," said Mordred, clearly lying, "but are we going to send the boy home or not?"

"You do know patience can be a virtue," Queen Pauline reminded him.

Priscilla was squirming fiercely, obviously wrestling with herself to overcome some inner struggle. Finally she rushed forward and hugged Greg. "Good-bye," she said, unable to keep the tears from her eyes. "You will come back to us, won't you?"

"According to Nathan, yes."

"But he doesn't know of another prophecy," Lucky said cheerfully. "Maybe you'll just come back to visit. You have the ring Ruuan gave you. You can get here anytime you want."

Greg tried to picture the circumstances that would make him want to pop between worlds into a dragon's lair. "Right."

King Peter handed over the clothes Greg was wearing when he arrived on Myrth, and Mordred conjured a screen of illusion while Greg awkwardly changed. A scraping noise near his feet caused him to notice Rake dragging a backpack across the stone floor.

"Oh, thanks, Rake," Greg said, pulling the bag over his shoulder. "I almost forgot."

Rake stood up on his hind legs and chattered so adamantly, Greg nearly checked to see if one of Myrth's monsters had crept up behind him. "Oh, sorry, you want to get in, don't you?"

The shadowcat circled around excitedly as Greg lowered the bag to the ground, and then dove inside before Greg pulled the flap half open. Greg closed the bag and cinched it tightly, remembering how Rake had spilled out the day the two of them were plucked off the Earth.

"You finished?" Mordred asked, pulling him toward the center of the room before Greg could respond.

"Wait," Greg managed to shout. "We were wondering if you could send me back earlier, say about a half hour?"

Mordred scowled for a moment but then consulted with one of the other magicians. "Yes, we could," he said eventually, "but probably not in the sense you are expecting. If we send you back early, you will not be in the body of the Greghart who left that world. He will still be there with you until we pull him over here."

"Oh . . . I see. Well, will people see me? Will I be able to do things?"

"You'll be going back in time, not becoming a ghost," Mordred told him.

"Okay, well, I guess I'll just need five minutes then."

"You want to go back five minutes early?"

"Yes."

"Very well." Mordred feigned a smile. "We *are* here to make you happy, after all."

After a signal from Mordred, the surrounding magicians left their positions along the wall and moved in to surround Greg, cutting out the light. Greg watched the faces of his friends disappear behind the many robes of black. Then the magicians began the chant that would open the portal between worlds.

Lucky's face reappeared next to Mordred's hip. He squeezed his way into the center of the circle with Greg, where he could signal the exact moment for the magicians to open the portal. Happy for the company, Greg waited anxiously for the transfer to occur.

Time lingered.

Greg was just about to ask what was taking so long when a flash split the air, revealing a window to another dimension. He watched in awe as world after world rushed by.

"Now," Lucky shouted, and Greg gasped as he was jerked through the rift. Four times now he'd made the trip between this world and his own, yet each time terrified him as much as the last. Try as he might not to scream, he just couldn't help himself.

"What the—? Hart? How'd you get here?"

Greg swallowed hard. He was standing in front of the school in the exact spot he'd stood when the magicians found him, just steps from the tree where Manny Malice was already hiding.

Maybe six minutes would have been better.

The huge boy stepped out from behind the trunk and rolled up his sleeves. "I asked you a question, Hart. What's the matter? Cat got your tongue?"

Greg observed the size of Manny's biceps and silently wondered how the boy managed to hide behind a mere tree trunk moments before. "I don't want to fight you, Manny."

"I'll bet you don't." Manny curled up his fists and took up a boxer's stance.

Sometimes it's impossible to avoid a fight, Greg recalled Nathan telling him. Queen Pauline, too, had tried to tell Greg there wouldn't always be a peaceful solution to his problems. Greg looked at the size of Manny's fists and hoped against hopes this wasn't one of those times.

"Come on, Hart. Put up your dukes."

"My dukes?" said Greg.

"You makin' fun of me again, Hart?"

"No, of course not."

Without warning Manny unleashed a punch that should have flattened Greg's face. Greg read the strike as if it had been dealt in slow motion. He moved his head no more than necessary to dodge the blow. Then as Manny slowly withdrew his arm again, Greg moved his head back to fill the space—or at least half the space—where Manny's fist had just passed.

Manny's jaw dropped. "How'd you do that?"

Greg noted a quiver in the boy's tone. He smiled, realizing the spell Queen Gnarla cast on him had not yet worn off. "You don't want to fight me either," he warned.

"I don't?"

"Not if you're as smart as I think you are."

Manny looked doubtful, and for a moment Greg wondered if Manny knew Greg thought he possessed less wit than a troll. But then Manny surprised him with a second blow, or at least he would have, if the blow hadn't been dealt with such unnatural slowness.

Again Greg dodged nimbly aside, but this time he reached out and flicked Manny's earlobe with a finger. Manny pulled back his fist and grabbed his ear. Greg was sure he spotted fear in the boy's eyes.

"How'd you do that?" Manny asked again.

"I told you, you don't want to fight me. Remember what happened last time?"

"Last time you got lucky," Manny replied, though his voice lacked its usual sureness. "And this time you don't have that stick of yours."

Greg glanced at the tree to his left. A branch nearly four inches in diameter extended about a foot above Greg's head. He reached out and used the strength of ten men to snap the limb off at the trunk, then broke off a section about five feet long and held it out in front of Manny's dazed face.

"I do now," Greg said, and Manny stammered something indiscernible as he took a few nervous steps backward.

"Uh . . . well, consider yourself lucky this time, Hart," said Manny. "I gotta catch my bus." He turned then without taking his eyes off Greg and dashed toward the row of buses just now pulling out from the curb.

Greg chuckled as he watched Manny go, but something about the sight of the buses pulling out concerned him. Then it hit him. This was when his alternate self had made his sprint across the yard.

He jumped behind the nearby tree and peered around the trunk, watching in amazement as his other self dashed across the lawn toward the waiting buses. A smile came to his lips as he realized this time he would reach the bus without incident. But then a sudden thought struck. What would happen if the other Greg got on the bus and left without ever passing through the portal into Myrth?

The possibility was too terrifying to contemplate. His other self was running full speed and had already passed the tree where Greg was hiding. Greg had to do something.

Fortunately Queen Gnarla's spell was still lingering on. Greg overtook himself within three or four strides. He tackled the other to the ground and threw one hand over his eyes. Struggle as he might, his weaker self couldn't hope to pull free from Greg's spell-enhanced grip. Greg dragged him back, kicking and screaming, to the spot where the portal would soon open.

In moments the air flashed and the expected rift opened. Greg didn't hesitate. He tossed his other self through the opening and watched himself disappear into the void of space, smiling at his own quick thinking. It was only then he heard Rake chatter behind him.

He spun to witness the shadowcat racing across the yard toward the school. Of course. Greg had forgotten about the shadowcat spilling from his knapsack when Manny stopped him before. Maybe this time Greg had tripped himself up instead of Manny, but Rake was loose again just the same, and the shadowcat was too terrified to stick around long.

Remembering his enhanced speed, Greg moved to chase Rake down, but the rushing wind emanating from the rift changed in pitch, and Greg knew there was no time. If Rake didn't pass through that gap this very instant everything that happened on Myrth would be changed.

Without contemplating the consequences, Greg ripped the pack from his shoulder and hurled it at the closing gap. Had he not had Queen Gnarla's spell to help him, he'd have surely missed his opportunity, but the knapsack flew through the gap without an instant to spare. It disappeared in a flash, and Greg could only hope it ended up on Myrth, not floating around space, too late negotiating the tunnel before the rift died away.

What would happen if Rake didn't make it?

For that matter, what would happen if he did? The Rake that was supposed to be heading to Myrth was hiding in the shrubs lining the schoolhouse wall. The Rake in Greg's pack was the same one who'd gone to Myrth before. He'd know all that was about to happen before it occurred. Did the dangers of knowing too much about one's future apply to shadowcats too?

Maybe not. Rake couldn't tell anyone else what was about to happen. The most he could do is try to warn them, perhaps with a shriek just before something bad was about to happen.

Wait, Rake was always doing that.

A demanding howl caused Greg to look down at his feet. The original Rake had come out of hiding. He rubbed against Greg's legs until Greg stooped to pick him up.

"Did you know what was going to happen to us, Rake?" Greg asked, but then he realized this Rake couldn't tell him even if he understood. This Rake had never been back to Myrth.

Greg picked up the knapsack his other self dropped. He opened the flap, and Rake jumped inside with alarming swiftness. Odd. Then when Greg went to sling the bag over his shoulder he could barely lift its weight. Queen Gnarla's spell was wearing off.

Behind, Greg heard the rumble of school buses. He used the last remnants of his heightened abilities to sprint for his bus and managed to catch it just before it pulled onto the street. The driver looked anything but pleased about having to reopen the door.

"Sorry," Greg said. He jumped inside, feeling as if his limbs had turned to stone.

Toward the back of the bus, Manny Malice sat staring Greg's way, eyes wide with terror. With a feeble shriek, he ducked his face behind the girl ahead of him.

Greg smiled and looked for an empty seat.

"Here, Greg." Ahead, Kristin Wenslow motioned toward an empty space in the seat beside her. Greg's weakening knees grew weaker still. Kristin's smile was sweet and genuine, but not half as wide as Greg's.

"Don't mind if I do," he told her. "I really don't mind if I do."

Acknowledgments

"Many thanks to Debra Dixon, Deborah Smith, Pat Van Wie, Brittany Shirley, and any nameless souls at Bell Bridge Books who have devoted their time and effort making The Journals of Myrth the best series it can be. I am so grateful for your many hours of help. And thanks to my wife, Nancy, for supporting me in my writing endeavors for more than two decades."

And I think I'm done with this one . . .

About The Author

Bill Allen may be described as an unusual man who has accomplished an unusual many deeds. In fact, it has been said that if you total up all the things he claims to have done, he cannot possibly be less than seven-hundred years old.

No one knows if this is true. All that is certain is that for a good many years he has been living in Melbourne, Florida with his wife, Nancy, writing software by day and, well, mostly sleeping by night. Every now and again he writes stories, too.

How To Save A Kingdom is Book Two in the Journals of Myrth series.

To find out more about Book One: How To Slay A Dragon and the upcoming Book Three: How To Stop A Witch, visit Bill at www.BillAllenBooks.com

Coming Next: How To Stop A Witch

CPSIA information can be obtained at www.ICGtesting.com
Printed in the USA
BVOW05s2022150415

396243BV00002B/534/P